POISONED

A CASEY CORT LEGAL THRILLER

AIME AUSTIN

AIME AUSTIN
www.AimeAustin.com

LOS ANGELES, CALIFORNIA

ALSO BY AIME AUSTIN

Judged
Ransomed
Caged
Disgraced
Unarmed
Kidnapped
Reunited
Contained
Abused

POISONED

A CASEY CORT LEGAL THRILLER

AIME AUSTIN

Poisoned

This edition published by
Moore Digital Media Inc.
1125 N Fairfax Avenue
Unit 46071
West Hollywood, CA 90046
www.aimeaustin.com

Copyright © 2021 by Aime Austin
ISBN 13: 978-1-64414-036-9
eISBN 13: 978-1-944179-74-8

Cover Designer: Wicked Good Book Covers
Cover images © Depositphotos, Shutterstock

Poisoned/Aime Austin. — 1st ed.

"To believe in "the greater good" is to operate, necessarily, in a certain ethical suspension."

—JOAN DIDION

1

Veronica Bonilla Garza

April 6, 2007

I singed my finger shoving a Pop Tart in the toaster oven as Tino brushed right past me.

"Strohmeyer comes first before us, then?" I asked. It was a continuation of the argument we'd started upstairs when I'd heard Ivy slam the bathroom door open and sounds of her retching had echoed. When I'd begged him to call off, and he'd refused.

If my eyes could have thrown daggers in his back, he'd have fallen right there in the kitchen. Instead, he grunted in response. Threw his coat over his shoulders. Fisted his way through the sleeves. Zipped the two sides together.

"Do you think you'll make it home early? I have back-to-back appointments until five thirty. Then I have to get Stella from day care."

"Yeah, maybe." His shoulders, made bigger and broader in his wool coat, shrugged and walked out the door.

Every single morning, my husband, Tino, got up and chose his job over his family. He would have said it was *for* his family, but that would have been a lie.

How a man could love a brewery of all things above his wife and daughters was a mystery I tried to solve every single day. None of that mattered right now. Today of all days I needed him to pick his family first.

"Tino!" I yelled. Maybe he was just outside shoveling snow or gathering firewood. I thought for sure he wasn't just going to up and leave.

Not today.

"He not here, Mama," Stella, my four-year-old, pronounced. Her little face was so serious I knew it was the truth.

"For real?"

Stella nodded. Pointed outside the kitchen window. Indeed there was a bald spot in the snow where his car should have been. How he had the gall to walk out when Ivy was sick—again, I'd never begin to understand.

The gagging sound from the bathroom told me that I didn't have the time today to deal with calling Tino to turn around and come back home. Instead, I took charge and did what I had to do: pick up the phone and call off.

"Juanita?" My supervisor was on the line after I made it through the automated menu and the receptionist.

I held the phone to my ear with one hand while trying to poke the Pop Tart into the toaster oven with the other. There were no hands left for me to soothe my youngest.

Stella was having nothing to do with the *mofongo* that I'd already heated up and put on her giraffe plate. I could practically see the yellow cartoon animal frowning at me in disapproval.

"Hi. This is Veronica Garza," I said formally. It was the best unaccented voice I could do right now. I always made an effort to sound as *blanquito* as possible when I was dealing with doctors, government offices, or in this case—work.

"No *quiero mofongo*, Mommy. I want Pop Tart," Stella wailed. My daughter shoved away her *platanos* like I was trying to poison her to death by way of tropical bananas.

I put my hand over the receiver, pointed to the toaster oven where her factory-made breakfast was heating half-heartedly. Tapped a finger against my lips in the vain hope that she'd take the cue to lower her voice.

"Veronica?" Juanita's voice called me back to the reason I was on the phone.

"Yes. Sorry for all that. My daughter…"

Juanita cleared her throat, impatient. It was clear that my boss did not want to hear about Stella's toddler tantrum.

"I can't come in—"

"The snow coming down over in Brighthill too?" Juanita interrupted before I could finish. "Your nine o'clock appointment canceled. As long as you make it in by ten, it won't be a problem. We would not want one of our best massage therapists to kill themselves on the four-eighty. No Rocky River stay-at-home mama's 'me time' is worth that."

Most of our morning clients hailed from the well-off suburbs. Brecksville was just south, Bay Village and Rocky River to the west.

I could hear the phone moving away from Juanita's ear, a shout down the echoey spa hall. I called her name, to get my supervisor back. To make sure she understood. When I heard her breathe into the receiver, I spoke before she was distracted again.

"No, not late, Juanita. Not at all. You know how Ivy's been sick," I started. Ivy had been sick for most of the time I'd worked at Spasy as a massage therapist. This was not news. "She's not good today," I continued. "I need to get her back in to the doctor."

"Veronica—" Her sigh was long, deep. "We talked about this."

We *had* talked about this. My missing hours and sometimes whole workdays while I was in the emergency room. Or nursing Ivy at home on some new medication cocktail that treated the latest symptoms but never the real problem.

I always found a sub, but there was a lot of scrambling on the spa's part to make sure that clients were okay with someone different, that everything was covered.

Spasy didn't like to scramble. My customers liked me— a lot. That was good for tips. But it was bad for a corporate spa business that was happy to substitute one cog of a massage therapist for another no matter what lip service they paid to how special we all were.

"Juanita. This will be the last time, I swear." This time, I thought, *this time*, I'll figure out what's wrong with Ivy. I'll get her the care she needs and cure whatever was making her sick once and for all. Everything will go back to us being a normal family like we were when we lived in Cleveland's Tremont neighborhood.

Sometimes I think this house was what made her sick. I hadn't said anything to the doctors, but I'd stayed up half of last night doing research on radon, worried the color-less, odorless invisible gas could be responsible for Ivy's symptoms.

Maybe this time I'd finally get the guts to bring it up to the doctors. As long as I didn't say anything about looking it up on the internet, maybe no one would laugh at me at the hospital.

"You were already on probation, Veronica." Juanita's voice broke into my thoughts. "There won't be any need for you to come in today. I'll shift your clients over to Samantha." My supervisor took a huge breath that ended on another long sigh. I didn't like the sound of that sigh. "We're going to have to let you go, okay?"

Though I sort of knew it was coming, her words were a kick in the teeth. Not one I had been expecting when I picked up the phone. I heard Ivy coughing and knew there wasn't a damned thing I could do to save my job, not at this moment.

"I'll get corporate to put your last check in the mail," I heard Juanita say through the landline. "Please let us know when you can return your uniform."

I looked down at the hot pink scrubs that had always been a little too tight around my ass. It was one thing I wouldn't miss. Didn't want the hassle of that damned job anyway. Though I couldn't reconcile my thoughts with the tears that had started smarting around my eyes.

Stella placed her chubby hands on my already stained but otherwise clean Spasy top and patted me to get my attention. Now, I'd have to wash the smashed plantains and garlic off these before returning them.

"What, Stella? I told you before you can get your Pop Tart when the toaster dings."

I could see her trying to keep multiple thoughts in her toddler brain. Her eyes shifted to the sound of throwing up coming from the hall bathroom. The loud chime of the toaster oven came next.

"Mommy. Ivy's sick again," Stella stated the obvious. "I'm hungry."

"Juanita. Sorry. Thanks. I have to go." None of what I'd said to my boss had probably made any sense, but I didn't have the brain capacity to add politeness to my vocabulary just now.

Before the toaster pastry turned too dark around its edges and Stella refused to eat what I knew was the last one in the house, I pulled the pastry from the oven. With the tips of my fingers burning, I tossed it on a plate in front of her, a smiling tiger's face this time. I poured her milk and hoped that somewhere in there all this added up to a balanced diet. She took a bite and chewed happily. I flicked on the countertop television and flipped through the channels until some kind of cartoon was on the screen.

One down.

More sounds of throwing up bounced off the bathroom's tiles.

One to go.

I dropped the phone and TV remote onto the laminate counter and hightailed it to the house's single bathroom. My ten-year-old daughter was hunched over the toilet, her own portion of *mofongo* emptied out of her stomach and into the ceramic bowl. I flushed the food down into the septic system and tried not to think of it stewing in that concrete container along with all the other waste we'd produced over the years.

"I don't think I can go to school today," Ivy said after she swiped the back of her hand across her mouth. Swallowing the bile that rose into my own throat with the smell, I jumped up and turned on the hot water in the sink. After I wet a hand towel in the warm stream, I turned off the water and pushed it toward her. Ivy didn't take it, shaking her head.

"Mommy!" Stella yelled from right outside the bathroom door. She had half a toaster pastry in her hand and half *on* her left hand. A hand that had just smeared strawberry filling along the newly painted bathroom wall.

"Thirsty!"

I tossed down the towel.

"Did you finish your milk?"

Stella shook her head so hard, her hair swished around the top of her blue roll-neck sweater.

"I want fuzzy water."

"It's called seltzer, Stella. The water is not fuzzy."

She disappeared back into the kitchen, probably to glue her eyes to the bright images that flickered across children's programming. That girl would not drink anything that came from the tap even when Tino added a filter. She claimed it tasted like very bad medicine. There was no convincing a four-year-old that highly mineralized well water was probably better for her than anything that came in a plastic bottle. Most of the time I just gave in, handed her the "fuzzy" water and hoped her baby teeth would last long enough for her to get her permanent ones.

"Mama?" Stella again.

I was about to run out and get the seltzer—anything to get Stella to be quiet for a minute—when Ivy's head nearly disappeared into the toilet. Again. The sound of her emptying her stomach bounced off the walls of the tiny room. I swallowed three more times to keep my own breakfast down.

"There's blood, Mama." This was from Ivy.

"Stella! Go find your coat."

I knew my younger daughter would heed this command. She was always looking for a reason to be outside no matter how hot or cold or rainy or snowy the weather.

My little one truly belonged in Puerto Rico. I blinked away the thought.

Tino and I had made the decision twelve years ago to plant roots in this cold, damp city. I needed to be okay with it once and for all. A pang of longing for home pierced me so deep the pain almost felt real.

I shook it off.

For now I needed to put blinders on. Get Ivy help so she could be better. So she wasn't sick all the time. Then maybe, maybe I could approach Tino with the idea of moving back. He'd dragged us up here all this way to get his foot in the door at Strohmeyer's main brewery headquarters. After more than a decade of him working and waiting and hoping for more than token advancement, I wasn't sure if it was worth it.

Stella ran back into the bathroom, her little pink coat zipped and buckled in all the right places. Her purple hat was tipped at a jaunty angle that surely wasn't intentional. She had a rainbow glove on one hand, a sparkly white mitten on the other. At any moment other than this one, I'd have wanted to hug and kiss her. Praise her for trying and nearly succeeding. Pat her on the head just for being cute. I never thought I'd love her as much as Ivy, but I did.

The hard part no one tells you about motherhood is that each of your children will need very different things from you. And sometimes…sometimes, you have to sacrifice one for the other.

"Can I go make a snowman?" A small hand encased in yarn awkwardly patted my thigh.

"Snowman?"

I tipped the flusher, wet the towel some more, and gave it to Ivy. I leaned over my older daughter's back, caught the cord in my fingers and pulled up the blinds. The snow was nearly to the sill. I tried to look beyond the window but was blinded by only whiteness. It hadn't looked that bad a half hour ago. I was sure that there'd only been an inch surrounding the space where Tino's car had been. That had to be a drift.

Snow that high would mean we were blocked in. My only way to get Ivy to a hospital would be by ambulance. My final check from Spasy wouldn't come close to covering that out-of-pocket fee. I tried to remember if the snow blew on this side of the house and the depth was an illusion.

Eight years. That's how long we'd been here, and I still wasn't quite used to having our little part of the American dream. Truth be told, I very much missed our apartment in Tremont. But when the young bearded guys with their coffee and the yoga-pants-wearing women with their cupcake shops had moved in, this house mortgage had become a lot cheaper than our last rent increase.

Most importantly, it made Tino happy. If Tino wasn't happy, no one was happy.

From our old apartment it would have only been two miles to the big MetroHealth hospital. I could have left Stella with any of the *abuelas* in our building. Focused on Ivy without the guilt of ignoring my other daughter.

Instead, I had to tell Stella that no, she couldn't build a snowman, though that was a very reasonable request from a not-yet-in-school four-year-old. Normally I'd have dropped Stella at day care before taking Ivy to the hospital, but if the snow was anything like it looked from that one tiny window, I wouldn't have time to get her there before Ivy needed that ambulance I couldn't afford.

I glanced out the window one more time hoping for some kind of salvation. None was forthcoming. I took a deep breath, closed the blinds, and got to it.

I worked hard to get Stella buckled into her car seat, something she vehemently hated. Then I needed to usher Ivy into the car and to the emergency room, something my older daughter vehemently hated.

All that with a thick layer of recent lake-effect snow on top.

Forty minutes later, we were all buckled in the car. The driveway was shoveled sufficiently for me to get down to the nearly empty street, but the fat flakes were still falling hard and fast. When I'd learned to drive as a kid in Ponce, my biggest worry had been dodging tree branches during tropical thunderstorms, not frozen water during a snowstorm. When I'd mentioned how beautiful I thought it was to our neighbors, here from Puerto Rico before us, they'd shaken their heads and muttered under their collective breaths. It hadn't taken me long to figure out that pretty was also treacherous.

As I carefully backed out onto our street, an SUV roared around the corner, nearly hitting us. I floored the gas until my spinning tires found traction and pulled us back into the driveway.

"Mama?" Stella asked. "I thought we were going to the doctor."

Ivy was silent, but I could feel her steady gaze along the side of my face from her spot in the passenger seat. I didn't say a word to either of them until my hands and feet stopped trembling long enough that I could put the car in reverse and try again.

Between the time the SUV had nearly sideswiped us and me backing out a second time, a Brighthill village plow had thundered down the street. Now I had to add getting over the hump of snow at the end of the driveway to my list of morning challenges. Once I did that though, the street should be smooth sailing. I took a deep breath, floored the gas, and got us safely onto the heavily salted pavement.

Three minutes into the drive, Stella said, "Mama? I have to pee."

"You're going to have to hold it, *niña*," I said. At the stoplight at the end of West Fourth Street, I flicked on the left blinker and looked between my older daughter in the passenger seat and my younger reflected in the rearview mirror.

I don't regret having Stella. It's not that I don't love her fiercely—just differently from Ivy. Two children are a lot, though. Especially when one needs extra attention.

After Stella was born, the number of hours in the day had not increased accordingly. I don't know how anyone did this, how my mother had managed three girls with only a year between each of us.

After Ivy, I hadn't wanted a second. Tino had pushed and pushed—for years.

"They'll play with each other," he'd said. "You'll have a break from being only Ivy's mom."

"Ivy shouldn't grow up alone," he'd said on a different night while whispering sexy words into my ear and saying there were no more condoms.

I'd finally given in on a night when I'd been drunk on Jamaican rum and high on love.

"When we're gone, siblings have each other," he'd huffed while he'd been thrusting, another time without any barriers between us.

Those were the sweet nothings he'd whispered in my ear right before we'd conceived our second daughter. When he hadn't been around to help care for her those first hard lonely months when my mother had already been promised to my sister and my new niece, he'd said, "I'm just getting a foothold at Strohmeyer."

When I'd pleaded for more help on the weekends, he'd claimed he was studying for his beer specialist certificate, while it looked to me like he was catching up on the Caribbean World Series. I'd turned away from him and the TV and changed Stella's diapers.

Blotting out my memories, I wove around a snow bank as carefully as I could. All I wanted was for the man I married to help raise the kids he'd brought into this world. I didn't think that was too much to ask.

A drive that should have taken twenty minutes took three times that. When we got to the hospital's parking lot entrance, I could finally take a breath, relieved I hadn't skidded and done a donut on the way. I looked away from the windshield for the first time in an hour.

Ivy was pale, sweaty. Stella was red faced, sweaty. I parked in the first clear space I could find and extracted my children from the car.

"Mama? Mama! I still have to pee." Stella tugged at my open coat while I held Ivy's shoulder and tried to close and lock the passenger door at the same time—a feat of acrobatics all my massage training had failed to teach.

"Let's get inside, honey. You can't exactly go out here."

Stella pointed to a yellowed bank of plowed snow.

"Somebody else did."

"That was probably a dog, honey. Let's not look at that too closely." I pulled her away before she could take off her glove or mitten and stick one of her bare hands into the urine-covered snow. I loved her curiosity...most days.

"Come here." I grabbed her mittened hand firmly. "It'll be warm inside. They'll have a bathroom."

I almost melted in gratitude when I spied the intake nurse. A familiar face was exactly what I needed right now.

"Mrs. Garza, Ivy sick?"

As I'd done too many times before, I lifted the form and clipboard from the desk. Wrote Ivy's name and the date. Added "vomiting blood" to the symptoms box. The intake nurse took the board and pulled it down near her keyboard.

"So sorry." She shook her head in sympathy.

"Can I ask you a favor? Stella has to use the bathroom. Can I leave Ivy here for two minutes?" I didn't wait for a response. I didn't have enough wipes or a change of clothes to deal with a Stella-sized accident. The way she was bouncing around told me we were less than two minutes from her bladder releasing.

I lifted my youngest into a football carry and hightailed it to the closest family-sized restroom with scarcely a glance over my shoulder. I figured that no one stole children from hospitals. Babies maybe, but not sick ten-year-olds. The emergency room waiting area was as safe a place to leave my child as any.

Ten minutes later, weighed down with Stella's winter coat, hat, and scarf, I trudged back to the waiting room while my youngest did some video-girl, ballet-tap-combo pirouette down the shiny linoleum floor. I dropped everything when I peered into the waiting room and found it empty.

"Mrs. Garza? Mrs. Garza?" the intake nurse called, putting a halt to the panic that had been surging inside my body when I realized I'd completely misjudged the odds of child abduction. "I put Ivy in number three. I didn't want you to have to wait."

"Thanks." I lifted my hands into a prayer posture, tipped them toward the nurse in appreciation.

"You might want to put a mask on the little one." She pointed to Stella. "Still seeing a few bad flu cases coming through here this spring."

I patted myself on the back for not commenting on these people's idea of "spring," and gave the elastic and paper contraption to Stella. She'd been to the hospital enough times to know how to get it over her own ears, nose, and mouth without my help.

I picked up the stuff I'd dropped, then headed straight into the treatment bay where my older daughter lay, small and tan against the stiff blue-white sheets.

"Ivy. How are you?" I asked while smoothing her hair back from her clammy forehead. "Has a doctor seen you?"

She nodded. "They're going to take me for a CT scan."

I turned away so that I could keep my worry from Ivy. The co-pay on the last CT scan had taken us two months to pay off. And that had only been with extra early morning and late-night shifts at Spasy. Now I wouldn't even have that. I couldn't even think about how I'd find another job with Ivy this sick. At least Tino's salary covered the mortgage and car payments, if not a lot else.

"I have a mask, Ivy." Stella pointed towards Ivy's bare face. "You don't have a mask."

"I'm already sick, Stella. They don't give sick people masks."

"Oh." Stella already had one of her little legging-clad legs up and over the metal rail at the side of the bed when she asked, "Can I sit next to you?"

Ivy, like me, had learned to move fast where the four-year-old's will was concerned. My older daughter leaned as far as the IV let her. They run a line automatically these days. It was probably in her chart somewhere that she was always a little dehydrated. Ivy put her hands into Stella's armpits and lifted her up until her sparkling boots cleared the bed's railing.

Then she tucked her sister right next to her. My big one and my little one were very different, but these moments of communion really warmed my heart. Let me know that when Tino and I were gone, that they'd at least have each other.

He'd been right about that one.

Their dark heads were pressed together. Stella was laughing so hard that she had to lift her mask over her head, and it now sat on top of her curly hair like a fat light blue headband or a weird nurse's cap. I dug my phone from my pocket and snapped a small grainy photo. It wasn't perfect, but I wanted to keep this memory vivid in my mind if things got hard. Harder than they already were.

"Mrs. Garza? I'm Doctor Richardson.... You can call me Kirsten. I don't know if you remember, but we met a few months back, when I was called in to consult on her case. I've been reviewing Ivelisse..." Dr. Richardson tripped over the pronunciation.

"We call her Ivy. You can just call her Ivy," I said like I'd done so many times in the past. To make it easy for the people up here who stumbled through my daughter's beautiful name. One that in its full form meant *life*.

The doctor pulled a pen from the pocket of her white coat and scribbled a note in the chart.

"I've been reviewing *Ivy*'s chart, and I think we could benefit from a new scan. I've put in the order. Just waiting for someone to take her up to the radiology floor. I don't want to make any kind of guesses about diagnosis until then, okay? Plus we're doing blood and urine, the full panel workup." Dr. Richardson paused, her eyes shifting left to right. "I think, though, you should call Ivy's father. We should have something more in the next couple of hours."

Dr. Richardson didn't exactly smile. Maybe it was more of a grimace. I tried not to read too much into it as I tried to remember her specialty, why she'd been called in before. It was pediatric something. They were all pediatric...something—immunology, radiology, endocrinology. Instead of worrying about what Dr. Richardson thought she'd seen in her initial workup, I kissed Ivy on the forehead when the orderly came to take her, then bundled up Stella.

"Where's Ivy going, Mama? Can I go?"

"They're doing something like an X-ray. Are you hungry? I think it may be close enough to lunchtime that there are some French fries down in the cafeteria."

"*Papas?*" My daughter's smile was beatific as if I were offering her sainthood and not merely potatoes.

"Yes. *Papas.*"

"Sauce?" Stella's voice went up like she was one of those people talking on public radio.

By sauce she either meant the hot sauce Tino liked or ketchup. Either way, I was pretty sure the cafeteria would be able to give Stella what she wanted.

When we got downstairs, I placed two quick calls to my husband. Left him a voicemail on his work and cell phones. Then, I let Stella help me slide a tray across the metal grille lines in the counter picking up fries from the fry cook and Boston cream pie from the dessert rack. Then I got two pints of milk—one chocolate, one plain.

While I waited to pay, I fingered my phone wondering if I needed to leave another message for my husband. As if someone had read my mind, it rang in my hands. The caller ID said it was him.

"Tino," I said by way of greeting.

"I just got your messages. I was down in the plant—lautering. We've got some great new brews coming down. Today I'm trying out one with fresh fruit and another with dried."

I hated to crush his enthusiasm for separating hops from wort, but our daughter was more important than getting Americans drunk on overpriced beer.

"You need to come to the hospital." I put it as plainly and directly as I could without giving in to the hysteria that was starting to bubble up in my chest now that no one had smiled for hours. Now that the fourth doctor in as many hours was examining Ivy.

"You got it? Right? My message." Tino's voice was heavy with impatience. "I can't leave right now. The brewmaster is coming down here in a few. Snow delayed him at the airport. I can't miss this meeting. It's crucial to my career."

He'd talked about the man like he was god descended from the heavens.

"That the cousin of Ed Strohmeyer you keep talking about?" I asked, mainly to prove that I'd been paying attention, not because I cared one bit.

Tino often accused me of not being supportive of his "career goals." But I'd uprooted my family and had moved to snowy, cold Cleveland. I didn't know what more I needed to do to show my support for him.

"Felix Braun is his name. Practically grew up in a brewery in Germany before coming over here after the war and setting up the recipes for Strohmeyer. He really knows his old-world techniques. He's all but retired and is thinking of promoting one of us to brewmaster when he moves back permanently. They say this is his last ever trip to the States."

I cringed at his use of the stuck-up phrase. *The States.* Neither one of us had a passport. Had never left *the States.*

"I gotta meet with him today if I want a shot at this," Tino continued. I sent prayers up to thank God that he couldn't see my face. I was guessing it wasn't a nice one. "It will make my career if I can head up my own craft brew brand. I think I have a good chance if I can convince Braun at this meeting that I have what it takes to make something unique that the average guy likes to drink."

"Sauce?" Stella piped up. I looked across the table where we'd sat with our trays of food.

I lifted the Tabasco from the little metal basket on the side. My little one shook her head. I hefted the glass bottle of Heinz, same headshake. I looked around at the tables. Found mustard just within reach, pointed to it. Another shake. This one came with a trembling lip. I was quickly running out of chances to keep this one on an even keel. I carefully pulled the phone from my ear and lifted my eyebrows. My daughter got the message.

"White sauce, Mommy," she insisted. "It's white."

Tino was yammering on about expanded distribution opportunities while I was trying to imagine what in the hell kind of white sauce Stella had experienced in her four short years on earth.

"'Naise." Stella clapped at the sudden resurgence of her memory. "Daddy called it 'naise."

"Mayonnaise?" I asked. The other "naises" were yellow.

Stella nodded enthusiastically. I was up and out of my chair about to pester the cashier. She must have overheard because she was ready with a handful of yellow and blue Hellman's packets.

"Go to the meeting or whatever," I said into the phone interrupting Tino's monologue on craft brew marketing. "I'll handle things here." *Like I always did*, I muttered under my breath before I pressed end and shoved the phone down in my bra. Then I used my teeth to open packet after packet, squeezing blobs of the gelatinous sauce onto Stella's plate. She dipped her potatoes, started humming and swaying in her seat. All the signs that she was happy and content and okay with life as it was right at this moment. I envied her that simplicity where only the present mattered.

Six hours and what seemed like dozens of tests later, no one was swaying happily or humming where they sat.

After more pestering phone calls from me, Tino had finally arrived. No one would talk to me until I'd summoned him here. He'd come under threat of divorce or barring that—death.

The nurses had long since left to move on to more acute patients. When the doctors had finally come back, it was dark outside. All of our stomachs were rumbling, but I didn't want to make a repeat trip to the cafeteria. Doctors didn't wait around.

Tino and I, with Stella fast asleep, had been ushered into a little room with a couch and a couple of upholstered chairs. I took a moment to glance at Tino, see if his dread mirrored mine.

We each sat like stone-faced statues on the furniture waiting for the doctors' pronouncement. Neither Dr. Richardson's face nor those of the two doctors to her right and the two to her left were an omen of good news.

"Mrs. Garza. Mr. Garza," she started.

I nodded. Grabbed onto Tino's strong hand. Our differences disappeared in the miniscule gap between our skin.

"I'm sorry to tell you this." She paused for a moment, looking toward Stella. The four-year-old was fast asleep in her father's lap. "We found a tumor in Ivy's right kidney."

For a long moment I didn't hear a thing. Just air rushing past my ears.

"A tumor? Is it cancer?" Tino's voice cut through the static. Stella's head bobbed with the force of his words, but my youngest didn't wake up.

"We won't know for sure until radiology makes a final determination. I've consulted with the urologist, radiologist, and oncologist on call, though," she said, her hands going wide. I looked at the man and woman on one side of her and the two men on the other. I was guessing these were the specialists. "...and we're sure it must be. We compared today's scans to ones you took six months ago and this mass...it's nonexistent on that earlier one. Nothing grows as fast as cancer."

The "C" word.

My biggest fear—realized.

"What can we do?" I blurted. "Is...is my daughter going to die?"

Though she was silent, Dr. Richardson's fierce headshake was enough reassurance for the moment.

"I think it would be best if you leave her overnight. I'll make sure she's checked in as a patient. Tomorrow the pediatric surgical oncologist can examine her. Get a final determination. We may take more scans. Then we'll talk about staging and treatment."

"You don't think he'll say it's a mistake, this diagnosis?" Tino asked, his voice high and tight, his accent more pronounced than I'd ever heard it.

"I'm sorry, but no. It's just a matter of getting the on-cologist's official sign-off."

"You won't take a...what do you call it? Veronica?" Tino turned to me, looking for some kind of excuse as to why this couldn't be real...some kind of lifeline.

"A biopsy," I answered. It was all I could offer. "Like with Abuela's breast cancer." I turned to the trio of doctors. "Why no biopsy?"

"The kidney is a very sensitive organ," a male doctor said. "We only do biopsies in the rarest instances. We'll leave that ultimate decision up to the pediatric surgeon, but it's unlikely he'll want to go that route. The blood and urine and scan results are pretty conclusive."

"What are the treatment options?" I asked. When I'd snapped that picture of my girls, I hadn't imagined that all that dark hair which had been in the way of Ivy's brown eyes might disappear with some kind of chemotherapy.

Who hadn't seen pictures of children's cancer wards? The little ones moving through the halls, IV stands in hand as they walked like pale, bald ghosts among the healthy.

"I don't want us to get ahead of ourselves, but I also want you two to be able to sleep tonight," Dr. Richardson said. "I want to emphasize that the prognosis on these types of cancers is pretty good.

"As long as there's no spread, and the lymph nodes aren't implicated, then there are a large number of treatment options. The least radical, though, may be laparoscopic surgery to remove the tumor."

Dr. Richardson and the others must have clearly read our blank faces staring straight back.

"It's pretty neat," the youngest doctor piped in. Her left breast read Joy Hanson, M.D. It did not have the alphabet soup embroidered after her name like the others. "The surgeon makes the tiniest incision, then uses a camera to visualize the tumor, then removes it. At Cleveland Clinic, they even use a robot."

A squeeze on Dr. Hanson's forearm from Dr. Richardson shut her up quick.

"What Dr. Hanson is saying is that there are many ways to execute the tumor removal. We'll tailor our approach to Ivy's stage and age and overall health."

"Can she live with only part of her kidney?" Tino asked.

"People are able to function normally for the remainder of their lives with only one kidney," Dr. Richardson answered. She sliced her hand through the air, hard. "That's enough for now. Go home. Get some sleep. Ivy's in good hands. She's already out—sedative."

Dr. Richardson took her charts and stethoscope and stood from where she'd been squatting in front of us. "Let's talk tomorrow."

She stepped from the room, the others bustling behind her without so much as a good-bye.

"What was it that you had to tell me?" Tino asked off-handedly. He did that a lot, half paid attention to the important stuff I said. Usually I'd soft-pedal the bad news, but I didn't have it in me today. I turned to him and said it plainly so that he would understand.

"I got fired today for calling off. I'm not sure we can even afford the co-pays for today's hospital visit, much less any kind of cancer treatment."

"We have the money, Roni. I wish you wouldn't worry so much about that. I'm able to provide for all of us."

"It's not just the money, Tino," I started. Though that was a *huge* part of it. Macho posturing and blatant chauvinism couldn't pay the bills. He seemed to have conveniently forgotten that half the reason I'd gotten the job at the spa was for the affordable insurance. Strohmeyer had a gold-plated plan that cost both arms and both legs. "It's the health insurance from Spasy. I'm going to lose that too."

2

Justin McPhee

June 3, 2007

"You can't fall in love with me," I said to the arm that Casey Cort had wrapped around my middle. From chest to hip, her warm skin was pressed against mine. Lying prone and naked on the right side of my bed, I could feel her breasts against my arm. I tried not to let that distract me from what I needed to say to her.

She peeled her arm from my middle and rolled onto her back. The lazy sweep of the ceiling fan was the only sound for a long minute. It had gone from near freezing to nearly eighty degrees in just a few hours. All the stupid phrases about waiting a minute for northeastern Ohio weather to change were true.

"There's no danger of that, Justin," she said, her reaction coming out on a long sigh. Casey's postcoital husky voice was disappearing like fog after the sun.

I wish I could say why her words hurt when they held the exact things I'd asked for: space, distance, understanding.

"I'm not marriage material either," I said. I needed her to know that what we were doing, what we had between us, was all there ever was going to be. I'd had too many women misunderstand sex with me.

They got attached.

I never did.

"No one's trying to get you to walk down the aisle, Justin, especially me. Morro, your dog, is your ride-or-die person…thing…being…whatever.

"You're not commitment material. Got it. I don't think a wedding ring is going to fall from the heavens and land on the third finger of your left hand along with a Catholic priest and a church full of our families. You're safe from me."

She lifted her right hand in a Catholic priest's sweeping absolution motion. "I pronounce you free from matrimony," she intoned.

The relief I felt was palpable. Casey didn't need me. She wouldn't be secretly planning a wedding, shopping for diamond engagement rings, or trying to tie me down.

"How is it going with Ron?" I asked. Just the mention of that guy's name made my gut twist. But he was the guy that Casey should marry. I didn't want her to forget that. I also wanted advanced warning if our time was going to be cut short by *that* guy's diamond ring landing on *her* left hand's third finger.

Casey lifted my comforter and pulled it up over her breasts. I tried to figure out if she was cold or if that meant there'd be no second round. In another ten minutes or so I'd be very much interested in a second round.

"Why are you asking me about this?"

She looked at me sideways.

"I don't *really* care." I heard my voice catch on that one. I cleared my throat. "Just curious."

"About what?" Her sex voice was all gone now. Midwest, friendly Casey, the one I had drinks with and shared legal gossip with was back. I immediately missed the other.

"What you're looking for," I said. "You've been engaged twice in the time I've known you."

Not that I approved of her choices. How did a defense attorney end up dating two prosecutors—one of whom was known to be corrupt when she was the exact opposite of that?

I'd never met a more ethical person than her. I figured they must have some other traits I couldn't see. Like big penises or something.

Or rich.

They'd both been that. I tried not to compare my modestly sparse apartment to digs I imagined were filled with smoking jackets and humidors. Rich was something I wasn't.

I hadn't even revealed to Casey that I was using a litigation loan to fund the Brighthill case. I'd be hellishly underwater without multiple settlements. Not only from the principal on the loan, but the interest wasn't favorable either.

In another world, the kind that cared for consumers, these litigation loan outfits would have been classed as loan sharks. But I lived in this world with its hypercapital-ism.

"I want to get married and have kids, obviously," Casey said, interrupting my thoughts. "If you've been counting my engagements, maybe you've also noticed that I'm thir-ty-six, not twenty-six like when you met me. Time is kind of running out."

"Time?" Casey had at least fifty, if not more, years be-tween now and death. "Is there something I should know?"

"Biological clock." Her sigh was deep. "It's ticking, okay? I won't be able to have kids forever. Not biologically at least."

I wasn't much older than her and I'd never thought much about it. The tabloids at the checkout counter were full of silver-haired male celebrities having kids. Now that I thought of it though, their wives were always well south of forty.

"And Ron Pinheiro is your choice?" I tried to picture her with my law school classmate...and couldn't. Instead I was somehow in the picture. I needed to clear that film loop out of my mind. Mentally, I played back our last few months, making sure we'd used a condom every time. I could only think of a single slipup, maybe two, but well outside any margin of error.

"I haven't ruled him out. He's available. He wants the same things."

"That doesn't sound like a lot of sparks, fireworks." That was something Casey and I did have. "When we're together it's like lightning in a bottle," I admitted.

"And what does that have to do with the price of tea in China?" Her squint pierced me.

"Nothing." I paused for a long second trying to think of why it was so important to me for Casey to admit that we were well suited. I couldn't think of a single reason. I turned the spotlight back on her. "You were saying?"

"Right. Ron. I like him a lot. We get on well. There's not much else I could ask for."

Butterflies?

Sparks?

I think she should have asked for those. In my mind, that kind of connection was essential. Would be essential for me if I ever found a woman I wanted to settle down with. One who had all of the qualities Casey had...plus that intangible something I couldn't quite put my finger on.

"Then where is he?" I asked.

"Beachwood, probably." Casey looked up at the ceiling. "Downtown in his office, maybe. Though he's trying to cut down on weekends. But he's on the cusp of junior partner, so he needs all the face time he can get."

"I didn't mean literally." Was she being deliberately obtuse, I wondered.

She turned back to me. Again, her hazel eyes were focused, intense. "Then what do you mean?"

I tried not to squirm under her scrutiny. Physically, I pushed back putting more distance between us. The sheets whispered across the mattress.

"If this is the guy for you, your future husband and all that, then why are you here in my bed, instead of in his?"

That got to her. Casey's face screwed up into a frown.

"You know what, Justin?" She lifted her left hand, spread her fingers wide, then lowered her pinky, then her ring finger then the others in quick succession while she counted. "In five, four, three, two, one, I'm not going to be in your bed either." Casey threw off the covers, stood, and pulled on her underwear. "Easy peasy."

"I wasn't trying to throw you out," I backpedaled. My hopes of a second go deflated at the same time a certain part of my body did as well.

"Could have fooled me," she said.

"Don't go." I was surprised to hear those words come from my mouth. I'd never said them to anyone before. This was getting confusing. I needed to talk to her again about Brighthill. I needed her help for my biggest case ever way more than I needed her in my bed.

Priorities.

"Why not?" Casey had her bra fastened tight and was pulling on first jeans, then a well-washed Ohio State T-shirt I'd found incredibly soft against my bare chest when she'd walked in my door last night. I'd hugged her long and hard once she'd gotten the dog greeting out of the way.

"I want to talk to you about the case." I hadn't mentioned it when I'd invited her over. But I'd planned to talk about it...after round two. Without that happening, it was now or never.

"Your big plaintiff's thing?" She was at socks and shoes. My time was running out.

"Have you considered my offer?" I rushed out. I got out of bed and copied her, pulling on my own underwear, then a Case Law T-shirt and some plain heather gray sweats. "I really need the help."

She didn't ask for clarification.

"It was two days ago. Have you asked anyone else? You must have some trustworthy friends from Case."

She was out of the bedroom and back in my living room. Casey sat on the couch, straightened her socks, then pulled on first one shearling boot and then the other. I'd always thought that Uggs were a play on the word ugly, but they looked cute and warm and snug on Casey even if it was creeping up to eighty outside.

I kind of wanted to scoop her up in my arms and keep us both warm. Instead, I channeled my energy into the case that was very much in need of better staffing. With Brighthill, I'd bitten off more than I could chew. My enthusiasm was not enough to make up for the sheer man hours I'd need to battle the firm representing Strohmeyer Breweries—Morrell Gates.

"I think I trust you more than most people I know." That was the absolute truth. "You never have an ulterior motive."

Casey cocked her head.

"You just accused me of having an ulterior motive."

"That's different."

"Is it really, Justin? Either you think I'm honest and truthful or you don't. When I told you I was only looking for something casual, I meant it. I haven't pushed you for anything more. I don't *want* to push you for anything more. We get along. This works between us. And if or when it doesn't, I'll pick up my toys and take them home."

"I very much want your toys here," I admitted.

"In what capacity?"

That one question made me feel uncomfortable. If I didn't shift something in the conversation, I was going to sweat or stutter or worse. Work was somewhere I could squarely land.

"Let's start with the case. Brighthill." I named the city with the growing childhood cancer cluster.

"A small city in the south-central part of Cuyahoga County. Yes, Brighthill."

"And Clearwater Park."

"Another tiny city. Are they towns? Villages?"

"Clearwater is a village. Brighthill is a city."

"Does that make a difference?"

"When it comes to this case? No. I want you on this. I want you to join me."

Casey's silence presupposed the big question.

Why.

"I know you're not the only lawyer in Ohio or even Cleveland for that matter. But I need someone with a strong moral compass. A clear sense of right and wrong."

"Me. You're talking about me?"

"Not a *Taxi Driver* reference is it?"

Casey shook her head.

"Our parents' generation—those were the moral and righteous ones. The greatest generation who fought the Nazis and ushered in a new era of civil rights."

I couldn't disagree. But our generation didn't have those big fights. Ours were of a different kind. For me, it was representing the little guy.

"You stood up for yourself against the Strohmeyers even though it was against your interest."

This was the thing I'd always admired about her. Whether it was Strohmeyer or Hudson, Casey always stuck with her principles even when it cost her.

"If I'd known how it would go, maybe I wouldn't have done it. It's easy to seem like a strong and moral person after the fact."

"Either way, the Strohmeyers are bad people." I paused. "They're killing children."

Casey blinked. She moved back just enough for me to know that what I'd said had hit the mark.

"That's a pretty strong charge. When I flipped through a few files, it seemed like a garden variety toxic tort case. God knows there's a history of those going nowhere in the courts. Look at the asbestos cases here in Ohio. The bar journal said there were like forty or fifty thousand in the court system. That was three years ago, I think. The federal EPA has to have hundreds, if not thousands of lawsuits going on at any given time.

"Honestly, Justin, dying kids or not, I'm not interested in signing up for something that's going to take the rest of my life. Is this your retirement plan? Is this why you're doing it? The payout?"

I tried not to be hurt by her reference to the nearly thirty-three percent payout I'd likely see from any settlement. Personal injury lawsuits and the large attorney's fees that resulted were a necessary evil. Someone had to advocate for the rights of the injured, and without incentivized lawyers to do it, no one else would.

"I have a Roth IRA for that."

"Then what makes this one so compelling? Something that's going to be worth putting all the time in? Because make no mistake...this will take *all* of your time, and if I sign on...a *lot* of mine too."

"It's the kids. I have thirty-five cases now. We have brain tumors, malignant bone cancer, astrocytoma, sympathetic nervous system tumors, neuroblastoma, malignant bone cancer, soft tissue sarcomas, acute lymphocytic leukemia, and so on."

"So on? I couldn't spell any of that, much less repeat it back in front of a judge and jury."

"Hopefully neither of us would have to."

"Your plan?"

"Settlement, of course."

"Seriously? Why would Strohmeyer settle? Have they given up their holier-than-thou, above-reproach attitude?"

Casey's huff of disbelief was a bit unsettling. I was used to our relationship having a certain balance. One where she came to me for referrals and advice, mentor/mentee conversations not one of working equals. Maybe if she were on this case with me, that part of our relationship would have to change as well.

"No. That's the problem. They think that if they throw all the paper in the world at me, that somehow I'm going to forget about the Mullinses, the Lowerys, the Beallses, the Serranos, the Poulins."

"Who are they?"

"The first families that retained me," I answered. When the first family, the Mullins, had contacted me, I'd thought they were off their rocker. Kids got cancer. It was no one's fault, or everyone's fault. But they'd invited me to their 'families of cancer patients' support group meeting, and when I'd gotten back to my office, I'd done some research and crunched the numbers.

One kid's cancer or two in a population was normal. Maybe not normal, but expected. Three or thirty strongly suggested an outside cause. Before I'd known what I'd be taking on, I had signed twenty families as contingency clients. Which meant that I'd fight for them, but that I'd have to finance that fight myself.

"It's Morrell on the other side?" Casey asked. I knew she was back to the same question as before—why did I want her on this case with me? Even I wasn't sure of the answer, though I knew somehow in my gut that she was essential to the future of the Brighthill families.

"You worked there."

It was one of the first things she'd told me about herself.

"For a single summer. Ten short weeks. The Strohmeyers got me fired, remember?"

"Do you want to know who's on the cases?"

"Is that going to make a difference?"

Hooking her into this was like fishing. I kept throwing out different bait and lures to see what would make her nibble. I wanted her any way I could get her.

"Maybe." I gave an exhaustive list of everyone who'd appeared on any pleadings.

"You have a photographic memory?" She raised her eyebrows.

"No. These cases are just important to me. I can't set it and forget it. I need to be down in the trenches."

"You want me in there with you?" Casey asked the obvious question.

"More than anyone." My answer was as honest as I'd ever been with her.

"No offense or anything, but what makes you think you can handle it?" Casey shrugged. "We're two common pleas lawyers and not even two full-time personal injury lawyers. I mean, I think I handled exactly one PI case and that was because the plaintiff had negotiated her own settlement and needed me to draft documents for her and collect the check."

Her thought process was completely logical.

From Casey's perspective, I wasn't the guy to do this. It could be handled better and maybe more efficiently by one of those firms who advertised in English and Spanish on bus benches and the glossy back cover of the yellow pages. It was time for me to lay all of my cards on the table. This hook had bait and a fly and a spinner.

"I worked at a big firm."

Her reaction was about what I expected. Her eyes had gone wide with shock.

"Wait? What? When? I met you at some bar association breakfast or luncheon...the domestic relations lunch, if I remember correctly. You were solo even back then."

She was right. I'd portrayed myself that way. Maybe even on purpose so we'd relate to each other better.

"I wasn't before, Casey."

"I think I'm going to need a drink for this." She made as if she were going for the fridge with its half bottle of wine left over from last night. Instead, she looked at her watch. Shook her head. "Crap, it's too early for a drink. Tell me."

I lifted and lowered a single shoulder, relieved I'd finally found the lure that was going to reel her in even if it was likely going to embarrass me.

"What makes you think there's going to be a story?" I asked. It was straight-up deflection. I was dreading the answer I'd have to give. Confessionals weren't fun when sober. Suddenly I too wanted to get myself a glass of that wine.

"Because this is Cleveland. No one leaves a firm voluntarily unless they're moving in-house or elevating to the judiciary. That's about it. You're not working as corporate counsel and I don't have to call you 'Your Honor.'"

"I did well at Case," I started. "Not like top-of-my-class good, but I was on the Health Matrix."

"What's that?"

"The law school's Journal of Law and Medicine."

"Seems apropos, then."

"How the law handles medicine has always been one of my areas of interest."

"So you weren't on *the* law review, but you were an editor on another journal..." She trailed off. I was giving her the edge pieces of the puzzle. She wanted the middle.

"I did on-campus interviews and got a summer associate job."

She rolled her hands in a "speed it up" motion.

"Where's the punch line?"

"It was at Dalton Lacey. Ron and I were in the same class there as well." Each new crop of lawyers was rigidly separated by their year of graduation at most law firms.

"Fuck me." This time she glanced at my kitchen clock. "I don't care what in the hell time it is."

She opened the fridge and pulled out a beer. She turned the label toward herself and nodded.

"Not a Strohmeyer brand." She opened the exact right drawer and pulled out the opener, popped the cap, then took a long swig. I was about to speak, but she held up a finger. Took the second longer pull.

"Dalton Lacey," she concluded, then took the tiniest burp. "That's how you ended up working on Hudson cases. Ron never mentioned it. Lulu certainly never did."

"I may not have left voluntarily."

"No. Duh. Did you rat out the son of a rich family? There aren't that many in this town."

"Not exactly."

"I don't want to pull teeth. Just tell me. I hate surprises. No doubt if I worked with you on these cases, I'd somehow be surprised. It's not TV. Let's get to it. I don't practice law in this way."

I swallowed. Embarrassment more than a decade old surged through my body.

"So. At a firm party, I met this girl."

"It's always a woman. Go on."

"At a party after the Indians won a game, I was sitting in a corner nursing a beer, not quite swigging like you. It was at some partner's house. They had a big screen before it was a thing. Anyway, this girl...woman, she came over. She was pretty and a doctor, a resident at the Clinic. I mentioned my article in the Health Matrix."

"On what?"

"Split parental consent in acute medical cases."

"So what, kid comes in to the hospital after falling off a mountain. One parent is a doctor and the other a Christian Scientist?"

"That's an extreme example," I said. I had to laugh because it was exactly the kind of hypothetical that would have been on a law school exam. They were always extreme when the real practice of law was anything but. "Basically, yes."

"So back to the woman who ended your firm career..." She did the "move along" thing again, only one-handed this time.

"It's not that complicated. We had some beer, some wine. Maybe a shot or two. We came back to my place..."

"I'm not sure I need to hear the rest of that sentence. I can imagine how it goes. Not that I'd have to use my imagination exactly…"

"We didn't have the kind of chemistry you and I do."

"And then…?"

"And then I went back to work on Monday. On Tuesday, I was called into the office of one of the big partners. You know the kind who have an office with a wall of windows that overlook the lake. I'd never met him. I thought I'd caught his eye, that he'd seen one of my memos, and he wanted me to work with him on some matter. Then…"

Casey lifted the beer bottle over one eye and her free hand over the other as if she were seeing something unpleasant. "Which was she, the resident? His daughter, his girlfriend, his fiancée, or his wife?"

"Wife."

"I don't need to hear more. They told you that you had no future. Gave you two weeks or six months' severance. You put in resumes everywhere else in town only to find your pedigree—now tarnished—opened no more doors. Then you hung out a shingle. Did I get that about right?"

Even with half a beer in her, she'd gotten it exactly right.

"It's why I sympathized with you at the luncheon. Not because what we did was even similar. You did something noble. I was just stupid. But the result was the same. Cleveland's top tier closed like an oyster. Nothing could pry it open to give us access to the pearl we knew was there and so close."

"You have the experience, then…for the case. To represent these plaintiffs against a big firm and bigger corporation."

"Just a couple of years. But enough to know how law firms work from the inside out. And everything they're doing on this case tells me that they have something to hide. Something big. Something so explosive that once I find it, they'll be willing to offer settlement in all the cases."

"What is that exactly? The exploding needle that's going to set the haystack on fire, to torture a metaphor. Bring Strohmeyer and Morrell to the table with buckets full of cash?"

"That's where you come in. I haven't found it yet. But it has to be somewhere in that office, hidden in plain sight. In one of those big boxes. I just need you to say yes, that you'll help me find it. The reward will be better than the pearl."

"Better?"

"'Millions of dollars on attorney's contingency fees' better."

In silence, Casey drank the remainder of the beer. Put the sweaty bottle on the counter with a resounding *thunk*.

With the promise of money and reprisal, I knew I had her.

3

It's been said that revenge was best served cold. I was starting to wonder if it was best served at all.

"Have you been listening to anything I've said?" my best friend, Lulu Mueller, asked. We were sitting on my couch. The windows were open and cool night air ruffled the leaves fat with early summer rains. One bottle of white and one bottle of red were uncorked on my new coffee table. I hadn't had a glass of either.

"No. I'm sorry. Please go back about a minute. What's up with Sinclair's divorce?"

"He's not pursuing it."

"Don't put that on me," I said. When Lulu and I had been in Poland and Germany chasing down my father's relatives, she'd passed on a request from Sinclair that I represent him in his divorce. I'd politely refused. "I'm not the only lawyer in Cuyahoga County, Ohio."

"I'm not putting anything on you." Her words said one thing, her tone the exact opposite.

"Your face says differently."

"When he asked if you'd represent him, I thought he was ready to move forward. To leave his wife and move forward with me. I thought when he insisted on leaving his family home and moving in with me that he was ready."

"And now you're not sure he's moved on?"

"If he doesn't love her anymore, if his daughter's in college, if he's moved in with me, why can't he leave his past?"

I shook my head. Women across the world for time immemorial have been having this conversation. How women ended up here again and again was a true mystery to me.

"Have you read any women's magazine printed in the last thirty years? I think every single pastel headline reads 'He's Not Going to Leave Her.'"

"I'm not the stupid side chick."

I fought to keep my eyebrows from my hairline. I'd very much agree with her on the first part at least—she wasn't stupid.

"What? I'm not. It's not like I'm his secretary or something."

"No, you're just the associate a partner schtuped."

When she frowned, I knew I'd probably overstepped.

"Casey. That's not nice."

"I'm sorry I said it the way I did. That doesn't mean it isn't true."

"Everything else in our relationship but that little thing is fine."

I didn't point out that a fully formed human woman with the title wife and the diamond band and joint home ownership to go with that wasn't "little."

"Is he still telling you what to eat, what to wear, and monitoring where and when you come and go?"

"He's just concerned," Lulu explained, though she couldn't figure out how to rearrange her face so it didn't reveal a tiny niggle of doubt.

"About what? You managed to feed and clothe yourself and get to and from work before you met him."

"He just wants me to dress more professionally so I don't kill my chances at partner for no good reason."

"Maybe. Maybe I could get on board with that, though I can't see why your...eclectic...style would be a hinderance. It's not like you show up in court with boho chic from head to toe."

For years Lulu had worn all the colors of the rainbow in nearly every outfit every day. She'd worn her clothes and used her put-upon speech patterns like armor.

"I'm not stupid. My mother's hand-me-down Chanel skirt suits are for the sexist judges."

"No one can discriminate against tweed," I acknowledged. "But what's with him wanting to drive with you everywhere and wanting to share a phone with you?"

These had been her most recent relationship grievances.

"The firm wouldn't allow that phone sharing, so it was a no go. That's just asking for a malpractice lawsuit for violation of attorney-client privilege."

"But the driving?" I asked in response to her non-answer.

"He just wants me to be safe. Winter driving in Cleveland can be a challenge. He cleans off the car and warms it up before I have to come downstairs from the apartment."

"He waited in the reception area of your salon while you were getting your hair done. Exactly how many car accidents have you had in the last twenty years you've been driving?"

"Well...zero."

"And how many has he had in his forty million years?"

"It's forty-seven years, and I don't know. Maybe half a dozen. Or a few more. He's been alive many more years as you've so kindly pointed out."

"So what in the heck is he protecting you from?"

"I think that's just an excuse. He's a man, you know? I think it's just hard for him to say he wants to spend time with me, so he uses this stuff as pretext."

I sighed inwardly. Lulu wasn't ready to call it quits or even call out Sinclair's behavior. I had so much on my plate that I couldn't really put her stuff on there as well.

"You can say no at any time. Okay? I just want you to get that. I'm here for you," I insisted.

"Are you?"

"You can call me. Anytime."

"But can I?"

"What do you mean? We're here now, not drinking the wine in front of us."

"But not Sundays. Not for a while like we do when you're in between fiancés."

"That's not fair." I wasn't going to take the bait. Yes, we'd often had brunch. Yes, Lulu and I had once spent more time together. But as life got more complicated and our careers got more complicated, I couldn't maintain friendships like I used to or even wanted to.

"Justin?" Lulu probed.

"Friend with benefits," I answered honestly.

"That's all?"

"Maybe colleague...for at least a little while."

"Colleagues?"

I told her about Justin's idea that I join him in his quest for justice for the injured children of Brighthill and Clearwater Park.

"Why would you do it?"

"Money. Experience. Revenge."

"Who's the defendant?"

"Strohmeyer."

"And the firm on the other side?" The way Lulu asked the question, I could tell she already suspected the answer.

"Nothing has changed in the last decade. Morrell Gates still represents the brewery. Ted is a partner. Shively's still there. The associates on the case are two people from my summer class."

"Oh, Casey. I feel for these kids. I mean, cancer, especially for kids, is no joke. But, honey, that's a lot. Morrell and Strohmeyer. Isn't Simon Brody in-house for them?"

"Yes to all of that," I cosigned.

"Oh, honey. Can Justin even do this case?"

"Why? Because he's just a common pleas lawyer like me?"

The resentment I'd held back for so long came rushing through in an unexpectedly blinding torrent. I was just about over being "fourth tier" Casey.

"No. I wasn't saying that. I went to law school with you. I worked with you on those pro bono cases. I know you have what it takes. I don't know anything about him. I grew up in a family of professionals. A degree doesn't mean as much as people make it out to be."

"He was at least high enough in his class to grade on to the second-best journal." If I was going to talk about Justin, then wine was in order. I leaned forward and gave myself a generous pour of red. I turned the full force of my gaze toward my best friend.

"Did you know he worked at Dalton Lacey?"

"*My* Dalton Lacey?" Lulu's hand was pressed hard in the center of her chest.

"There isn't exactly another that I know of."

"He isn't there now. He left to hang out a shingle?"

I took a large gulp. Then another. Then I told her the story.

Halfway through, Lulu had pulled the chardonnay and white wine glass close. She'd poured the golden liquid nearly to the brim and drank it down—twice. Lulu stopped drinking when I stopped talking.

"That sounds monumentally stupid." She shook her head. "Jesus."

"You're a Jew. Save the invocation of Jesus for the rest of us."

"Jesus *was* a Jew."

"Touché."

We clinked glasses and laughed like we used to when life wasn't so serious.

"Are you feeling some type of way about this?"

I loved that she'd slipped into her old speech pattern, even if it was for just a moment. I'd always cringed a little inside...thinking that it was put on. Never thought I'd miss it as much as I did.

"He fucked up and paid for it," I said. "I didn't fuck up and paid for it. I guess that's the very definition of life isn't fair. But maybe joining him on these cases could make things a little more fair."

"That kind of brings up a lot, Casey. Not gonna lie. That's like confronting your whole past. You ready for that?"

"It's been ten years. I'm tired of running. Morrell isn't going anywhere. The Strohmeyers aren't going anywhere. The Brodys aren't going anywhere. Neither am I. I was born here. Raised here. My ageing parents are here. I can't stay the victim. I can't keep hiding in juvenile, in criminal, in domestic relations. I don't know why I've conceded that big cases are for big firms."

"I never said that, did I?" Lulu took another sip. In my mind she was swallowing her guilt with her wine. It *was* her and everyone else, but more than that it was me. I needed to let both of us off the hook.

"The referrals you guys gave me, for example—and I'm not saying that I'm not grateful—but they were always small matters you didn't want to handle."

"But big for you, right?"

"Maybe in the beginning. I'm thinking that was my lack of confidence in myself. I got it into my head that somehow working at Morrell was going to confer some kind of training or knowledge or anoint me with oils or something. I kept pointing my fingers out in blame, but maybe I should have been pointing in. During our third year my real interest was in doing labor and employment. Why didn't I do that? There was no one keeping me out of that."

"Is that what you want to do? Labor and employment? Or is it personal injury. 'Cause that's what we were talking about. Whether you wanted to sign on to work with Justin while you're in the booty call business."

"The sex is not the point. It's very much beside the point, really. The point is that I limited myself. I've limited myself for ten damn years. I think maybe it's time to stop doing that."

"This is a three-glass-of-wine discussion," Lulu said before refilling her glass with white and mine with red. "What do you want, really?"

"I think that's what I need to decide. If I sign on with Justin, maybe the constant work and a big payout will give me the breathing space to make the big decisions I need to make. I've been so damned busy limping along, trying so hard to hold on to my pride that I haven't ever taken a breath. I could have, maybe should have ten years ago, moved back in with my parents. Taken more time to look for a job or figured out a way to open my practice on more than a shoestring."

"Woulda. Coulda. Shoulda. Casey..." Lulu shook her head.

"Yes and no. Going back and living in regret. That's stupid. Going back and thinking about why I made the decisions I did and not doing the same things again. That's wise. At the beginning of all this, all I wanted was a steady job in law that was rewarding and a family life that was even more rewarding. And you know what, I don't really have either."

"Those self-help books sometimes say if you don't have something, maybe you don't really want it."

That stung, hard. It was time to hear the hard things, though.

"Maybe that's correct. I keep saying I want marriage, but I'm half in with Ron and half out with Justin. I say I've wanted a legal career, but the cases I've taken have been tantamount to self-sabotage."

"Brighthill isn't that? Self-sabotage? It feels like Hudson all over again. Bright idea, but without the underpinnings to make it a successful endeavor."

I took another hit of wine. It was hard to hear, but she was probably right. I'd jumped from one legal specialty to another looking for the unicorn. This time, though, I felt like I was finally getting on the right path.

"No," I reassured both her and myself. "It's the wedge that could give me breathing room."

"But what if it's not. What if it's a case that goes on forever? Costs you everything. Money. Time. You keep sleeping with Justin and it muddles the guy thing even more. I think your idea that this is the way out is faulty thinking."

"Something's gotta change, Lulu. I've got to get off this roller coaster. Ten years has made me sick of it. Sick of dating. Sick of losing at love and at the law. I have to get off the fence and start making actual choices in my life."

"Oh, hon." My best friend looked at me like I was one fry short of a Happy Meal. Brighthill and Justin weren't perfect. I knew that. But maybe they could be a way forward.

"Nope." I shook my head vigorously. "No pity. Let's just drink to moving forward."

"Sounds like you made a decision."

"Two actually."

"You're going to do the cases."

"I'll talk to Justin a little more about his theory of the cases. Do some of my own research. If it all checks out, then yes, I think the change of scenery will be good."

"Number two?"

"I'm going to go all in with Ron. He's nice. I like him. I could probably love him. But I have to give it more than half a chance. So the next time he asks me out, I'll say yes and come to it wholeheartedly and with bells on. If he wants this like he says he does, then I'm ready to call his bluff."

"That's a lot of metaphors. Does that mean you'll cut Justin off?"

"I didn't say I'd made three decisions."

I don't know if it was the wine—we'd each had way more than half a bottle each—or just the relief of coming to some decisions, but we laughed together in a way we hadn't in ten years. Somewhere along the way it had all gotten too serious when it didn't need to be.

Life was too short for pity parties.

4

My daughter was going to die. I was sure of it even though not one doctor had said that out loud in the last two months. I doubt anyone in a white coat ever did. On television they used words like "terminal" and "hospice" instead of death. In real life, they didn't say anything at all.

I'd had to stop watching all of those shows. Kids on their death beds with beautiful actors running alongside gurneys had stopped being entertaining.

It was deathly quiet in the upper floor conference room. The young doctor, Joy Hanson, had called and asked us to come to a meeting about Ivy's care. I'd never heard of such a thing. Nothing had been happening while all the doctors talked around and around about having a care plan.

I kept hoping that one day very soon we'd just show up with Ivy, they'd run her into some surgical room that looked like a cross between *Star Trek* and *Star Wars*, a futuristic robot would operate, and then the cancer would be all gone. Maybe that was what was going to happen. Tino said I was too pessimistic. Everything was going to be fine, he'd promised before running out the door to get in more face time with Felix Braun before he went back to Germany.

When the last doctor arrived, closing the door behind himself, I pulled down my blouse and sat up straight. I was at the end of a twenty-person table in a large conference room. The chair next to me, one they'd probably reserved for Tino, sat empty, gently swaying back and forth on its metal seat pole. I put my hand on the chair's plastic arm to stop the movement. Then relocated my purse from my lap to the seat which kept the chair still. I was already nauseous enough without something spinning in the corner of my eye.

"Mrs. Garza," Doctor Richardson began. "Thanks so much for coming here this morning. Like Dr. Hanson said to you on the phone, we like to gather a care team when presented with a case like your daughter Ivy's."

"Care team?" I knew it was rude to interrupt, but since I was alone, I needed to make sure that I understood everything. There was no one else I could bounce questions off or compare notes with later.

"Care team. Multidisciplinary team. Treatment team. Health care team. We sometimes use those designations interchangeably."

"Are we here to talk about that laparoscopic kidney surgery you guys were recommending?" I was proud of myself. I'd practiced that word—laparoscopic—in the mirror until I'd gotten it right and could say it without a stutter.

Everyone at the table shifted uncomfortably. If my daughter weren't long for this world, if that was the reason for all the delay, I wish they'd just tell me. I was bold in my questions, but not that bold. My grandmother had always said not to invite death through the door. Instead, I just watched Dr. Richardson open and close her eyes slowly. Finally her brown eyes met mine, and she spoke.

"Yes and no."

"Okay. Oh my God—is there something else wrong?" I couldn't imagine what would be worse than death but was thinking I was about to find out. "Is it something no one told me about my Ivelisse?"

"No. I'm sorry. There's no alarm. We just want to come together and discuss the best treatment options available given the circumstances."

"Options? Circumstances? Aren't we here to schedule the surgery? Does she need more tests or something?" There'd been so many tests over the last weeks, I was starting to worry that her veins would collapse like a heroin addict's.

"Mrs. Garza." Dr. Hanson's voice was low and urgent. "Are you sure your husband can't be here?"

"I don't know. I don't think so. He's nearing a promotion at work, and it's been hard for him to get time off. When you guys called this meeting and canceled the surgery date, he went in, so he could save his off days for when we really need them."

"Oh. Okay." Dr. Richardson placed her hands flat on the brown fake woodgrain table. "Well, I just want to introduce you again to everyone, so you're familiar with what each person on the care team does."

Richardson went into a lengthy introduction about herself and her specialty in pediatric oncology, then she pointed to the doctor who'd called us and followed Richardson like a shadow, Joy Hanson. The two from the other day were an attending radiologist and oncologist. The newest were two different kinds of urologists. A hospital insurance administrator and a social worker made up the rest in the horseshoe formation around the table.

I shifted in my seat, straightened my blouse, then took a gulp from the sweating water glass in front of me.

"Okay," I said through still-parched lips.

"Let's talk about staging, first. Ivy's cancer is stage two renal cell carcinoma. There's an eight-centimeter tumor T2, which means it's remained local, no spread to the lymph nodes or any other organs. It's G2 well differentiated."

"Is that good or bad?" I could barely breathe. My heart felt like it was going to beat right outside of my chest. Through all that, I managed to spit out my next thought. "Isn't it the higher the number, the more serious."

"That's more or less true. It starts at zero and goes to four with some fractions in between. Ivy is at stage two, but an early stage two. Yes, an earlier diagnosis is always better, but this is not bad. We have a lot of treatment options ahead of us. Like we may have said during our last discussion, there's localized radiation and chemotherapy. That can shrink and kill the tumor and eliminate the effects the cancer's having on her. The alternative is a radical nephrectomy."

I searched through my brain. None of this was making any sense.

"Radical? Doesn't that mean removing the whole kidney? So she'd only have one in the end. One for the rest of her life?" I barely paused to suck in air. "Wait. What about the lap-laparoscopic—" This time I stuttered just a little on the long and complicated word but pushed on. "The surgeon would make a super tiny cut, then take out the cancer. I read up on it when I went home," I said without using the dreaded words "internet research." "Of course, I'll do what's best for Ivy."

"Here's why we wanted to talk. While your care team would go one way, the insurance company has different ideas."

I looked from Richardson to Hanson to the woman they'd introduced as the insurance company's hospital administrator. The pale woman with short red hair couldn't meet my eyes.

"What do they want?"

"Amalgamated Consolidated Health and Casualty—" the redhead spelled out before I could interrupt.

"ACHC," I abbreviated. That red and blue waving flag logo was on the corner of the cards I had in my wallet. It was at the top of all the explanation of benefit letters that came fast and thick in the mail, giving me a list of costs I was responsible for, bigger and bigger numbers with every new envelope opened.

"ACHC wants to balance cost and efficacy," said the woman who'd been introduced as the hospital insurance administrator. She finally looked me in the eye. "We think that the radial nephrectomy is the best balance of those two. Kidney removal will eliminate cancer and future risk of recurrence in that organ."

I looked between the doctors. The stone set of their faces didn't make me feel good. There'd been so much talk of the importance of saving her organ, giving her the best chance to live not only cancer-free but disease-free going forward. Lowering the chances that she'd be chained to a dialysis machine sometime in her life while waiting for a transplant. I'd researched the numbers. Eighty-four percent of the people waiting for a transplant wouldn't get one. I wasn't a betting woman, but those weren't good odds.

"Do you, Doctor Richardson, think that the removal is a good idea?"

"It's certainly a treatment option that's viable."

"Is it the *best* option, though?" I had to ask how something that was a last resort last month was suddenly the top treatment option this month.

"Given her age, preserving her organs would be our medical priority, but as the urologist can speak to, many people can live a long and healthy life with only one functioning kidney."

"Is that the cheapest option?"

"The radical option would be only a single procedure. There would be no need for further treatment. We think a single treatment would give you a jump on healing. It's the standard of care at the majority of America's public hospitals."

"Public hospital" was a stand-in for poor people. The first thing I'd learned when I'd moved north was that people paid lip service, but really didn't care about the poor or anyone who struggled. I turned to Dr. Hanson. Something about the young doctor's face made me think she'd be the one to tell me the truth.

"What's the downside? If she can live a long and healthy life with one kidney, why didn't you recommend it?"

"Every procedure has risks."

There was so much and so little in that. I was feeling like I had to pull the truth from the people in this room a single letter at a time. I wanted to get loud. I wanted to call them all liars to their lying faces. Then Ivelisse's face came before me like a vision. I tucked the roaring lion back inside, took a deep breath. Summoned the polite girl my parents had raised.

"What are the risks of her having only one kidney?" I asked, my voice calm and smooth even to my own ears. Even my grandmother would have been proud.

"There's the possibility of cancer recurrence from the same idiopathic cause. With only a single remaining kidney, it limits our treatment options."

"What else?"

"Sometimes the burden on the remaining kidney ends in kidney disease."

"And that's not cancer, this kidney disease?"

"No, it's reduced kidney function."

"That doesn't sound as bad as cancer. What happens if she gets kidney disease?"

"She'd get medication for hormone and blood pressure regulation. Also, she'd have dialysis."

"Dialysis? For how long? Until it healed?"

"No. Until a transplant donor could be found."

"Transplant?"

My mind spun. One minute it had been a tiny cut with a tiny probe to remove her cancer, maybe followed up with chemotherapy and radiation. Now they were talking about removing her entire kidney and all the possibilities if her remaining kidney didn't survive.

"Transplant is a worst-case scenario. Don't get fixated on that," the insurance administrator said. "There have been huge strides in transplant procedures and medicine. Anti-rejection drugs are a lot better."

I shook my head. I wasn't ready to hear any of this. I needed Tino here. He'd ask better questions. Get them to give our daughter the best treatment, not the cheapest treatment.

"What would you do if it were *your* daughter?" I pointed my question at Richardson, at Hanson, and any of them who had a child they'd loved and held close since birth.

"I'd appeal ACHC's decision," Richardson said as if she'd rehearsed the answer.

"Appeal?" I turned to the insurance administrator.

"That's certainly your right," she said. "But I think you need to consider the time this could take, your daughter's health, your policy caps, and her future ability to get insurance because of this preexisting condition." Probably realizing how negative she sounded, the administrator softened her tone. "We want Ivy to get better, obviously."

"How long do I have to make a decision?"

"We'll expect you to make a decision about the course of care within the next week," Richardson said.

"Will she be okay?" I'd been battling guilt so hard I hadn't been able to sleep. If I'd brought her in February or March instead of giving her ginger ale and crackers to ease her upset stomach, then maybe they'd have found the tumor when it was smaller. When this life-or-death decision wouldn't be on my shoulders.

"Tumors grow, but they're not mushrooms. Yes, you need to make a decision, but one week shouldn't make much of a difference," Richardson said.

"Thank you, I guess. I need to get home. Talk to my husband."

"Let's talk soon, then," Richardson said. "Circle back on your treatment options."

Everyone stood before I could, scurrying out the door like mice caught in the light.

5

"Thank goodness you're here. There's a blizzard of papers coming my way." I nearly wilted with relief, but didn't because I wasn't interested in emasculating myself. I needed help and she was here. That was enough.

"I'm not one hundred percent signed on. There's a lot I need to know before I hitch myself to your wagon."

I wanted to tell Casey, queen of metaphors, that she'd already "hitched" herself to my wagon more than once. Didn't seem like a good idea, though. Sexy, jokey Casey was long gone and serious lawyer Casey was in her place. I liked both of those Caseys well enough. Would integrate them if I had any say in the matter. But right now, I'd pick lawyer Casey if I had to choose.

Whenever someone came into my parents' house when I was a kid and they stood around boots on, coat at the ready, my mother would ask them if they were staying for tea. The tea was metaphorical, of course. It was more likely that she'd offer up Folgers coffee and then an Entenmann's pound cake that had been hastily pulled from the freezer and stuck in the oven for quick defrosting.

With that in mind, I motioned to the couch and Casey, raised with good Catholic manners like me, took the hint. She dropped her beat-up leather messenger bag, purse, and jacket on the plush surface.

"Everything still in the conference room?"

I took a key from my blotter and placed it in her palm.

"You not coming?" she asked.

"In a sec. Got lunch delivered. Need to check the reception area."

"Lunch." Her smile lit up her face. Warmed my heart. Made me grateful I'd thought ahead. "That's nice of you. What did you get?"

"Chinese green beans."

"Did I tell you that was my favorite?" Her smile, if possible, was even wider.

"You must have. Take a pad and pen from over there on my credenza. I'll be in with you in a couple of minutes."

I could smell the food before I saw it. The tip envelope was gone. My stomach growled a little, and for a moment I regretted skipping breakfast. I pulled apart the paper bag. Two staples skittered across the rug. I left those for the cleaners' vacuums and peered in.

Two little plastic soup containers sat atop green beans, and after tilting those to see under, my own favorite awaited: kung pao chicken. There was rice as well as chopsticks, forks, and napkins. Satisfied, I took my haul down the hall and to the conference room that was rapidly filling with paper-stuffed bankers boxes.

Casey was walking around, lifting and peering into each box methodically.

"Food's here," I announced after I propped open the door. The sole window wasn't enough to keep the room from feeling stuffy. It being a weekend meant we were in here alone. The violation of attorney-client privilege would be of little concern in an empty suite.

Casey took the bag, helped herself to the egg drop soup—choosing that over the wonton, which she offered to me. I took a seat across from her.

"What do you need to know?" I was ready and willing to do whatever it would take to get her on board.

"How many cases right now?" she asked.

"Thirty-two."

"Are all the kids under eighteen?" Her pace was rapid fire. I dropped the plastic soup spoon into the container. Now wasn't the right time to sink my teeth into a meat-filled dumpling.

"Yep."

"What's your theory of the case?"

"What is Strohmeyer most known for?"

"Other than the jingle, *You'll be a highflyer if you drink Strohmeyer...beer...?*"

"Not that."

"This isn't law school, Justin. I have no desire to engage in the Socratic method. Can you just answer the questions straight up?"

I ate a dumpling, then slurped at the broth giving myself time to formulate a perfect answer.

"One of the benefits," I started after I put the nearly empty plastic container on the faux wood table, "that they tout of the beer is that it's made from Ohio's purest well water. Not city water like a lot of other beers, but well water. My working theory is that while they're using that water, they are simultaneously contaminating the same water by causing stuff to seep into the groundwater and flow down to the few residences in Clearwater Park, and even more in Brighthill."

"What's the contaminant?"

"Mycotoxin."

Casey abandoned her own soup and spoon and picked up a pen. She clicked it open and started to scribble. She asked, and I spelled it for her.

"What is that?"

"It's a fungus."

"How does it grow?"

"You know how beer is made?"

"I vaguely remember the standard Strohmeyer tour from elementary school. God knows they wouldn't do anything like that nowadays. But isn't it just water added to hops and wheat, then that liquid is fermented? Hops make it bitter and the other stuff makes it less bitter, maybe? Obviously not. Just tell me."

"You're basically right. It's barley, water, hops, and yeast. The grains are steeped in hot water for an hour in a process called mashing. The liquid called wort is drained out and boiled with more hops and whatever flavorings there are. That's strained to get out the solids, then put in another stainless container with sugar and yeast for a week or two. Then it's shot with carbon dioxide for fizz or left to get fizzy from the leftover yeast."

"What's the waste from this? I feel like I remember the Strohmeyer tour guide stressing that it was a perfect process because there was no waste. The grains went to pigs or cows or were buried or something. But it's not like plastic or spent nuclear fuel that yields waste that won't degrade even after a thousand years or whatever."

"That's the hype that Strohmeyer still promotes. Don't believe it."

Life experience had made Casey a skeptic. It was one of the reasons I thought she was a good lawyer. She took nothing at face value.

"What are the dirty details, then?"

"The waste? It sits in pools on the Strohmeyer site. In the stagnant liquid, various fungi grow. These are the mycotoxins. They're a known carcinogen."

"Then how do factory farm animals eat it and not die? Is it because they don't live long enough to get cancer?"

"No, that's not it. It would kill them quickly. The spent grains are bound with clay or some other binder which neutralize the fungi. Animals eat it and don't die...not from that at least."

"Then how are you alleging it gets to these kids and has enough time in their systems to disrupt cell growth and cause cancer?"

"Those pools I just told you about? They sit. Often for days or weeks while it drains. Because it's often wet here, the ground can be saturated for a long time. In the summer, they sometimes spray it with water to keep it cool, so it doesn't get hot like compost and rile up the neighbors with the off-putting smell. Sometimes it's just rain. Drenches it, seeps right into the ground, through the porous soil, and down into the water table. Which isn't that deep, not in this part of Cuyahoga County at least. It's how some municipalities are able to survive on well water alone without Cleveland city water and sewer services."

"What do the folks in Brighthill do for sewage?"

"Septic."

"Seriously? I thought those were only in very rural areas. Not a couple of miles outside of the city."

"Strohmeyer doesn't use septic, of course. They have too much waste. They have a special sewer hookup."

Casey scribbled, turned to what I think was page three on the pad, and scribbled some more. She opened her green beans, lifted her fork, and chewed thoughtfully for a good five minutes while her mind processed the information.

I followed her cue and added white rice to my chicken, mixed them, and ate.

"So let me get this straight," she said after she put down her fork. "You're suggesting that these mycotoxins...fungus...*fungi*...grow on the spent grains. Water washes it all down to the water table and it enters the well system. Then what? The little kids drink this contaminated water and boom—cancer?"

I finished chewing the small piece of chicken I'd picked up with chopsticks, swallowed, then nodded.

"More or less."

"What experts do you have lined up?"

"I have a few names, have even had a few conversations with one woman, which weren't free. I haven't bitten the bullet yet and paid a full-on retainer for her services."

Casey took a few more bites of her beans, then replaced the clear plastic lid and moved her half-eaten soup, the rice, and the fortune cookies aside, leaving a large clear space before her.

"What's the oldest case?"

"You mean which was filed first?"

Casey stood and patted her hand on the boxes. I jabbed my chopsticks toward one that was on top of a stack.

"Ciara Mullins. Parents, Todd and Marianne."

She hefted the box with their names clearly displayed on the side, moved it to the closest chair. Lifted the lid.

"You filed a complaint. Any service problems?"

"No, thank goodness. They're local and unlike every other corporation, they are not 'headquartered'"—I air quoted—"in Delaware or Nevada or some other corporate tax haven."

She shuffled through some more paper.

"They filed an answer. No counter claims or joinder."

"Yes and no."

"Motion to dismiss, rule twelve, subsection 'B' six. Did you file a brief in support of your motion in opposition?"

I hesitated.

"I got an extension."

"They agreed?"

For as long as I could remember, it had been local practice and common courtesy for defendants to give plaintiffs a single extension without need for excuses or reasons. But it was becoming more common for defendants to push back, especially in cases that were likely to be publicized or highly contentious like this one had the potential to become.

"In exchange, I think, for me giving them a preview of how many more plaintiffs I have on deck."

Casey rested her elbows on the table, then put her chin in her cupped palms. I tried not to shrink back as she scrutinized every inch of my face.

"So what are you doing? What's your plan here?"

"I'm not sure what you got exposed to at Morrell, but at Dalton, there were a ton of insurance defense matters. It was their bread and butter back in the day. Basically, the big car manufacturer we represented would just settle every case as it came down the pike. I figured we'd do that. Take our third, and then move on to the next. Same experts, same basic discovery, and so on."

Again, Casey was quiet for a long moment.

"You remember Lulu, right?"

I nodded. Lulu Mueller was a close friend of Casey's who worked at Dalton Lacey. She'd probably come in a couple of classes behind me. Had started a few months after I'd left.

"Who could forget her sparkly rainbow winter coat? She always stood out at young bar functions," I recalled.

"Are you too old for those now?"

"Sparkly coats?" She gave me a comically withering look. "The young bar is for lawyers under forty, Casey. I'm not that old yet."

Her gaze swept over the top half of my body. I studiously ignored the tingly feeling that overtook me for a second too long.

"Anyway," she continued, "I was talking to Lulu and I think the biggest problem I've had over this last decade is that I let the past cloud my judgment. My goal this year, starting right now, is to level up. If you want me in this, then we can't do it like some run-of-the-mill, bus-bench-advertising ambulance chaser."

I tried not to be hurt at the less than charitable observation.

"So what magic pixie dust do you plan to sprinkle over
this?"

"I think we—"

"We?"

"You. I think *you* need to consolidate these cases. Make
it a class action."

"Class action? Jesus, those are a lot of work."

"One time. You'd have to only do the work once. The
hardest part would be, I guess, recruiting more families. If
you have more than thirty, then I think you have that part
down."

"You think it could work?" I loved Casey's mind, and
cursed my own for not thinking of this simple but elegant
solution to these cases.

Her nod was emphatic.

"So what was your plan, to get a few thousand here
and a few thousand there? How would that compensate
the families? How would that get Strohmeyer to truly stop
doing this polluting?"

"You have a point."

"Okay, I'm going to put this stuff away. Let's finish
lunch in your office away from all these papers, then we'll
make a plan to draft the rule twenty-three motion."

I stood and went around to her side of the table.

"Can I kiss you first?" I asked after I'd already pushed
my lips against hers.

"What's that for?"

"Bringing you on is the best decision I've made in a
long time." Cancer and fungus forgotten, I leaned in for a
second one, then swept the stuff from one side of the con-

ference table to the other, slammed the open door shut with my foot, then took her into my arms. Courts were closed on weekends, motion drafting could wait.

6

"Tino, come here. You should see this."

I had Ivy's laptop on my thighs. The hot plastic was nearly burning a hole through my nightgown, but for a moment I didn't care about the heat. Tino had bought the computer for Ivy last Christmas. It was supposed to help her with her schoolwork. She hadn't been to school much since before Easter, though. Since we'd gotten the diagnosis, school and nearly everything else had come to a grinding halt. Now the school year was all but over, so she didn't need it anyway.

Day after tomorrow was the decision deadline. Once again, we were meeting with her "team" of doctors to set a path forward for her treatment. I still hadn't made a decision on which path that would be—the easy one that could leave her vulnerable to lifelong dialysis or the hard one which would involve a health insurance company death match.

When the doctor was handing Ivy to me moments after she was born, I never would have imagined this...cancer. My thoughts had been full of first birthdays with cake on her little chubby face. Her first day of kindergarten. Her quinceañera. Her first boyfriend. Her first broken heart. Tino walking her down the aisle.

Nowhere in those first moments of motherhood did I think about emergency rooms or cancer wards or a nephrectomy—a word I'd never wanted to learn. A word I didn't want to know now.

Never kidney removal. There had to be no mom ever who'd thought of that while trying to put a newborn baby on the breast for the first time.

Tino finally wandered in to our bedroom a few minutes later, his Blackberry in hand. He was still wearing his button-down work shirt, khakis. It was like living with the dad on that black-and-white show...*Leave it to Beaver*.

I always wondered how that TV dad could eat dinner and play with his kids, all the while in a shirt and tie. The short answer was, he didn't. Because that dad wasn't more than a cardboard character playing a role.

Tino didn't because he was more concerned with work than the girls he'd helped to create. I mostly left food for him, under foil, in the oven. What had started out as a rare thing—Tino's absence from family dinner—was now a regular weekday occurrence. I assumed he ate when I was doing bath time or story time or bed time, because there was always a dirty plate on the kitchen table in the morning.

"What do you need, babe?" he asked, never once looking up from that tiny plastic gadget in his hands. I wanted to snatch it away, throw it out the window into the never-ending rain and snow Cleveland delivered for more than half the year. "The kids are asleep, right? I wanted to catch up on emails," he continued still not looking me in the eye.

Not spend time with me. Never time with me. We were more roommates than co-parents. And more co-parents than a married couple. Now that both girls could sleep for ten hours a night, if not more, I thought things would be different.

I wanted to kiss, to cuddle, to watch a movie. To whisper and laugh in the dark like we used to in those early days when spending time together had felt like the world's most precious gift.

Not to mention sex. I missed that too. My thoughts about us as a couple seemed stupid and ridiculous in light of what Ivy was facing which is why I directed much of our conversation toward our daughter and not ourselves. Fixing us would have to come later, I guessed.

"How many emails can you have?" I grumbled. "Aren't you in the brew room most of the day?" From what I could figure, they added water to grains. Fermented it. Put beer into bottles, rinsed and repeated. How many emails could there be about what amounted to one of the world's oldest and simplest ways to get people drunk?

"That's why I have a lot of emails." Tino barely glanced in my direction. "Mostly Felix Braun asking me questions. I really think that he's going to recommend my promotion. It would mean enough money that you wouldn't have to think about going back to work."

I was so done with that "barefoot and pregnant" broken record. I *wanted* to work. Somehow working bruised Tino's fragile male *quien es más macho* ego and around and around we went. He never seemed to understand that the same pride he had in his job I had in mine.

After Ivy was born, and certainly after Stella, he didn't understand why I wouldn't want to be at home all day carpooling, chasing kids, cleaning, and cooking. Behind his back, I called it the four fucking Cs. Although with a fifth fucking big-ass cancer C, I missed worrying about just the other four.

"I was thinking of calling Juanita again," I admitted. "See if I can get back on at Spasy."

"You shouldn't have to do that. Give me a couple of weeks. They're going to make a decision by the end of the month."

"Tino, we don't have until the end of the month," I said. "Once we go back to the hospital, no matter what we decide treatment-wise, the bills are really going to start coming in. Co-pays. Medications. Who all knows what else."

Money was always the excuse I used. The almighty dollar ended conversations quickly. There was no denying the collection letters that arrived in the mail. Tino's pride couldn't pay the bills. Although I didn't know why I was pushing this now.

Cancer treatment and a full-time job did not go together, and I knew that. No matter how much I missed my autonomy and missed having money I didn't have to account for, all of my attention needed to be focused on Ivy. I gave Tino the evil eye until he looked at me.

My husband sighed, put the phone in his pocket. Looked me full in the eye for the first time in days.

"You said you found something?"

I turned my own email account toward him.

"You see this?"

"I can't read it at that angle. Just tell me."

"Our insurance will end in two weeks. They say we can keep it with something called COBRA. But we have to pay for all the insurance ourselves."

"How much could that be. It was only a couple hundred per paycheck."

"It says here fifteen hundred sixty-three dollars."

"Give me that." He snatched the computer from my lap. Scrolled up and down through the email two times before he handed the laptop back. "That's crazy. We'll just switch to Strohmeyer. It was kind of expensive before, but we don't have a lot of options now."

"I went through the papers downstairs. I think that's an answer, but there's a ninety-day waiting period before it will kick in. Dr. Richardson said we could wait a week before we decided what to do, but not three more months when it's already been two."

Tino turned and walked out of the room.

"Where are you going?" I knew my voice was too loud, might wake up Stella, but I needed my husband. I couldn't just wave a magic wand.

Google was turning into a sort of magic answer cube. Maybe those fast-forwarded movie scenes where the characters did research had a grain of truth. Maybe there was always a needle in a haystack, I just needed enough patience to look for it. I only took a beat before I started typing.

I typed "cancer" and "Brighthill" into the laptop. The result was surprising. When Tino came back in, I dropped my shoulders. Waved him over. "Come here."

Tino got on the bed next to me, his weight on top of the comforter pinning me in place under it. I turned left, caught his eye again. He let his own shoulders down. Fixed the pillows so he was propped up like I was.

"What's that?" He pointed toward the monitor. "Did you figure out a better treatment the insurance company would be willing to pay for?"

"I was looking on Google. I put in cancer and Brighthill and this came up."

I angled the laptop toward him so he could see what I had. He glanced at the screen, then at me.

"You're going to burn your legs."

Tino got up and returned with the lap desk from the corner of the room. He lifted the laptop and propped the cool Styrofoam bead-stuffed cotton on my hot legs marked with bright red welts. The computer's fan went from a whirring, high-speed jet-engine sound to a lower, car air conditioner sound.

"It's this website." I pointed.

He looked at the banner at the top, white letters on a fire-engine red background. "Brighthill/Clearwater Cancer Cluster," he read. The picture of dark and ominous-looking smokestacks against a dark Cleveland sky went without comment. "What's all this about?"

"This lawyer..." I scanned the page again, my eyes pinging from the injury stuff to the smokestacks to the word cancer until they landed where I needed them to. "Justin...something Irish. McPhee, that's it. He's looking for people who have kids who've gotten cancer and live in Brighthill or Clearwater Park."

"Looking for them? Lawyer? Not a doctor? What is he going to do with them when he finds them?"

"It says here that he represents them."

"Who is he going to sue, God?"

"God is not responsible, Tino," I huffed. "This is Cleveland. One of the manufacturers in Clearwater Park or here in Brighthill or maybe even Independence or Brooklyn Heights probably poisoned the air or soil or water."

"Veronica," he said in that voice I hated. The voice that said I wasn't smart enough to understand the ways of the world or men or beer and now cancer.

"Don't 'Veronica' me. It says here, 'Our toxic tort attorneys can help you hold the liable parties accountable for the harm their negligence has caused you and your loved ones. We can aggressively fight for your rights in a variety of cases. No family deserves to suffer in silence.'"

"Toxic tort. What does that mean?"

I quickly looked the term up on Wikipedia.

"It says here that it's when someone's been injured by a chemical or dangerous substance or something."

"Everyone who has cancer doesn't sue. It's not like she was rear-ended by a tractor trailer. It's just a thing that happens."

"While you've been busy brewing, I've been researching. Cancer is not just a *thing that happens*. It's caused by carcinogens. That's kind of a known fact now. Maybe not a hundred years ago. But now.

"All the chemicals in the air and water and food get into our body and make us sick. It's always caused by something. Old people can't sue because they've been exposed to every single bad thing in the environment for a hundred years. Ivy is different though. She's a kid. Her life has been limited to here and San Juan. That's not a lot of exposure."

"God just—" he started again as if being a Catholic made it so that we had to accept cancer like we had to swallow the host at communion.

"God doesn't give cancer. It's not some punishment handed down for sinners or the unbaptized. But any number of these manufacturers might have. I'll send an email to him. I just want to meet with him. It says here on the website there's a cancer cluster. If that's true, then I might want to do this."

"This? What's *this*? Sue? We're not those kind of people."

"What kind of people is that?"

"The kind who try to blame others for their problems," he said.

"Cancer is Ivy's problem. My problem. Our family's problem. But it's not our *fault*. It's not pointing blame fingers. It's someone taking responsibility. Who's going to pay for these bills?" I vaguely gestured to the little desk that sat in the corner of the dining room a hallway away. The one I used monthly to rob Peter to pay Paul. "Who's going to pay when the insurance runs out? Who's going to pay for the good expensive treatment that can make her well instead of the cheap bad treatment that may leave her sicker than they found her?" I swallowed hard. Held back the tears that had yet to run dry. "Us? We didn't cause this. The person…people…business responsible needs to help pay for this."

"Veronica—"

"Don't 'Veronica' me like you're my dad." I paused, then realized I'd probably made up my mind for good. "I'm going to meet this lawyer."

Tino did a double take. I knew he'd thought I'd been consulting him. Looking for his buy-in. I might have married young, but I was growing up. I was an adult who could make her own decisions. Who didn't need her husband's permission for anything.

"When will you make an appointment?" he asked.

"Tomorrow, if I can."

"Who'll watch Stella?" He asked this as if I were going to leave my four-year-old home alone with a pointy knife and electric sockets for company.

"Day care."

"I thought they didn't take drop-ins."

"They might do me a favor."

"So why did you ask me if you have your mind made up?"

"I don't have it made up. Not like you did when you decided that we had to move to Cleveland and you accepted a job before telling me. Not like *that* at all." I stopped for a moment. Tried to scrub the old resentments from my voice. Tried for a softer tone. "I'm telling you because I want to find out more from this lawyer. He might be able to help us." My shrug was a little bit exaggerated, but it was to protect us both. Me from disappointment. Him from emasculation. "Maybe it won't be anything."

"And Ivy, what about her?" Tino asked, ticking his fingers like the children were solely, one hundred percent my responsibility.

"She's going to her last week of school. She feels well enough."

"You've got it all figured out."

"All figured out. You mean child care?" I couldn't help that my voice was getting louder. "I have to have it all figured out because you are the opposite of helpful. Move to Cleveland away from our families. Move away from Tremont because Brighthill is closer to Strohmeyer. You've isolated me from anyone who could help me. I have to *figure it out* because I'm alone here. I love my girls, but I can't give up my whole life to make sure someone feeds them and wipes their butts."

"Isolating you? Wiping butts? Is that how you see our marriage and motherhood?"

"How should I see it, Tino? I haven't seen my parents since Christmas two years ago. Mrs. García? Mrs. Suarez? The two *tías* I got close to in Tremont. Haven't seen them since Christmas. I'm here in Brighthill. Not another Boricua within spitting distance. Just a bunch of people who think I'm weird and too brown and too loud and too different."

"I bought a house for our family. That's the American dream. I'm killing myself for a promotion so you never have to work again and this is the thanks I get?"

"The thanks *you* get?" I slammed the lid of the laptop shut. Put it on the nightstand. "You have all the answers. Maybe you should give Ivy chemo or radiation or take out her kidney. Since you're such an expert, maybe you're a surgeon now. I'll see this McPhee guy and you finish medical school. Let's see who can heal our daughter first."

7

Instead of Ann, I was starting to think that "self-sabotage" should be my middle name. I shoved my cell in my coat pocket as I made the two-minute walk from my office building on Public Square to Justin's.

The partners at Dalton Lacey had just come back to Cleveland from their annual meeting in St. Croix. Nothing had been made formal yet, but the good word was that Ron Pinheiro was going to make partner. Only junior partner, he'd said on the phone just now, but a law firm partner nonetheless.

In today's economic climate, a partner of any kind was a big deal.

A really big deal.

It wasn't tenure at a school or university, but it was the closest a lawyer could get to permanent job security besides being a federal judge. I knew firsthand how someone could fuck that up.

Ron had wanted to celebrate that with me—right now. He'd proposed a long boozy lunch that would have likely led to a long late-night date night at his place. But I'd turned him down. That was the reason I was kicking myself, not literally of course, but I was yelling at myself nonetheless.

All that celebratory together time would probably have solidified my place in his life as a woman with the title "girlfriend." It could all have led to something more like fiancée or even wife.

That's what I wanted, something more than casual with a man like Ron. Someone who was smart and rich and successful.

There, I said it.

I glanced up at the sky to see if God was going to strike me down with lightning.

Waited a beat.

Nope.

Not today.

My freshman roommate in college—Amrita Reddy— she'd wanted to become a doctor. She'd been from one of those immigrant families that was more success focused than mine had been. While I'd been doing a little too much post-girls' school partying and blowing off boring gen ed classes, she'd diligently been attending biology and chemistry labs at eight in the morning, freshman year.

I'd been in awe. With a work ethic like that, I knew she'd get her medical degree no problem. She wouldn't be waylaid by boys or sex or babies like so many other women were.

Or so I'd thought.

My freshman residence hall had been littered with the stories of daughters only there to fulfill their mothers' abandoned dreams. Amrita was supposed to have been different.

On the same day my college boyfriend had dumped me at the end of first quarter senior year, Amrita had come into the dining hall sporting a diamond on her left hand. We hadn't been in each other's pockets the way we'd been during freshman year, but I'd been shocked as shit to see a huge rock on her finger when she hadn't been dating anyone at school. Because even at a school as big as Ohio State, gossip was a varsity-level sport.

When I'd rushed over to congratulate her, I was surprised to hear her say to her table of friends that she'd be getting married right after graduation and that she'd pulled her medical school applications.

"Wait—why?" I'd asked, not caring that I was rudely butting into someone else's conversation and ignoring every etiquette lesson from my strict Catholic education. "You made it through all the pre-med classes, and aced the MCATs."

She'd looked at me then. Square in the eye. It wasn't a look I think I'll ever forget. It was equal parts amusement, anger, and resignation.

Deep resignation.

"My father says he's going to use the money he'd have spent on school for my wedding. There's no need to send me to school to *be* a doctor when they've arranged for me to *marry* a doctor." She'd twisted the ring around while she'd talked, the sparkle disappearing and reappearing.

Amrita had never become the doctor she'd wanted to be, even though I kept waiting for it to happen, for someone's mind to be changed. Instead, she'd stayed in Columbus working in various state senate staffing jobs while her holiday cards filled up, first with a husband, then with three children in quick succession. Then she'd moved to some suburb of Cincinnati in northern Kentucky and had given up on working outside of the home altogether. I couldn't help but think the medical profession was worse off for her father's decision.

After she announced her engagement, I'd prided myself on being different. I doubled down on school after that meeting in the cafeteria. I'd applied to law school, graduated with honors, and when I couldn't get a job, had hired myself.

Amrita, I thought—not that I'd ever say it out loud in a room full of feminists—had failed herself. Not stood up for what she'd wanted. Not that she probably didn't love her kids, or even eventually found love with the husband her family picked out for her, but with every holiday card or the occasional group email with the women from Lincoln Tower, my freshman dorm, I wondered if she'd given up.

When someone brushed by me on the sidewalk, I blinked and tuned back into my surroundings. I had no idea how long I'd been standing there going down memory lane. I needed to stay away from lingering in my past; it was a virtual minefield.

Ron's call had brought all of that back, though. That internal debate, the struggle most women only have surface conversations about. I'd had it with myself dozens of times.

I'd be embarrassed to admit it out loud, especially to someone like my best friend. Lulu came from a family of women with educations, who'd always worked high-powered jobs. But I'd had fantasies where my dad walked me down the aisle.

First it was to give me away to Tom, then Miles, and now to Ron. In those daydreams, all my problems with money and loneliness were solved after I said, "I do."

Everything got better.

I liked that fantasy a lot. I could see myself married to a man with a solid income. Living an upper-middle-class lifestyle. Having the kids I still thought I desperately wanted. In the dark of night when I lay awake in my bed, I was happy to trade my search for passion, and a soul mate for the certainty of stability, predictability.

In my waking hours, I'd just turned Ron down. And if I were honest with myself, completely fucking honest, I was falling for Justin.

He'd laid his cards on the table. We weren't anything to each other. Could never be anything. Which begged the question: Why was I on my way to 75 Public Square and Justin's office, instead of on a tram headed east toward my destiny?

I shook my head to clear it of everything that had just jumbled up in there, unwelcome.

Ron.

Amrita.

My feelings for Justin.

What my life might look like a year from now with or without Justin.

I vacated my spot on the sidewalk to which I'd probably gotten squatters rights, then entered Justin's building and took the elevator to his sixth-floor suite.

"I'm here to see Justin McPhee," I announced to his receptionist.

She nodded.

"Casey Cort, the attorney, right? You've been here a few times. I'll remember you and your cute name from now on, because Justin said you're working on a pretty big case together. If you know your way, you can go on back. He's expecting you."

"Your name again?" I asked. I think I'd been too preoccupied with my own case crises every single time I was here to remember if she'd introduced herself. I used to feel bad about my not-so-great memory. Now, I just asked again and moved on. Found out that no one was ever offended. I'd wasted too much of my late twenties and early thirties worried that they would be.

"Ernestine Butler," she answered. "Everyone calls me Ernie."

I took the hand she proffered and shook it over the high reception counter. She stood, released my hand, and turned to a man who'd come in with two white plastic bags that looked to be filled with Styrofoam containers.

"That for McPhee?" Butler asked.

The man nodded. She handed him a few singles and he gave her the bags and then a jaunty salute before going back to the elevator.

"These are for you." Butler handed the bags to me. "Mind taking them back?"

"No. Thanks. I think this is our lunch," I said, lifting them high and turning toward the back of the suite.

I weaved my way through the waiting room chairs, and followed the hall to Justin's office. I knocked with my elbow. It smarted a little, but the soft noise was enough to get his attention. He opened the door.

"I come bearing gifts," I said.

"Lunch. You're just on time, then."

Justin nodded at me, then he looked at me for a split second too long as if he'd expected a different type of greeting. I realized then when I showed up at his apartment with food in hand, I usually kissed him hello.

I leaned in, kissed him square on the mouth. I probably needed to have a conversation about the two different relationships we might have. Work was work and that other thing we did was something else entirely, and probably shouldn't be mixed with our lives downtown.

Later.

We could talk about that...later.

"I ordered a fried fish sandwich, cod, a tuna melt, coleslaw, and fries. You can have your pick of whatever you like," he said. "I'll get us something to drink. Pop okay?"

"Is there iced tea or something like that?"

"Yeah, I'll be right back."

While he was gone, I fiddled through the bags. Looked at all the choices. Pulled out the fried fish. Took the coleslaw over the fries. Potatoes were never a good look on my hips. Cabbage had to be the lesser of the two evils even with all the mayonnaise to drown it all.

I was trying to figure the best way to arrange everything so as not to make a mess on Justin's couch, when he came back in brandishing a 7 Up in one hand and the promised iced tea in the other. He set my tea down carefully, then put a hand on my cheek and pulled me in for a kiss. Not a trivial kiss either, but one with a lot of tongue suggesting he wanted a repeat of what had happened between us only a few days ago in his conference room. Not my proudest professional moment, for sure.

I pulled away, because his office, on a weekday, seemed like the wrong place and time.

"Justin...I don't think—"

"I'm sorry," he apologized. "I just can't be in the same room as you without wanting to kiss you. I know we should keep work and the...the other separate. But I just had to do that."

"We need to talk..."

"Won't happen again," he said in a way that suggested it would happen again and again if I didn't do something to change the dynamic between us. I decided my best bet would be to lob in a mini-grenade of sorts.

"Ron made partner. It's not official yet, no *Crane's Cleveland Business* announcement or anything like that, but it's for sure going to be announced on July first."

"I'll call him."

When my hand flew up, Justin's own lifted in a halting motion.

"After the official announcement comes down. Don't worry. Your secret's safe with me."

"Thanks." I'm sure my relief was palpable.

"So partner. Dalton Lacey. What do they pay? Maybe a couple hundred thousand, quarter million a year. More than they paid back when I was there. Either way, that's not bad for Cleveland. He could buy a house, get married. His wife wouldn't have to work."

I put aside the half-finished food, tucked the Styrofoam closed.

"Not good? I thought you liked fish?"

"Very good. I'll have the other half for dinner, later," I said. I didn't share that only eating half of restaurant portions was a weight loss tip from a magazine I'd picked up in the dentist's office.

He'd already seen me naked, but I didn't want to bring any more attention to my hips than necessary. Give him an excuse to cut our other activity short.

Not until *I* was ready.

I was definitely *not* ready.

"So, Ron...you need to go?" Justin asked after he took a last bite of his own lunch and balled up his napkins.

"We agreed on meeting...later." I waved my hand in dismissal.

"What do you have for me?" Justin's palms were up, ready to receive.

"I did the research. That's here." I handed him a huge banded stack of precedential cases printed off from Lexis-Nexis just this morning. "This is a draft of the class action certification motion I think we should file." I handed him my second copy of the twenty-page motion. With a table of contents and a list of the cases I'd just handed him, the complete document would be about thirty pages in total.

"Everything's in the war room. Let's go in there," he urged.

I plucked a brand-new yellow legal pad from my bag along with the Cross pen my parents had given me for graduation—sporting fresh new ink—and followed him to the conference room at the end of the hall.

He stuck in a key and turned the lock.

"Oh, I forgot," he said before he pushed the door open. He fished in his pocket, the change jingling. "These are for you."

He handed me my own key ring, three newly made shiny brass keys gracing it along with a tiny steel book. I took them and brought the book up to my face for closer examination.

It read *Boke of Saint Albans* in tiny raised letters.

"Oh my God! That's so cute!" I screamed. My voice was loud enough to wake the dead, or bored lawyers. Sometimes those two looked the same. The hug I couldn't help but give him was spontaneous and curiously one-sided after that last kiss. I tried to subdue my reaction a little with what I said next. "I love it. How'd you get it?"

"There's this new site online that my sister, Stacey, likes. You can order practically anything that's handmade."

"Thanks so much." I kissed him lightly on the cheek. That seemed like a non-rule-breaking move, unlike the hug. "What are the keys for anyway?"

"Front door of the suite, my office, and this room here. In case you want to work when I'm at court or something. I don't want you to be locked out. Ernie knows, so you're all good there."

I glanced around at the stacks of boxes. It looked only slightly more organized than last time. Unlike my first visit to this room, the bankers boxes were now labeled, fat-Sharpie-style, with the plaintiff's name, various numbers, and place of residence.

Another box was labeled pleadings. It was from this box that Justin extracted a stack of stapled papers.

"These are the newest."

"Tell you what. Let's trade. Why don't you read the motion and I'll look all this over."

"Now come the plaintiffs, by and through their counsel," he started out loud. I busied myself with the new pleadings, two new plaintiffs and their parents had joined Justin's crusade. One plaintiff six years old had leukemia. The second a two-and-a-half-year-old boy, who only had a single mom advocating for him, had been diagnosed with a pancreatoblastoma. I shook my head as I read. The only sound in the room was that of a wet highlighter being dragged across various passages.

"I think I last saw this laundry list of certification requirements in some bar exam study guide," he said after he turned the last page. "And that was more than ten years ago."

"The law moves like molasses which is both good and bad depending on what you need from the courts. Not much has changed, Justin. Numerosity, commonalty, typicality, and last but not least, of course, fair and adequate representation are still the standards," I recited from memory, then skimmed the motion's introductory paragraph on my copy to make sure I hadn't forgotten anything. Those were the same headings I had used to argue in favor of certification based on each of the factors.

He looked up. "I'll take this home to read, refresh my memory on the case law. Run me through it, though. What are your thoughts?"

I could have just briefed him. I realized, quite suddenly though, that I didn't really have a good idea of Justin's skills as a lawyer. I'd always thought he was probably a better lawyer than me just because he'd gone to Case, a tier-two school, while my alma mater was a tier four. Add to that my new knowledge about his tenure at Dalton Lacey and I was a bit more sure of him. More equal than I'd previously thought. Sure that between he and I, we could definitely handle prosecuting this case in the way it needed to be pursued.

Now that I was considering hitching my wagon to his, so to speak, I realized I needed to know just a little bit more, like whether he could argue persuasively. How well he knew the law and could answer questions off the cuff. Three things that would be critical to success in a case like this. If he didn't have what it took, I had to know that he'd be okay with me taking the lead. That's one thing of which I wasn't sure at all. I didn't want our relationship to be stuck with him on top and me on bottom, so to speak. I wanted our working relationship to be much more like our other one…one of equals.

"What's the burden of proof, first of all?" he asked.

A lot of my practical legal knowledge had been hard won and self-taught. The burden of proof made a huge difference on how any case was handled. The highest was, of course, beyond a reasonable doubt in criminal cases. The burden in civil was lower. In juvenile and domestic relations, it was the middle standard that reigned—clear and convincing evidence. Where a fact finder, judge, or jury had to think whatever a party was putting forward had a higher probability of truth.

"Preponderance of the evidence," I answered. That meant Justin and I only had to convince the hearing judge that what our side was saying about class certification was more likely than not to be true. It was the lowest standard, the easiest hurdle to jump. If the scale were to total one hundred, then we only needed fifty-one.

"Okay, go on." He looked down at the motion, then back up at me. "Numerosity. I see that you left some blanks."

"How many plaintiffs do you have now?" I gestured toward the new brown bankers boxes that had showed up in the days I'd been absent from his office.

"Forty children fifteen and under who have atypical childhood cancers. Thirty-seven live in Brighthill. The other three live just over the town line in Clearwater Park."

"You think that's enough?" I asked. Many class actions were small, as only a certain group was affected. But some like the billion-dollar tobacco litigation or even the Ford and Firestone one involved hundreds if not thousands or millions of plaintiffs. Given those, forty wasn't very many, but most cancer clusters are very small. "Most of the case law suggests that the minimum is forty."

"Do you think we're skating on thin ice on that one? People drop in and out of cases all the time," he said. "They're small towns. I don't think it's fair to expect thousands. Brighthill has just under seven thousand. Clearwater Park, fourteen hundred. I think in this case the complexity of the challenge in finding the specific cause of the cancer should overrule that."

"And if it doesn't?" I wasn't sure if I was playing devil's advocate or if I were trying to convince myself.

"Then we'll have forty different cases. But given how similar they are, I suspect we could do what I said before, turn it into a trial machine that practically runs itself. Same amended complaints from us, same defenses from them. Kind of like those medical device cases or even Firestone from back in the day before it went national."

"Class action would probably get a bigger settlement. That would be good for the families and good for us by extension."

"Us?"

"You. The attorney or attorneys of record on the matter."

"Exactly. Either way, though, I'm not worried about the case not being able to pay for itself."

Which was a relief. Like I'd said to Lulu, I wasn't interested in being on the bad side of any more cases. Leveling up meant considering the positives and negatives and not just jumping in to what seemed like a good idea without proper vetting.

"Alrighty then, moving on…. Common questions of law and fact?" I probed, taking over the questioning. *I* needed to be sure.

"Causality in this case. Whether mycotoxin or some other resultant pollutant is the cause of the kids' cancer."

"Okay," I said. I jotted down "hire expert" and "pin down causality" on the blank spaces I'd left in the motion's argument section. After a moment of thought, I scratched two big stars on either side of the page. Whether the case was certified for class action or if they were prosecuted individually, nailing down causality or at least a plausible theory that could survive a challenge from Strohmeyer was top priority.

"That one may be the hardest," Justin admitted. "Here's where I am on this. Not all of the cancers are the same. There's leukemia, brain, and central nervous system cancer, and others. But according to the experts I've consulted, an epidemiologist and two pediatric oncologists, all could be related to exposure to environmental contamination."

"So the plaintiffs don't have a lot of cancers in common?"

"Yes, but the papers on this, most of them out of Tom's River, suggest that carcinogens don't affect every person in the same way. It's kind of like how a different cologne would smell different on each person."

I pulled my mind away from how Tom Ford's Black Orchid cologne smelled on Justin's neck. I don't ever remember noticing cologne before, not beyond my father's Old Spice. But Justin's got my attention enough for me to have looked for the bottle when he was in the bathroom one time.

I put my hand back on the table, picked up the pen, tapped it on the pad to get back to the matter at hand and away from the inside of Justin's bedroom.

These kids had cancer and Strohmeyer was to blame. We, Justin and I, could be the bridge between life and death. Money made a big difference in our private for-profit health care system.

"What about being fair and adequate representation? That's the last leg of this little class action table. Did you see what I put in the brief?"

"Think we're good there. So far, I haven't found any outliers nor have any other parents contacted me from any of the surrounding towns. Based on alluvial groundwater flows, it's been super specific to a few square miles."

I decided to add "alluvial" to what I was going to have to look up later to add more detail in the causation section. I was glad that I'd come here to Justin's little war room today. I think he may have stumbled on the sort of magical place young lawyers always wanted to be, the warrior who can help people get what they deserve, get what they couldn't get for themselves in the legal system.

"Who would we be arguing this to? Don't you have a bunch of judges in the cases you've filed so far?"

The so-called judge stack should have yielded a random assortment of the thirty-four sitting judges for the cases he'd already filed.

"Presiding judge," he answered.

I couldn't keep my loud groan to myself. Sometimes, sometimes, I just wanted to live in a place like New York City or Los Angeles where you didn't run into judges you knew or judges who held a grudge every time you turned around.

"Tom's dad." My voice carried the heavy sarcasm the situation warranted. "Yay."

"You said Patrick Brody likes you."

That was true, Tom's dad had liked me. Had been more than fair to me the times I'd appeared before him.

Had been true.

May not be true any longer. Not with my defense of a pimp who'd outed Tom's illegal behaviors and lost him his prestigious prosecutor job. I couldn't imagine Patrick Brody liked me much anymore.

"A lot has happened since then." I didn't have to explain to Justin. Between me fobbing off one of the defendants from my last case on to him and the *Plain Dealer* piling on when the salacious details of my ex-fiancé Tom's proclivities came to light, there were no secrets in Cuyahoga County. "I'm not sure I'm still on his favorites list."

"Tom landed on his feet though. Who knows, maybe he'll be on this case."

"Wait. What?" I wanted to turn the clock back. Get that meal with Ron. Not be bombarded with constant surprises. I was still young, but I wasn't sure my heart could stand this.

"Tom. Morrell Gates," Justin stated as if I were omniscient or at least graced with the knowledge everyone appeared to have except me.

"Repeat this slowly for those of us in the peanut gallery, if you please."

"Morrell Gates hired Tom. He lost his job when the tape came out."

"I thought I'd read 'indefinite suspension' in the *Plain Dealer*."

"Maybe. Sounds like a 'save face' kind of move. The kind they save for cops who shoot unarmed black men."

For a long moment I tried to remember if that's what Marc Baldwin'd had. Pushed my past farther back. I couldn't put everything that had ever happened to me in

Cleveland in my rearview mirror, but I'd be happy if at least some of my past stayed there. Wasn't looking like that was going to be the case here.

I sighed.

Braced myself.

"Who's on this case, Justin? Obviously, I wasn't listening quite as closely as I needed to the last time I asked you this question."

He extracted another stapled stack from the box. Looked like an answer and a rule twelve motion to dismiss in one of the cases I hoped to consolidate.

"The partner is Miriam Shively. The associates I've seen on pleadings are David Cummings and Patricia Ritchey."

"And in-house?"

"Simon Brody."

"Well, this lottery ticket just turned into my worst nightmare."

I shook my head. Closed my eyes. Was happy that I hadn't finished my lunch because what I had eaten sat like a stone in the pit of my stomach. Old adages were adages for a reason. If something looked too good to be true...

"Do you know any of them?" Justin's wide eyes looked especially innocent right now.

"You're kidding, right?"

"I haven't worked for a firm for a long time. What I remember was an endless revolving door to me. People leaving after a couple of years, going to a new firm, then doing it again. Rinse and repeat and all that."

"Miriam was my mentor when I was a summer associate. David and Patricia were in my summer class. I imagine now that they're all competing for partnership, they'll be upping their game like never before. Plus you can't discount Ted. He's a partner there now. I'm sure his fingerprints will be all over this."

"This is good." Justin nodded like a wise old Jesuit priest.

"How is this good?" My stomach was still in knots over the idea of all the people from my not-so-great professional past coming to haunt me in person.

"The devil you know is better than the devil you don't."

"And other clichés no one ever wants to hear," I muttered, not quite *sotto voce*.

"Why not?"

"How many people want to revisit their devils? They're all in the place I was supposed to be. And now you're telling me that Tom's there too. I swear to God, Justin, I'm pretty sure this would be most people's nightmare."

"Is it yours?"

"My what?"

"Your nightmare?"

"I don't know, Justin. It certainly wasn't what I expected when I walked over here today. I'm starting to think Ron would have been a better bet."

"Are you still in love with Tom?"

"I'm not in love with anybody, right now." I wasn't sure that was the most honest statement I'd ever made, but I didn't want to discuss those kinds of feelings I'd had in the past and maybe even had now, though very much directed toward the wrong person.

"Not even Ron?"

"You know what?" I swung my left arm in an all-encompassing arc. "From now on, Ron and Tom and even Miles for that matter are off-limits. We never need to talk about any of them ever again."

"Why not? I think the fact that you said you're not in love with Ron is telling."

He was right. It was telling. And if I wanted to tell a different story, I needed to get off my ass and change the story, so I did just that when I stood and lifted my pen, pad, and new set of keys into my arms and turned for the door.

"Thanks for lunch," I tossed over my shoulder as I opened the conference room door.

"Wait? Where are you going?"

"To see if Ron's still up for a celebration. This...this can wait until tomorrow. I'll see you at one. After lunch. Why don't we do that part of our day on our own from now on."

If my goal wasn't to be with Justin, then I needed to stop spending so much time with him. I marched down the hall determined, from now on, to be in charge of my future. I was sick and tired of letting everything happen to me.

8

I smoothed down my designer Luis Antonio blouse for the hundredth time that morning as I walked into the lawyer's office.

I'd felt out of place from the moment I'd stepped off the sixth-floor elevator. The bright flowers on the rayon top and the tight-fitting skirt made me look like a peacock in a dark gray wool world.

Even the lawyer, Justin McPhee, was wearing a navy sweater vest over a lighter blue button-down. A pang of longing nearly took my breath away. I missed the color of the islands. Even the lawyers and doctors on my home island of Puerto Rico kept it bright. But this lawyer was like everyone else here in Cleveland who dressed like they were mimicking the weather.

I tried my best to smile when the receptionist left me with the lawyer.

McPhee took the clipboard from me, then shook my now empty hand.

"Thanks for filling out the form. Sorry to delay you, but I'm prepping this case down the hall in the big conference room and Ernie doesn't always remember where I am."

It was a cold fifty degrees outside, and this man's hands warmed me in a way I hadn't felt in a long time. I made my smile bigger as I pushed away my sudden discomfort.

"It's not a problem," I said, pulling my hand from his and waving his apology away. "I'm glad that you agreed to see me."

He gestured for me to sit in one of the two chairs across from his desk. I folded myself into one. I could feel air on my chest as my breasts pulled against the blouse buttons.

Regret and embarrassment surely tinged my tan face with pink. If he saw any of my crazy display, he didn't say a word. He sat in his own high-backed leather chair, then rolled forward and picked up a pen, clicking the ballpoint out.

"Tell me about..." The lawyer looked at the form. "Your daughter Ivelisse."

I did a double take. "You pronounced it right. Her name..."

"I went to Catholic school," the lawyer said. "My sister, Stacy, had a friend Ivelisse from Puerto Rico."

"Do you know where?" I asked. My nerves calmed down at the same time my heart sped up.

"Cleveland. I went to St. Ignatius." A slow smile spread on his face, making it much more handsome than I'd originally thought. "But I think you mean in Puerto Rico?"

I laughed at his attempt at humor. I nodded, interested to see if he was just blowing smoke. I'd met people like that here. Insurance agents, used car salesmen. They'd tell a little joke. Claim to know a lot about Puerto Rico to try to get our business. Then after I fell for the dupe and bought what they were selling, I'd quickly realize they knew just enough to make me wish for home, and the rug would be pulled.

"Bayamón." McPhee paused. "Did I say it right?"

"You said it perfectly." It *was* nearly perfect and not an awful imitation of the kind of thing Spanish-speaking newscasters did and *Saturday Night Live* skits made fun of.

"Her quinceañera was the hands down best party I've ever been to." The smile on his face was warm and genuine.

"Really?" I sat forward a little, placing my hands on my side of his desk.

"Her dad got a spit," he started. The lawyer gestured while he talked, his hands going as wide as a spit roaster. "He built a fire in a hole in the ground in her backyard and put coals in it. Then he got an entire pig somewhere— maybe the Westside Market—and roasted it. Then her mom did something to the meat or skin that made it super crispy."

"Bayamón." I nodded, my own hands flying from the desk even though I usually knew better than to talk with them up north. "It's known as *El Pueblo del Chicharrón.*"

"The city of..." he translated.

"Fried pig skin. Like pork rinds, I think that's what you call them here. But not quite that stuff in the plastic bags on the supermarket shelf."

"It was the best barbecue I ever ate," he enthused, his own hands making another circuit in the air. "I had a huge crush on her, Ivelisse, but I was her best friend's pimply younger brother." He paused, his face going red. McPhee rolled back his chair a bit creating some distance between us. I was a little sad about the newly created space though I couldn't pinpoint where that kind of emotion was coming from.

"Sorry," he started. Then he cleared his throat. The color receded from his face as he got control over himself. "Wow. That was TMI. That name, it just brought me back. Her mom and dad used to talk about Puerto Rico whenever I saw them. Ivelisse went back every summer. My sister even went with her for a couple of weeks when they were in college."

"It's a pretty place," I said, trying to smooth over his embarrassment and my own at our instant and unusual camaraderie. I'm sure he didn't like me seeing him that way. But it gave me so much confidence in him. Someone who was that passionate would probably be a great lawyer for my Ivy. "I miss it. My own Ivelisse was born there."

"How is your daughter?" he asked, all traces of a smile gone.

"Okay...not that good, really." I took a pause, swallowing the tears that could bubble up at a moment's notice. "She has cancer in one of her kidneys."

"I'm so sorry." He sounded so genuinely sorry that my carefully contained tears threatened to spill over again. Justin McPhee pushed a tall square box of tissues across the desk. I pulled my hand farther into my lap determined not to use a single one of them.

I'd already cried my way through two boxes at home. I was done crying. I wanted to do something. To fix it. To make it better somehow. Crying had done nothing but make my head hurt and my eyes puffy. Ivy was still sick.

"Last week I thought that it was going to be okay. They were talking about laparoscopic surgery. They have a ro-bot that makes a tiny cut and removes the tumor, stitches her up. After that she may not have even needed chemo or radiation."

"You said last week…"

"Then things changed. Turns out my insurance doesn't want to pay for that special surgery. They'll pay for a full kidney removal."

"That's cheaper?"

"A lot cheaper. They cut her open like a butcher would and remove the kidney. All the cancer would be gone too."

"So why don't you like that as a course of treatment? Is it that your husband disagrees?"

"No. It's not that. I'd be all for it if it were a cure. But it's one of those things where the cure is worse than the disease."

"How so?"

"One kidney can do well, but not always. Sometimes there's strain on it and if it fails, then she's on dialysis until a transplant could be found. If a transplant could be found. That relies on someone *else* giving up their second kidney or hoping someone's child dies. Who wants that? Then it's another even bigger surgery and anti-rejection drugs."

I had to stop. Research and Google had taken me down into a pit of despair.

"That's a lot of what-ifs. Maybe I could possibly help you if you decide to appeal. I'm not promising anything, but maybe I could lend you a little help with that."

"I'd appreciate it. I'm just worried because my insurance is about to end."

"Are they threatening to cancel coverage?"

"No, nothing like that exactly. I got fired from my job when I called off. I couldn't really take any more sick days to care for Ivy, so they let me go."

"I'm so sorry. I think I may have some ideas to help you, but let's talk about what I'm doing here first. We're planning a large collective lawsuit against the company that's polluting the water of Clearwater Park and Brighthill. We're investigating the possibility that there may be a cancer cluster downstream. We're looking to contain or stop the pollution. Possibly get it ameliorated or cleaned up. Then get compensation for the families. Money they can use for co-pays and treatments and all the medical expenses that insurance doesn't cover."

"Thank you," I said. "Thank you for taking up for us."

For just a moment, he looked unsure.

"What do you hope to get from a lawsuit?" McPhee asked after he pulled himself together. "I hope to help you and the other families get money, but that can't cure your children."

"Cancer is not natural," I said. I'd prepared for that question. To let him know that just because Ivy could be better. Maybe never sick again if she got the right surgery. That it didn't mean she wasn't as deserving of a settlement as any other afflicted family would be. "Cancer in children is even less natural."

"How long have you lived in Brighthill?" His voice was brisk, all business now. The pen kept moving across the paper. I wondered how he could write so quickly. I'd always had to think before I was able to actually put anything down on paper.

"We bought the house in 2001. Around Christmastime." Tino and I hadn't exchanged presents that year. The house and all its costs had been our gift to each other. He'd insisted I turn right around when I'd started to head out to the mall a few days after we'd moved in.

"Why did you choose Brighthill?" The way the lawyer looked at me, I felt like my answer was going to be very important. I paused to make sure I was saying it just right in English. I'd grown up bilingual like almost everyone I knew, but I still thought in Spanish when I was stressed or upset.

"Tino...that's my husband...Celestino. He works at Strohmeyer. That's why we came up to Cleveland to begin with. When the Tremont hipsters made our rent get too high, we came over that way. The house's mortgage, even with taxes and all that, was cheaper than renting. It has a big yard. Tino can get to work in less than twenty minutes most days."

"So about seven years," McPhee summarized. "Ivy would have been almost three when you moved?"

"That's about right. Her first nursery was in Brighthill. Then I put her in the pre-K program when that opened up."

"How do you get your water?"

I was quiet a moment when I couldn't quite follow his line of questioning.

"From the faucet," I finally answered. "Is that a trick question?"

"No. I'm sorry. I have a list of questions I ask everyone. Skipped around because you'd answered some others in the flow of conversation. I just have to make sure I don't miss anything. That nothing takes me by surprise. The worst thing that can ever happen in a legal case is...surprise. What I mean is, where does your water come from? City or well?"

"Well. It was on some paperwork we got when we bought the house. I think that's—good—well water. Supposed to have more minerals, make your teeth and bones stronger and all that."

"Do you think you have that paperwork?" he asked. He'd stopped writing and was looking up at me, eyes squinted.

"Probably." I'd always kept important papers. My parents had said it was critical not to throw anything away. Especially things about the house, the car, all the kinds of insurance and the like.

"Do you mix a lot of water-based drinks at home?"

"Water-based drinks? Like lemonade or Kool-Aid?" When our eyes met, he nodded. I continued. "Yes. Though I moved away from those kinds of sugary drinks I grew up with, 'cause they say those are bad for you now. We mostly drink one hundred percent juice now. But it's juice from concentrate. You know, in the freezer section. Cranberry cherry is her—Ivy's—favorite."

McPhee drew a bold blue line across the light blue page in front of him. Scribbled something below that could have been my younger daughter's name. "You mentioned you had another daughter?"

"Stella. I have to pick her up when I leave here."

"What does she drink?"

To think a few weeks ago, I would have thought that was the weirdest question and now it didn't even faze me. Anything that could get at the source of Ivy's problem was something I was willing to probe, no matter how out of left field it seemed.

"This one only drinks bottled water," I said. "She says the water tastes funny."

"Has Stella shown any of the symptoms that Ivy has?"

"No. Do you think it's the water?" I didn't give him a chance to answer as a certain understanding crept into my brain. "You think it's the water. I don't drink water. Didn't grow up that way. I drink Diet Coke. It's my worst habit. Tino drinks milk. His mother was like that and he can't drink anything else. Ivy. Ivy's the only one who drinks the water." I paused a long time while the fact that something as innocent as water could be killing my kid.

"Jesus," I breathed.

I closed my eyes as, out of habit, I did the sign of the cross.

"We're not sure." The lawyer stopped scratching on his pad. The look in his eyes when they met mine, was serious. "We're having an expert do testing. I don't want you to jump to any conclusions."

"What conclusion? That my water is dirty, polluted, poisoned? That whatever is in there caused my baby's cancer? How can I not jump straight there after what you've been asking me."

"I don't want to put the cart before the horse. We're in the information-gathering stage of this case. I don't want to sound any alarms if it's not necessary."

"Who do you think polluted the water—the city of Cleveland? The township? One of the plants? There are so many smokestacks around. Everyone talks about that like it's a good thing.

"People are working, they say. Money is going into the economy, they say. It was the same at home. Some people thought industry coming to Puerto Rico was its savior. My parents thought it was its death."

I cut myself off. I could hear how hysterical I sounded in this law office that was as quiet as the library. The lawyer didn't bat an eye. I probably wasn't the first agitated woman to step foot in his office. This place was probably hysteria central.

"On behalf of the other parents," McPhee declared, "we've filed suit against Strohmeyer Brewing Company."

"Wait. What?" I looked at the lawyer, the ceiling, the chair I was sitting on sure I had misheard him. "Strohmeyer? You think they polluted the water? They're not even in Brighthill. They're in Clearwater Park."

"Pollution doesn't respect political boundaries."

"How could this be? It doesn't make any sense, you suing them. I know a little about brewing. My Tino is hoping to be a brewmaster there. He always talks about how it's one of the cleanest industries there are. It's just water and grain that goes in the beer and some kind of stuff on the way out, but basically water mixed with grains. They feed it to cows and pigs afterwards. Nothing toxic."

"Have you ever heard of mycotoxin?"

"My...co...what? No." But the other part of the word—toxin—I understood loud and clear.

"Our working theory is that the toxins thrown off from the effluent are entering the groundwater systems downstream. Clearwater Park is at a higher elevation. That plus gravity..."

I didn't know what "effluent" was. I didn't ask that though.

"How do the cows and pigs not get sick?" was my question. Nobody was talking about pig cancer.

"They add binding agents, basically clay particles that can be passed through digestion but neutralize toxins and fungal growth. They don't do it for people, neutralize anything. From what we can figure out, Strohmeyer thinks that after tossing their waste into the water, it will be neutralized by the soil or just dissipate."

"That's kind of gross." I tried not to think of the gray-green foamy water you'd sometimes see near a clogged sewer grate after a hard rain.

"Animals in captivity can't be picky, I guess," he said. "Plus industrial farmers don't let them live nearly as long as people."

"How would this work? Could we even sue Strohmeyer?" I asked.

"Why wouldn't you?"

"Because of Tino...surely there's some kind of conflict of interest thing."

When McPhee shook his head vigorously, I thought I'd made some mistake though I was almost sure I'd used the right words. But when he spoke, I realized that headshake was about something different.

"His employment wouldn't limit your daughter's cause of action."

"Sorry...cause...?" I shook my own head at the unfamiliar legalese. Some I got. Some I didn't. But as with all the medical terms that had been thrown at me over the years, I was willing to learn.

"I'm sorry. I...basically your husband's employment may limit his rights in any number of ways depending on what agreements he's signed with the brewery. But these can no way limit the rights of his daughter."

"Then I think I want to do this." I leaned forward. Put my palms on McPhee's desk to show him I was very serious.

"Are you sure? Do you want to think it over? Talk to your husband? Is he coming down to my office today? I usually like to speak with both parents before we proceed." He paused. It looked like he was thinking of what to say next. "I want to be clear that I'm not pressuring you here. I'm not that kind of lawyer. It's that I need clients who are all in because this is a long haul, a lawsuit."

"Tino was supposed to be here, but it's hard for him to leave work. So, no, I don't need to think it over. What can we do? I want my daughter to not have cancer, for her to get well. I can't control that first part anymore. But I also want the people who are responsible to pay for their actions. It's not fair that they get to do whatever they want, toss whatever they don't want into our drinking water, and my Ivy has to suffer the consequences."

"Exactly." The lawyer nodded his agreement. "Let me go get the necessary documents from my paralegal."

He stood. I stood too. I pulled down my blouse hoping I hadn't been flashing him for the last half hour. He'd made me feel so at ease I'd forgotten about how uncomfortable I'd felt when I'd first walked into his office.

"What's next?" Suddenly I felt a sense of urgency to do something to move this forward, to get justice for my girl. If I couldn't win with the insurance company, maybe I could get a win in the courtroom.

"Follow me and I'll get the paperwork for you. Fill it out and give it back to her. I'll call you in a week or so. I have to ask you, though, to keep our theories of the case confidential."

"Theories?"

"What I said about the mycotoxin. I don't want to tip our hand with the defense team."

"If it helps Ivy, I promise to keep my mouth shut." I mimed twisting a key in my mouth like I was Ivy's age and not a thirtysomething-year-old woman.

"I'm not sure how you're going to manage that with your husband, but I'll just have to trust you to gauge that one on your own."

He shook my hand and gave me over to a thin woman in a pink shirt and khakis.

"Yes, yes I will," I said. Tino would be unhappy to say the least. I just needed to figure out how to explain it to him so he would understand that our daughter was more important than some rich company's bottom line.

9

"Is this okay?" Ron asked. We were seated in a bar of the newest "it" place on Fairmount in Cleveland Heights. Half French bistro, half California fusion, it was intimate, cozy, and didn't take reservations.

"It's perfect." I sipped my complimentary champagne and took in the surroundings.

Dark wood.

Fine furnishings.

Shiny brass accents.

For a moment I felt like I belonged. After I'd come home from that shitshow in Justin's office of crazy mixed-up feelings and a legal quagmire I didn't yet understand, I'd changed into dark jeans, tall boots, and my latest everyday fashion item, a sheer V-neck cashmere sweater.

I didn't have the perfect accessories—while the bistro was arguably French, I wasn't. But I was at least one hundred eighty degrees from a time when I had zero idea what to wear. They were very simple, my choices now, but at least they were easier.

"I'm glad you like it," he said while nodding. A faint smile played around his lips. "I have to admit that I wanted to impress you."

"You don't have to do that," I responded.

"I do. I haven't been the best boyfriend over the last few months."

I pressed my lips together to keep my mouth from gaping open in shock.

Boyfriend?

I think I'd imagined something more in a boyfriend. Someone who spent nearly every weekend with me. Who was my permanent date. Someone I didn't have to wonder about. I didn't say any of that, though. Instead, I posed a huge open-ended question because if I needed anything, it was more information.

"How so?" was my bright idea in that regard. I sipped more champagne and waited for an answer.

"I'm not dense, Casey. I asked you out for New Year's Eve because I've wanted to go out with you since we met in Lulu's office months ago. I just didn't see how dating and working to become partner could go hand in hand."

"But you asked me out anyway."

"Because my attraction to you won out over my common sense."

"Okay…" I had to admit it felt good that someone had lost their common sense on my behalf. Very good to be wanted by someone who was into me and not prostitutes or his mother's dreams for him or his dog.

"But I've leaped over the hurdle, Casey. I've won the race. I'm a partner now. The heavy lifting is done for a while." He was almost out of breath after his little speech. I looked into his brown eyes. They were earnest. I'd never seen that kind of look directed at me before. I very much liked it.

"Congratulations again," I gushed. "I'm super proud of you. It must feel amazing."

"It does feel amazing. I have only a few goals, and this ticks a huge box."

I may have not yet been a master at high-stakes adult conversation, but I didn't leave that one dangling. I sipped again. A refill was at my elbow and my nearly empty glass swept away in one swift and efficient motion. I took another sip from the new glass.

"What are your other goals?" I tried for subtlety, probably failed.

"I think you know...buy a house. Marriage. Kids. All of that. I'm a pretty traditional guy. I think that's something we have in common."

"Sure...that's true." I nodded in agreement. Took a large gulp of champagne. This conversation was teetering on the cusp of everything I'd ever wanted. That was scarier than I thought it would be.

"So what I'm saying, Casey, is that I want to pursue this with you."

"This?" I asked. I wasn't being deliberately obtuse, it was just so very unexpected. It had been that kind of day, that kind of week, that kind of life. I kind of wanted to turn the clock back and start over again making sure this time my loins were sufficiently girded or guarded.

Either one.

"I want us to be exclusive, Casey." Ron looked directly into my eyes. I tried not to shiver in anticipation. "I want to see where we can go from here. I think you're smart and beautiful. I thought that the moment I met you. Now I'm at a place in my career that I can genuinely support a wife and kids, now's the time to finally go after what I want. And what I want is you."

A glass and a half of champagne usually wouldn't make me tipsy, but I felt lightheaded as the host led us from the bar, through the split in the black velvet curtain to a small wood table near a window.

Once we were seated, I looked at him, still at a complete loss for words. I studied the clouds coming to cover the moon. Fat raindrops would soon follow.

"I need to think about what you're saying. I..."

"Of course. You couldn't have known what I was thinking when I called you today and told you my good news. So let's talk about something else."

"Okay," I said, relieved. I'd be lucky to get more than a half hour of sleep later. I already knew that my mind would be spinning with indecision about my future. My gaze drifted back from outside to Ron. I didn't have a damned thing to say to my "boyfriend." Fortunately, he picked up the conversational ball.

"How's your work going now?" he asked. "That last case was a doozy, but it looks like everyone got what they deserved with Tom and your former clients going to trial in federal court. You've got to feel like the outcome was fair...considering."

Considering they were guilty but found not so. Considering a well-connected prosecutor apparently lost his job. Considering I was merely a pawn in a big game of three-dimensional chess.

"I guess that was one resolution. I'm doing less criminal right now. Mostly divorces, and I've picked up a new case. A big one."

"What's that?"

"You know Justin McPhee, right? You guys were in the same class at Case..." After Ron's confirming nod, I continued, glad that we could skip over Justin's legacy at Ron and Lulu's firm. "Well, I'm working with him to get a class action certified. It's personal injury."

Ron's eyes widened a little. Happily, I wasn't the only one surprised today.

"That is both big and a little bit outside your wheelhouse. Have you done anything like that before?"

My bolder, more confident self made a huge effort not to be offended. I was changing faster than people could keep up. I'd give them a minute to catch up with me.

"Never. But there has to be a first time for everything."

"Can I give you one piece of advice from the defense side?"

"Please do."

"Pick the class representative well. They're going to be the first line of defense because the plaintiffs will go after him or her—hard. That person needs to be solid. They can't be easily compromised or a quitter."

"Thanks, I think." I didn't mention that I didn't know if I would be on the front lines making those kinds of decisions. I thought about the pile of documents waiting for me in my office where I'd dropped them off before cutting out early to come home and get ready for my date with Ron. There was so much I didn't know about Justin, about the case, about our likelihood of success no matter which strategy we chose.

"There are a lot more," Ron said. "But that's the most important. The others all boil down to knowing the law and the facts better than anyone else."

He leaned forward as if we were about to share a confidence.

"The big law firms, the in-house people, the business people, they all get siloed easily and lose sight of the big picture. If you can master the case, big picture to minutiae, then you've increased your chances of success—however you define it. Whether that's a big settlement or a big jury award."

"You said there were other tips. I know this wasn't supposed to be a business dinner, but I'm not too ashamed to say that hanging out a shingle is not the same as law firm training."

Nearly ten years into this and I was confident about some things but still tentative about so many others.

"In this economy, I'm not sure training is a word I'd use. All the partners talk about the go-go eighties and how cases were staffed to the hilt. How they could bill for the hours an associate learned on cases and the clients would pay. Now, there's a lot less of that."

Every single one of my law firm friends did this. They minimized the money, the perks, the training they got as if that would make me feel better somehow.

All they got was something I would have killed for. Something I did kill myself for...for three long years until the Strohmeyers and Morrell Gates pulled the rug from up under me.

I never argued the point out loud, but I knew and they knew that having a one-woman firm and working for a two-hundred-lawyer firm were not functional equivalents.

It was the difference between being a bank teller and being a bank president. Sure both people worked at banks, but their jobs were as different as night and day.

Whiny was how I was starting to sound to myself. Maybe I'd be the bank teller who became the bank president. My newfound if floundering confidence shouldn't get in the way of taking my career to the next level.

"But the other stuff? I really need your help if you don't mind. Justin and I could be out of our depth without even knowing it." That last part was to save face for Justin should he and Ron talk when that congratulatory phone call finally happened. Men's egos were a fragile thing. "I think I'd like to know that sooner rather than later."

"Have you hired experts?"

"Justin has at least one on board that I know of." That was probably an overstatement. I was starting to think Justin had taken a couple of phone calls with experts from one of those consulting firms that barely disguised an expert-for-hire mill. I'd been afraid to ask but committed to making sure I did before I signed on. My new motto, or one of them at least, had to be no more surprises.

"You'll want to hire early and often," Ron was saying when I tuned him back in. I took another sip to make it seem like I'd been thinking deeply about the man in front of me and not the one I was sleeping with. He continued, "You can be sure whatever law firm is defending the cases will hire experts immediately because they have the funds and want to keep the best ones from working for you. They'll be expensive, but it's something that can't be avoided."

"Experts, got it. What else?"

"Understand the business."

"Business?"

"Whomever you're suing. Know how they're run. Corporate structure. Is whatever product you're targeting something they can do without or a core business."

"How would I know about the core business?" I asked. Beer was Strohmeyer Breweries' *only* business as far as I knew.

"Fanta, you know the orange soda? Coca-Cola makes that. I'm ninety-nine percent sure if they stopped making Fanta, their stock price wouldn't drop three cents. But if they had to stop making Coke or had to pull Coke from the shelves, or needed to change the formula, that would be a different thing entirely."

"What's the difference?"

"Any corporation that answers to shareholders would kill off the small thing, even if only temporarily, pay you a tiny settlement and move on. But if it's a big thing, then you have way more leverage to get a big settlement."

My mind whirred. Beer was a core component to Strohmeyer, obviously. Whether they were a public company, I wasn't sure. I was almost certain the Strohmeyers were like the well-known Mars family brand—privately owned.

I nodded, prompting him to continue. If it wasn't an entirely rude thing to do with a *boyfriend*, I'd have pulled the pad and pen I'd abandoned when at Justin's office after lunch. Actually, if I'd had it, I would have. Which gave me an idea. I excused myself, got an extra pen and paper from the host and came back.

"Did you just leave to get a kid's menu?"

I held up the paper. Flipped it over. Indeed there was a brunch-time activity page on the front.

"Yep. I'm in it for the word search."

When Ron squinted, clearly puzzled, I smiled. "Just kidding. I really need to take notes."

"I'm not saying anything all that revolutionary..."

"Still." I put my head down and scribbled everything I could remember from the last few minutes.

"Okay, where was I?" He was obviously game, at least for the moment.

"Small product versus big."

"Right. Expect a motion to remove to federal court."

"Really? The plaintiffs and defendants are in Ohio."

"They'll make a case."

"Even without diversity?" This wasn't about race or gender, but the federal court being set up to settle controversies between people of different states.

"Big firms will do anything to get into federal court. It's more corporate-defendant friendly. Years of Republican appointments have made that happen. The judge quality is more even too. No one's up for reelection. The rules are uniform. I'm not saying they'll win that motion. I'm saying be ready."

I swallowed past the lump in my throat.

"Anything else?" I asked, though I had more than enough to chew on for days if not weeks even if I didn't have that long. My casual approach to "helping" Justin was quickly ramping up to a fifty-hour-a-week commitment.

"The only other thing I can think of," Ron said, "is to figure out an efficient way to handle discovery."

"Efficient? There are like thirty bankers boxes in Justin's office. I figure we can knock that out in a weekend."

"Did the defendant deliver a USB or some other means of electronic discovery for emails, memos that were never printed, and the like?"

"I'm not sure." Forget fifty. Work was ramping up to seventy. Even if Ron was my *boyfriend*, I wasn't sure there was going to be much boyfriend-girlfriend dating time in my immediate future.

"You're going to want to get sure. Most plaintiffs' firms nowadays use some kind of software. They can sort, code, and segregate what's relevant."

"Electronic discovery?" I took a couple of deep breaths trying to swallow down the panic that I'd jumped into the deep end of a pool without basic swimming skills—only toddler bravado. "I think I saw something in the Ohio Lawyer about that a few months ago..." I was starting to feel like a rookie lawyer again or even like an alien who'd landed from another planet altogether.

"It's what we do or the client does before even sending discovery documents to the plaintiff. I have no idea what kind of cost or budget, because for the most part our clients are not too price sensitive, but it's probably worth it. Otherwise you'll spend too much time looking at people's email jokes and porn saved on their hard drive and not enough time figuring out if the big bad defendant is really responsible for the thing you're alleging."

I scribbled and scribbled until my hand was tired. I felt young, naïve, stupid. All the things I hated about being a solo practitioner. All the things I'd allowed to keep me small for the last decade.

Clearly, I'd spent too much time being waylaid by Justin's kissing and not enough time thinking about what I was getting into by getting into bed with him—*workwise*. I wasn't quite ready to back out, because his Hudson referral had given me a taste of a big payday. I'd liked it.

This time I'd pay off my loans once and for all. I'd bought clothes and furniture, little luxuries, when I'd thought big money coming was a sure thing. Having to take a car from my retired parents had been a hard lesson in bad budgeting.

Lesson learned.

I needed this case, though. More than I wanted to admit.

But I wasn't sure two of us alone were well enough equipped or armed for this. I'd thought we were going to a street fight, but it looked like I needed to be ready for a shootout with semi-automatic guns blazing and at the ready. I had no gun, much less ammo.

I folded the paper, stuffed it into my purse. Turned back to Ron waiting for something akin to a flare of attraction to spark. Instead, a feeling of ease and contentment washed over me.

I had to wonder if that was enough to sustain a relationship long term. If I were a betting woman, I'd have assumed that half those polled with the question would agree and the other half wouldn't.

"Did you know Justin well in school?" I changed the subject to the second of my twin concerns. My date had enlightened me about the Strohmeyer case; maybe he'd have some insight on my temporary law partner as well.

"Yes, and no, I guess. The class at Case is small. Ours was a hundred and ten."

That *was* small. When I'd started school, law school class sizes had started to swell just as the need for lawyers was starting to shrink. It was one of the many economic ironies of the nineties.

"Why the yes and no?"

"Everyone knew everyone. It was hard not to in a class that size. Especially after winter hit and all that lake-effect snow kind of kept us on or near campus twenty-four seven. My life was a little different from other students, though."

"Why?" The lives of law students were far more the same than different. "The only people whom I never saw were those who had kids or were…"

"I was married." He spoke the words when I didn't.

The pressure behind my eyes throbbed to the beat of the smooth jazz drums in the background. I signaled the waitress for more champagne. I might regret it in the morning, but I needed something now. I gulped the remainder of what was in my glass and traded it for the new one the waitress bought.

"I'm sorry?" I said in case I'd misheard.

"I'm divorced now, nearly ten years."

"You were married?" I'm not sure if it was the alcohol or the shock of new information. I'd had too much of both today. "How? Why?"

I regretted the question words. They were stupid where the answers were obvious.

In front of God and family.

Because he'd been in love.

Enough in love to make a promise of lifetime commitment. I'd never loved anyone that much, otherwise maybe I'd have made it to the altar at least one of the times I'd been on the precipice.

"Long story short?" he started. Then he hesitated.

Obviously, we both wanted to abide by the rule that new lovers didn't talk about old. I nodded my affirmation that a violation was okay in this case. He took a sip of his own champagne, maybe only his second. Then he put both hands on the table.

I braced myself for the wave of jealousy that I knew was sure to follow. Just like the first that washed over me when Tom got engaged to the beautiful socialite Lizzy

Cofrancesco, then again when I saw him walk into that motel.

The wave that washed over me when I started seeing Miles while he was seeing my client Claire Henshaw. The one that always washed over me at the thought of Justin being with anyone but me—though his obvious experience told me there had been quite a few people before me and maybe even someone else besides me now.

Maybe I didn't have a wrong-man problem, but a jealousy problem. I'd have to think about that one day when I had time for self-reflection. For now I wanted to hear his backstory.

"We were college sweethearts," he said when he finally spoke after a long sigh. "Met our first year at Carleton. We were very much in love in the beginning." I closed my eyes as the wave of jealousy hit—hard. Looked back at Ron both ready and not to hear the rest. "I'm not so sure about the 'being in love' part as we got to the end of college," he continued. "But there was nothing wrong with either of us or our relationship except maybe for a lack of passion, so we got married because it was the next logical step."

"Logical?" Felt like the opposite of logic to me. He shrugged as if to say what could any of us expect of the brains of early twentysomethings.

"I think we both thought that was the best way to fix us. To infuse something new. The wedding did that...for maybe a year or two. Our relationship became better than I could have imagined."

I nodded, kept my mouth shut instead of doing what I wanted which was to stand up and yell, "TMI!"

"The third and last year we were on life support," he said, his eyes glued to the knife and fork he kept rearranging. "The last months, no pulse. I thank goodness she had the nerve to call it quits. I might not have. I really think marriage is too important to walk away from without a backward glance. I really wanted it to work out."

"And you think you want to do that again? Marriage?" He didn't sound like he was once burned, twice shy. I think I would be, though. I agreed with him on one thing. Marriage was that important. I wanted to think it was my Catholic upbringing, but I kind of believed it deep down. That belief had stuck even when I'd long abandoned the rest of the Catholic church's teachings.

"I'm ready." He said those words with such emotion that they hit me squarely in the heart. He continued, "I learned a lot, Casey. I learned that love doesn't conquer all. I learned that relationships take work. I learned that self-awareness can go a very long way in a relationship."

"Were your parents upset? My parents still whisper about people in the parish who couldn't or didn't or wouldn't stick it out."

"Yes, I think they were. But I'm a man well into my adulthood, and I make my own decisions. I told them when they have to walk a mile in my shoes, then they can make the decisions, but until then..."

Silence stretched between us like a taut string for an interminable minute or two.

"Thanks?" I shrugged a little. "For telling me."

"I want to be honest with you, Casey. One hundred percent honest. That's the only way to move forward. My honest self very much likes you. Very much adores you. Very much thinks it'll be very easy to fall in love with you."

His words lit me up in a way that nothing else had thus far.

"Wow...I didn't..." Know what to say.

How to take that in.

How to respond.

"I didn't say that to get some kind of response," he said as if he could hear my inner monologue. "This is me, Ronaldo Salvio de Vieira Pinheiro putting all of my cards on the table. If you know what I want, I think it'll be easier for you to make a decision if you want the same thing— a future with me."

I was grateful when our server came to talk about specials and ask what we wanted...to eat.

When she put down a complimentary bruschetta board and left, he asked, "Do you want to keep working?"

I tilted my head after chewing and swallowing the bread and goat cheese that would no doubt go straight to the hips I was trying to keep more straight than curvy.

"As long as I like to pay my rent and eat three meals a day plus snacks..." I held up the bread as a live demonstration. "I don't really see any other option."

He tilted his head and gave me another quizzical look. I was sure he was saying one thing, but I was saying another. We were both trying to make important points.

I clamped my lips around a second slice of bread, this one topped with sliced figs and prosciutto. Eventually he leaned forward as if to emphasize what was next.

"If we got married, I'd be able to support us both. You wouldn't have to work. Maybe part time to keep your hand in it, but you could do whatever you *really* wanted."

"I'd never thought about it," I lied right after his almost proposal left his lips. Of course I'd thought about it. I assumed in law school, *when*, not *if*, I'd married Tom that I'd take time off with our kids, little curly blond moppets I'd imagined so many times, they'd felt real.

Then I'd have come back as some kind of powerful partner at Morrell Gates. Maybe be the first partner there to succeed at the delicate dance of a work-family balance.

Or quit.

Like Amrita.

"It's something you should think about, Casey. What you want in the next five years, ten even."

I sat back while the server laid the entrees on our table.

"I will…I'll think about all of it," I said. Then I pierced one of my sea scallops with a fork. I had no idea what the future held. That was like peering into a Lake Erie fog. I did know one thing, though. I was taking Ron home with me tonight. I wanted to see up close and personal what that admiration and adoration felt like.

10

When the receptionist buzzed Veronica Garza's call through, I was fully expecting a litany of questions regarding the case. I'd been more than a little surprised when she hadn't sent back the engagement letter right away. Of course, I'd required that the engagement forms were signed by both her *and* her husband. I wondered, but didn't really want to know, what she'd have to do to convince him to sign on the dotted line so his daughter could sue his employer.

Strohmeyer was the sole support of that family, and even if there was no *legal* conflict of interest, it didn't mean that the next few months or years wouldn't morph into a very uncomfortable situation for them.

The light blinked on my extension, and I hesitated for a moment longer than normal. It was a shame that no one talked about the truth of the so-called prestige jobs of lawyers and doctors. That we were essentially in a client service industry. Better paid than some, but more stressful than most.

There were two types of clients. The first kind accepted whatever advice I gave and did exactly what I said. When I pressed them to make their own decisions, they would just tell me to make the decisions for them.

Those clients were hard. I never liked to make decisions about other people's lives, even though I did it every single day, because when you're suing someone—and especially when you're being sued—inaction isn't an option.

Then there were the second type of clients. The ones who liked to call every single day for an update. It had been a quiet week with few of those calls, but with Veronica's daughter facing major surgery for childhood cancer and a potential insurance fight, I didn't yet know into which box Ivy's mother would fall.

"Justin McPhee," I answered when I pressed the small plastic button and Veronica clicked onto the line. I tried to interject authority into my voice. No matter what kind of client they were, no one wanted their lawyer to be a wimp.

"It's me. Veronica. Ivelisse's mother."

"Are you okay? How is Ivy? I know that you emailed that you might have surgery scheduled—"

"Can you come?" Her question interrupted what was going to be a string of platitudes meant to placate.

"What? Something wrong? Where do you need me to come?"

"To the hospital..." Her voice trailed off, then erupted into a huge hiccoughing sob.

Her sniffle and cough stopped my questioning in its tracks. I looked at the calendar on my desk. Flipped it open to today's date—June 20—and found it empty.

Most lawyers, including myself, make money by billing, but I'd been a little light on the hourly cases while I took a deep dive into the Clearwater Park/Brighthill cancer cluster and Strohmeyer.

The payout from a single one of these personal injury cases could be more than I could conceivably bill for a decade assuming I worked eighty-hour weeks and never once got sick or took a vacation. That single fact alone made the priority shift worth it, at least in the short run.

I didn't wager at casinos or travel to Vegas. And I knew full well that the bigger the personal injury case, the bigger the chance of success. Also, the bigger the chance of failure. I was betting on myself—or myself and Casey Cort. I was starting to realize this potential class action was too big for a single shingle-hanging lawyer.

I was glad that Casey was going on this ride with me even if she hadn't fully committed in writing. The fact that she'd done extensive research on how to structure the cases and had all but drafted a class action certification motion made me believe that her agreeing to be co-counsel was merely a technical hurdle to overcome in the next few days.

Parents of children with cancer were a completely different kind of client than I'd ever had before. There had been no money in holding the hands of parents in juvenile court—not at two hundred and fifty a pop—so I'd avoided it at all costs. Business clients had businesses to run. So unless it was a bet-the-company kind of case, I rarely heard from them. This potential class action, with parents unfamiliar with the legal system, was a completely different beast. This was a kind of client management I'd have to learn on the go.

My eyes ping-ponged all over the scattered files in my office. There were no blue files. The color I'd used for pro bono and juvenile for years. Service to the community was an ideal I hadn't held dear in a few years.

Veronica Garza wasn't exactly a charity case, but maybe holding her hand for an hour or two would fill my compassion quota for the week. I closed some files I'd been planning to work on, locked my desk drawers, and gathered up my raincoat and car keys.

"I can't believe you came," Veronica said when I found her at the hospital's twelfth-floor nursing bay. I almost hadn't recognized her. Gone was the woman in a fitted skirt and half-buttoned blouse, not that I'd thought of her as anything more than a client, but I was a man who wasn't at all blind.

Before I could extend my hand all the way for a shake, Veronica's peasant-blouse-covered arms came around me along with some kind of fruity perfume. I hugged her back even though it was awkward. Clients usually hugged me when I kept them out of jail or got them custody of their children, not in greeting. I let go first.

"You really came," Veronica reiterated. Her voice was full of awe. Her brown eyes were warm, sincere, grateful.

"Why wouldn't I?" I shrugged to try to dial down the emotion, keep her on an even keel.

"Because you're a busy lawyer," she said. "Hospitals are not courthouses."

"It's my job to get justice for you...and the others in Brighthill," I said quickly. Because, of course, neither she nor her daughter Ivy were actually clients. She'd yet to sign on the dotted line of a retainer agreement. Ethics made it important that I keep this distinction clear. Lawyers had been disbarred for that kind of mistake, when clients gave up their opportunities for redress because they thought they were represented. I punted. "This is part of my job."

"I'll get the papers back to you ASAP," she whispered, her eyes shifting to the nurses who were surreptitiously watching our interaction. "I'm sorry. I meant to bring them by yesterday..."

"If you say you want to hire me, I'll take your word for it," I said, immediately contradicting my good judgment from a moment before.

God save me if her daughter died and she expected something from a settlement she'd never opted into. I hated having a job that made me see the potential dark side of every situation. "You seem to be an honest woman who keeps her promises."

Veronica looked away from me, blinked a few times. I took her elbow and led her to the little family room a few feet away. I pulled out one of the chairs that rounded a small wood laminate-covered table. I pushed the door halfway closed before I located tissues on a side table. I put them on the larger table, then pushed the small upright square box toward her.

Politely, I kept my eyes averted while she pulled tissues and dabbed at her eyes, blew her nose.

"Is that Ivy?" A small girl with tan skin and dark wavy hair rolled by in a wheelchair, IV bag swinging from a pole on the back of the chair.

Veronica glanced through the doorway of the hospital room, then patted my arm. I could feel the heat of her hand even through the thick Oxford cloth.

"Come meet my daughter." She stood.

We both came into the room while Ivy's IV bags were moved from the metal hanger on the chair to another pole anchored to the bed.

A man in scrubs thumbed a dial, then pressed a couple of buttons. Nodded when he was satisfied with what he saw, then left the room without a word.

"Hi, Ivy. Ivelisse." I extended my hand toward the girl. What should have been awkward wasn't. She was one of two dozen kids I'd met since I'd started work on this case. Veronica's daughter took my hand and gripped it like she was an adult about to have a job interview. "My name is Justin," I started. "I'm a friend of your mom. I'm a lawyer who helps people. I just wanted to come meet you today."

"Hi." Ivy was all dimples and smiles. If I hadn't met her in a hospital room, I'd never have guessed she was a cancer patient. She was nothing like the other children from Brighthill and Clearwater Park—pale ghosts, shadows of who they'd once been. "You got my name right," she continued, interrupting my moribund thoughts

"You're the second Ivelisse I've met," I echoed what I'd said to her mother days earlier.

"Cool. In Cleveland?"

"She used to live here. Not anymore, though. She's in New York City now."

"My sister's name is Stella."

"Can't say I've met another Stella, though."

That made her smile even bigger. I was probably the first person to say that to her, I'm sure.

"They're going to use a robot to take out the cancer from my kidney," she piped in. The IV tube shook as she pushed herself up in the bed to get a better look at me.

"I know. Your mom told me. That's a big deal. You have two though, right? So, one to spare while the other one heals?"

Ivy nodded vigorously. "Lots of people live their entire life with one. There are even babies born with only one. If I have one and a half, I'll be almost as good as a regular kid."

"That's pretty cool you know that. Great club you're going into, then."

"I have cancer today." Ivy's face went from smile to sober in a second. "But pretty soon I won't. I want to be in that club. The 'kids with no cancer' one."

"Doctors are kind of like magicians, huh?" I said as a string of them came into the room as if my words were some kind of siren song. I tried to think of a grouping word, something Casey would find funny, but pack of doctors or even school of residents didn't have the right ring to it.

I'd have to work on something funny to say to Casey the next time I saw her. Even though we were no more than friends with benefits, I very much wanted to keep seeing Casey Cort. I shook the thought from my head and looked at the white-coated men and women that surrounded Ivy's room like a scene from any of the popular medical dramas.

"Can you please excuse us? We need to prep your daughter for a procedure," someone in blue scrubs announced.

"I haven't made a decision, yet. I haven't signed anything about the surgery the insurance company wants."

"You'll need to do that soon," one doctor said. "Either way, though, we need to get up-to-the-minute information on the size and scope of the tumor. If there's any spread, the decisions regarding procedures will be out of your hands."

"What do you mean?"

"Mrs. Garza." The doctor's mouth was thin lipped in what I assumed was frustration. "I understand your hesitancy, but cancer isn't something that we can debate *ad nauseum*. There is no perfect treatment. No perfect answer. It's a disease where the cure is sometimes horrible because the disease is fatal. Decisions before death. Now, if you'll excuse us."

The doctor turned her back and started scribbling on Ivy's chart. The remaining doctors and nurses closed ranks around Ivy's bed.

"Sorry," Veronica said, trying unsuccessfully to get out of the way. I felt her pain when she kept bumping into different people who all seemed to be working as a synchronized team to do their jobs with a single pinball of a mother out of place.

"You and your husband don't need to leave," someone else said tuning into her discomfort. Someone who'd make a good doctor someday. "You can wait right over there by the window. We just need space to—"

I shook my head. "I'm not—"

Veronica shook hers. "He's not—"

I could see the compassionate doctor squint in confusion.

"Let's just get out of the way," I interrupted our marital status confession. I put a firm hand on Veronica's arm and steered her toward the huge window overlooking the university campus.

With a couple of feet between us and the medical workers, I watched Veronica as she looked down at all the college-aged kids walking around. It didn't take any mind-reading skills to know what she was thinking. That she wanted her daughter to live long enough to be like the students, no bigger than small dots, who moved around below. I joined her in watching them take their life and health for granted.

I turned away from the window before Veronica did, listening to the medical jargon that passed between the team as a kind of shorthand.

"Dr. Richardson, I was reading a paper a few weeks back about juvenile kidney cancer originating from arsenic. Is that the case here?" the doctor whose nametag read Hanson asked.

"The idiopathic cause is unknown at this time, doctor," she answered through her teeth. I had to assume the younger doctor was still in school or residency and hadn't yet learned patients weren't invisible.

Someone kicked something mechanical under the bed, and the wheels were disengaged a second time. Someone else pulled up a kind of handle in the back, and started to wheel Veronica's daughter away.

"*Te amo, mi niña*," she said, grasping her daughter's hand in a grip that turned both their hands white.

"She'll be back in about three hours," the doctor with Dr. Kirsten Richardson embroidered on her breast said. "We always advise caregivers to go home, shower, get some rest. We have your number and your husband's in case we need to call you, but we don't anticipate any issues."

"Thank you." Veronica held her hands in front of her mouth in full prayer position. "Take care of her."

"We will, Mister and Missus Garza. We will." With that, they all gathered around the bed and rolled her daughter right out of the room.

"I'm sorry about the mix-up," Veronica apologized.

"Don't be. It's a natural assumption maybe." That two parents would be at their daughter's bedside before life-saving decisions were made. "Your husband at work?"

"Always." Veronica shook her head. For the second time in as many hours, it looked like she was going to cry. Most good men, I mused, good fathers would be at her side as their daughter was going in to major cancer surgery. Maybe it was too much to handle, I thought, giving Ivy's father the benefit of the doubt.

"He was planning to be here, though," she said, her eyes pleading for understanding.

"What happened?" It didn't really matter *what* the excuse was. But I tried to put myself in the shoes of a jury who'd have to judge whether a child's cancer was worth putting a seven-figure price tag on. If a girl's father didn't think cancer treatment was important enough to interrupt his busy schedule for, it was going to be a leap of sorts for a jury to take it seriously. I was rethinking having Garza as a client.

"There's this guy at Strohmeyer, the craft beer brewmaster. He normally lives in Germany where I guess the best beers are made. He's retiring or leaving or just going back to Europe permanently. I'm not sure which, but he—his name is Felix Braun—this Felix is supposed to pick the person who gets his job before the end of the month."

"Ah," I said to fill time. Beer was a yes with a Cleveland jury, but job over family was still pushing this kid's case into the loss column. "Have you talked with him about the case? Does he know that Strohmeyer is the defendant?"

"Not yet. He hasn't been home long enough lately."

"Is that going to matter?"

"It doesn't matter to me. If Strohmeyer requires this kind of time and loyalty from its employees when one of the kids of the employee has cancer, then how much can they care about any of this? It won't matter to him."

I wanted to believe her. I think the addition of Ivy to any potential class action would make the case that much stronger.

Pretty girl who moves to a house in Brighthill. Her parents from Puerto Rico now here in Cleveland seeking out a better life. She does nothing more damning than to drink the water.

It was liquid gold.

"Are you going to take that doctor's suggestion? Go home?" I asked. Veronica looked exhausted, and it was only inching up on eleven in the morning.

"I can't." She shook her head so vigorously a big hoop earring got caught in her hair. "I can't go far from here knowing my baby is here being probed and prodded," she said while trying to get hair out of the gold hoop.

I reached across the space between us, stilled her hand. Quickly and quietly I unwound her springy curls from the gold jewelry. I pulled my hands away when the deed was done, but not before I felt her shiver at my touch.

"When is the last time you ate?" I asked as I stepped back into the safe zone some two feet away.

"I don't remember. Stella had an Eggo. Ivy couldn't eat last night or this morning. I didn't want her to feel alone, so I skipped dinner and breakfast too. It was hard for her watching Tino and Stella eat McDonald's in front of the TV."

I glanced out of the window, then back at her.

"Do you like Chinese? There's a place near here that would be a good place to talk some more about the case."

It was a lame excuse, but I could see her crumbling despite all the effort she was putting into holding up a big showing of maternal strength.

I could see the no that was coming my way in the way she stiffened her spine, but then her stomach growled as if on cue, and just like that her posture softened.

"I think that would be good," she said. "Let me just tell the nurses' station where I'm going and I'll meet you."

I gave her directions, then let her go to check on Ivy one last time while I took myself to the restaurant. Even my stomach growled at the smell of freshly steamed rice and exotic meat broths. I raised my hand from a back booth when I saw Veronica stand hesitantly by the front door.

"What's good?" she asked after she'd scooted across the vinyl bench seat across from me. I'd be the first to admit that the menus in front of us looked overwhelming, filled with endless variations of rice and noodles and meat and vegetables.

"You eat anything?" I asked.

She nodded. "All that hipster stuff about avoiding wheat or carbs or meat isn't for me. I grew up strong and healthy on good, filling meals."

When the waitress came, I took the lead and ordered family style. Beef and noodle soup as a starter. And sausage fried rice. While we waited, I debated a bigger question in my head, but asked her about growing up in an American territory instead. Once we finished the soup, I plunged in.

"Have you ever heard of a 'name plaintiff'?" I asked.

"Name...no..." Veronica shook her head. I watched her hair swirl, but this time it didn't catch on her hoops.

"I didn't think so, but I never want to make assumptions. When there are big cases, class action or even big Supreme Court cases, the lawyers need a face. A face that the judges, jurors, news organizations, and the public can sympathize with."

"Would I recognize any of them, these...name plaintiffs?" she asked before she took a large forkful of the rice. The pleasure on her face was enough that I felt the decent thing to do was turn away. I took a bite of my own, chewed, swallowed before answering.

"Dred Scott, Norma McCorvey—"

"Norma?"

"Jane Roe in Roe versus Wade, Ernesto Miranda, Miranda rights. Or even Amber alerts after Amber Hagerman."

"That's a sad one."

"Indeed it is," I conceded. "But what's important about that one girl's death is that something good came from a horrible tragedy. Something that can save other kids from being kidnapped and having the same terrible crime happening to others."

"So, Ivy?"

"I want Ivy to be our name plaintiff. I want the consolidated case to be called Ivy Garza versus Strohmeyer Breweries."

"Why my Ivy?"

"She's strong. Once she has surgery and recovers, she'll be able to, with your and your husband's permission of course, speak out on how childhood cancer has affected her. The other kids...some of the other kids are pretty sick. Doing everything they can just to hang on. Chemo and all of that."

I didn't say the obvious. That her daughter was likely to live where the others were maybe going to die. A living plaintiff, someone a jury can well sympathize with was better than a dead one.

For the first time that morning, Veronica Garza hesitated. "I don't know—"

"You should ask Ivy. Talk to your husband. Think about it all. Not today of course, or while you're making a decision about Ivy's treatment. But after that, please think about it and let me know."

She nodded and took another bite. I knew that I had her. That Ivy would become the face of this case. I scooped up rice and sausage with my own fork. This morning had not been a time waste after all.

11

"You don't have to come back with me." I realized too late that I'd taken too much of the lawyer's time. Doctors and lawyers were really busy people. Ivy and I weren't their only priority.

"I just want to say good-bye to Ivy," he insisted. "Maybe have a quick chat with the insurance people informally on your behalf."

"You'd do that?" Despite all that business, he had time for me. I could feel nothing but grateful for his generosity.

"If you want the expensive robotic surgery that would lead to the best outcome, it's time to figure out what it would take to get that."

"I need more time to think, maybe..."

"I'm not sure you *have* more time. When does your health insurance expire? You mentioned you lost your job.

What's the COBRA cost? Can you guys swing it, at least until you can figure out insurance with Strohmeyer?"

"No, I can't swing it. I just worry that I won't make the right decision."

"Time isn't on your side, Veronica. You have to know that."

"I know. I know. I'm sorry."

"Don't apologize to me. Don't get mad, Veronica. Get even. Get what your daughter needs."

"Now?"

"No time like the present," he said. Justin McPhee grabbed my hand tight. Squeezed. I took that energy transfer and used it to push at the elevator button. Got to the administrative floor faster than I wanted to. When we got off the elevator, I faced the same receptionist from days ago. Asked for the hospital's insurance administrator.

"Do you have an appointment?"

"Justin McPhee." He didn't wait for me to hem and haw. He took charge. "I'm an attorney here in Cleveland. This was the only time I could spare in my schedule today."

"She's just off the phone now." The receptionist stood as if her chair were on fire. "I'll let her know that you're here."

Not two minutes later we were in her office. Unfortunately, any sway Justin McPhee had stopped right there. She let us come in and take a seat. But after that it was all the same words that added up to no.

"The bottom line, Mr. McPhee, Mrs. Garza, is that Amalgamated Consolidated Health and Casualty only covers procedures generally accepted in the medical community."

"But they do it at Cleveland Clinic and Mayo Clinic and Johns Hopkins. I checked."

"Those are an elite...a different kind of hospital. This is a teaching hospital. Their job is to first and foremost, of course, provide excellent care. Their other job is to teach generations of future doctors. Highly experimental care is not always the best care.

"I'm sure that a robot sounds new and shiny, but you really need to consider what your daughter needs. From listening to the doctors the other day, Ivy—that's her name, right?—Ivy needs to have her cancer removed before it crosses from stage two to stage three. All the evidence points to very high rates of survival if she gets the complete nephrectomy."

"She's so young. You heard them, right? You said it yourself, that there's a possibility her remaining kidney will become diseased."

"I'm not meaning to be glib when I say this, but kidney disease is not cancer." The insurance administrator kept her voice calm, cool, pleasant like she were talking about the next Fourth of July picnic and not my daughter's life. "It's not pleasant. Often it can be downright unpleasant. But it's not always fatal. Cancer kills, no doubt about that. You can't make a decision about today based on an unknown future."

"I'm only here on an informal basis, but can you please explain what Ivy's appeal rights are in this situation. What formal procedures do you have in place for denials?"

"When the receptionist let me know that you were here, I retrieved the information our own in-house counsel recommends we share with attorneys. There are about fifty pages there, but the bottom line is that under ERISA law, Amalgamated is the administrator of a self-funded plan and therefore exempt of any appeals process. We've heard Mrs. Garza out as a courtesy. You understand, though, that we're not liable for any consequences of an adverse determination. My advice, mother to mother, is to get the surgery your daughter needs."

She stood, her red hair orange in the fluorescent office light. Justin McPhee shook her hand. I followed their lead. With the attorney's hand at my back, I walked from the office no better off than I'd been. It was hard, but I was quiet all the way through the offices, past reception, until we were on the elevator. Then I couldn't hold back any longer.

"Is she right? I can't appeal?" I asked the moment the metal doors swooshed shut.

"Yes, she's correct. There are a few different kinds of insurance plans. Long story short, since your company pays for all of the health care, they don't have to give you whatever *you* want. They can give you whatever *they* want within acceptable medical parameters."

"How is that legal? I thought insurance was government regulated."

"Those *are* the regulations."

"That makes no sense at all. How can we live in a country that cares more about businesses than the people that work for those businesses?"

"You're not the first to ask that question," he said on a sigh. The elevator doors opened on Ivy's floor. I stepped out ready to make the only choice I truly had left. Get her the lifesaving surgery the health insurance company was willing to pay for. I just had to hope and pray she would heal, that she'd be well. That our family would look back on this one day as just a thing that happened, that we'd moved past. I wanted to imagine that quinceañera, that college graduation, that wedding where she was happy and healthy and thriving here in Cleveland or Puerto Rico or wherever she settled. Even with the lawyer by my side, I suddenly felt very alone.

"I just wish Tino was..." I started. Then I couldn't believe my own eyes. "Tino!"

I shouldn't have been so surprised to see my daughters' father striding down the hall to the children's cancer ward, but I was.

It was as if he were starring in a mob movie or something, because there were three men in dark suits walking behind him. I had no idea what to make of it, but stopped short. I turned toward the lawyer. In my silence there was a question: Had he made arrangements for my husband to be here?

Justin McPhee's raised eyebrows told me that he didn't have any more clue than I did. I shook my head slightly as I tried to figure out what was going on. I broke away from McPhee and ran to my husband. I put one hand behind his head, the other on his chest.

"You're here," I breathed.

"Of course." My husband pulled me closer. Hugged me tight. "Of course, I'm here. I brought some people that we need to talk to."

I assumed he was talking about the mystery men behind him. I looked behind me and waved for the lawyer to step forward, meet Ivy's father.

"Oh, this is Justin McPhee, the lawyer I mentioned. He's been helping me out today."

That was the cue for Tino's companions to join our little group.

"Simon Brody," a tall man with blond hair said, then extended his hand toward McPhee. "I've seen your name on quite a few pleadings lately."

"We've met before," McPhee said.

"Sure. Of course. Cleveland *is* a small town. I'm here on behalf of Strohmeyer today," Brody said. "I think I have some news Mrs. Garza is going to want to hear. Can we find a more private place to talk?"

"There's a room just over there." I pointed to the place where we'd gotten the bad news on Ivy. It felt a little unlucky, but I didn't say anything. If the important people from Tino's work were here, it wasn't time to show our superstitious side. I didn't want to give anyone any reason not to give him the promotion he'd worked so hard for and deserved.

I didn't say anything as Justin bustled into the room with us. When we were all in, the other man introduced himself.

"Wynell Trudeau." He extended his hand toward mine. I shook it gratefully. More because it belonged to a black man than any other reason. It was nice to not be the only brown person in a room sometimes. "I'm over in benefits at Strohmeyer Breweries."

"Benefits?"

Simon Brody stepped forward a little. "Strohmeyer is more than just a large corporate employer, and one of the largest in Cleveland. We truly care about each and every person who works for the brewery, from janitor to brewmaster."

My head snapped toward Tino. Had he been promoted? Is this why these men were here? No, that didn't make any sense. Tino's eyes didn't meet mine, so I turned my eyes back toward Brody.

"When Tino came to Wynell to sign your family up for health insurance, your daughter's situation came to our attention. First, I want to say that I'm thoroughly sorry for what you are going through. Cancer is always a tragedy, but for young children it's truly something no parent—or child, for that matter—should have to live through."

"Thank you," I said. Then before I thought better of it, I took Brody's hands between mine, so grateful for his words.

"You're welcome. What I came here to tell you, though, is that starting today, you're going to be covered by Guidance Health. We've reached out to our contacts, and as soon as she's clear, Ivy can be transferred to the Clinic. The top pediatric oncologists, urological surgeons, and others will be building a team to manage her care. We did find out that they have a Da Vinci system there, so if the team gives the go-ahead, she can get the robotic surgery which may give her a better outcome."

"Oh my God. So she doesn't have to have her entire kidney removed? I can't thank you enough." I gripped Brody's hands hard, hoping my gratitude was coming through. "This is...my God...my prayers have been answered."

"In order to get it done today, we're going to need you to go with Wynell to hospital administration so we can get the paperwork going."

"How long. How long will it take?"

"Since you'll be signing out, probably not long. Transfers from here to the Clinic probably happen all the time."

"I can't thank you enough," I repeated, because it was true. "All of you."

Trudeau looked a bit uncomfortable, but I didn't care. They were going to save my daughter's life.

An hour later, Ivy was ready to be moved, and I had her discharge and transfer papers in hand. Tino was carrying records for the new doctors to review. McPhee had gone as well as Brody and Trudeau. It was just me and Tino and the young woman doctor, Hanson.

"I just want to thank you for all you and Dr. Richardson have done. I couldn't be more grateful."

"I'm sorry that we weren't able to provide the care that you wanted. But there are some limitations to any medical decision. We'd love to treat everyone with experimental procedures or the most cutting-edge care in the world, but that's not the system we live in, unfortunately."

"That feels very 'every man for himself,' what you're saying."

"I'm still young in my career," Hanson said. She shook her head. "And according to Richardson and others, a bit idealistic."

"I think you're a good doctor. I like that you think of things that no one else is thinking about."

"Can I tell you something in complete confidence?"

I looked at Tino, across the room making Ivy laugh. "What do you mean?"

"What I mean is, what I'm about to tell you is something that I think is important for you to know. But I can't be associated with it. If anyone were to ask, I'd deny it to my dying day."

"If it can help Ivy…"

"I think Ivy's going to be okay with Strohmeyer stepping in. But I think that it could help the other kids."

When my eyebrows lifted, Hanson nodded.

"I heard what your lawyer said about other plaintiffs. That must mean some kind of big lawsuit. Either way, this is what I wanted to hand you." Hanson pushed across a plain manila folder. There was no marking on the outside or on the center tab.

"What's in here?"

"It's about the arsenic. There are some lawsuits from the EPA about arsenic pools Strohmeyer is leaving on the ground. Also, there's a photocopy of a journal article showing a possible link between arsenic and childhood cancers."

"I don't know what to say." I didn't want to tell her that I wasn't part of the lawsuit. That with Ivy getting treatment, I didn't know if I should sue. Strohmeyer was doing right by my daughter. May soon be doing right by Tino. Who was I to complain, to ask for more? "I'll just say, thank you, for all that you did." I gave her prayer hands and a head bow.

"You're welcome. I wish Ivy and the rest of your family nothing but good health."

12

"What's going to happen, Mama?"

Ivy looked so tiny. Her tan skin made the sheets look so white. The big hospital bed made her look so small. It was like an optical illusion but without the fun house.

"I'm not sure," I said. I shifted my eyes away from my little girl hoping I could somehow stop all the disaster scenarios running through my head.

All those stories that started with her dead or dying, her getting paler and paler until I couldn't tell where her skin stopped and the sheets began, were like a bad movie loop.

"Let me answer that for you," Dr. Mira Ames said. She must have been standing in the doorway. I hadn't noticed her. When I did look up and away from my daughter and met the doctor's warm brown eyes, she stepped in.

Dr. Ames had been amazing in the last seven days Ivy'd been in the hospital. She'd counseled us through a redo of all the imaging and blood tests. While the new doctors did have all of her test results and reports from the other hospital, they insisted they wanted to run their own so they could have up-to-the-minute results to interpret. It was hard watching my daughter being poked and prodded again and again. Since all of it had led us to today—the day her minimally invasive robotic surgery was scheduled.

"Hi," Ivy mumbled so quietly it was almost inaudible. Even after all these years she was still a little bit intimidated and a lot shy in front of doctors.

Folding her white coat under her backside, Dr. Ames sat on the bed next to my daughter.

"It's good to see you this morning. You look well rested. Where's your sister?" Dr. Ames said while lifting Ivy's hand. I knew it was a subtle way to check her pulse. The good doctors were like that.

"She's at day care right now," I answered for Ivy like I often did. It was a habit I was trying to change, but not today on the day she was *finally* going to have her surgery. I had to make sure that she was not misunderstood.

"Are you going to leave, Mama?" Ivy's eyes grew wide.

The question seemed to take Dr. Ames as much by surprise as it did me.

"Leave? No, *mija*. Why would I go anywhere? I'll be right here with you the whole time." I took her other hand in mine and squeezed it to reassure her.

"Who's going to get Stella, Mama? Day care closes at seven," Ivy continued.

"Your father will get her."

Ivy shook her head so hard, the IV stand bobbled, and I had to reach over to steady it.

"He never picked *me* up, Mama."

"Of course he did." I patted her hand. "Shush now. You're being silly with this."

"No, he *never* did," she insisted, her voice loud and sure for once. "One day you said he'd come and pick me up. Then all the teachers left until it was just Mrs. Brown and me. Then you drove up in your pink work clothes. The ones that look like the nurses' clothes here." Pink scrubs were popular in this children's ward.

Another doctor came in, picked up the chart. Caught Dr. Ames' eye and paused before coming any farther into the room.

"Ivy, we have a policy here in the children's ward," Dr. Ames started, tugging on Ivy's hospital gown for emphasis. "Kids only have to worry about one thing."

"What's that?" I think my daughter had taken on worry as her primary job no matter how many times I tried to take the burden from her.

"Getting better," Dr. Ames' eyes were serious, but her voice was soft. Ivy was riveted. "Healing takes energy. So all us doctors want you to do just that. Focus on sleeping. Eating. Big squeezy hugs from your family when your stitches heal. Getting better so that you have to stay here the shortest time possible."

"Okay." Ivy was tentative, but I could tell she was listening.

"Can you do that?"

"I can do that." She nodded in confirmation.

"Let your mom and dad worry about your sister and all the adult stuff."

"Thank you," I said to Dr. Ames. Grateful was the only way to describe how I was feeling. I hadn't realized that

Ivy knew her father that well. I thought I'd glossed over how much Tino had delegated parenting to me.

"Now." Dr. Ames' voice got more serious. "Let's talk about today. First, this doctor is going to check your wristband and use a marker to draw on your stomach."

"Why is her coat shorter than yours?" Ivy pointed to the young woman who was still standing by the door as if waiting for an invitation.

"We train doctors here so they can go on and take care of other boys and girls like you. We have almost two thousand doctors studying here to become better doctors. This is Dr. Cook. Can she go ahead?"

Ivy nodded, intrigued with the fat Sharpie in the young doctor's hand. Cook did what Ames had done. Asked Ivy her date of birth, what she was there for, then with my daughter's permission, lifted her thin cotton gown and drew a big blue X on her right side.

"We're going to take you for one last scan," Dr. Ames said after she and Dr. Cook had a brief whispered talk.

"Again?" Ivy asked.

"We need a picture of your insides and your kidney as it is today. Bodies change, and we can't use last week's or even yesterday's pictures."

"Then what?" Ivy asked.

"Then another doctor is going to come in. He's an anesthesiologist. His job is to put you to sleep during surgery. He's going to ask you and your mom a bunch of questions and look at your chart."

"Why?"

"So that you get the right dose of medicine to put you to sleep. Adults get one amount. Children get a lot less."

Ivy nodded. I caught Dr. Ames' eye. Gave her a tentative smile as well.

"Then the surgeon will come in. He will want to talk to you too. He's going to control the robot and the really small tools that will remove your tumor and sew your kidney back together."

"That's a lot of doctors." Ivy's words echoed my thoughts.

"Each doctor does a special thing. We're like a car. There's a starter motor. An engine. Windshield wipers. They're all separate. But when they work together, you can drive a car. Doing an operation is like that, all the parts coming together."

"Cool. It's like a bunch of mechanics working like you see on NASCAR."

I couldn't hold back my spontaneous laughter. Tino had often said that doctors were like plumbers. Mechanics was a new one. I'm pretty sure they didn't go to ten years of school or whatever to be compared to mechanics.

"A lot like that, Ivy." A man in scrubs came into the room.

"Radiology is ready for you," he said. "Mama, take a breather. She'll be back in about forty-five minutes."

After I let go of Ivy's hand, the orderly wheeled her bed out and the doctors followed. I sat in the chair next to the space that was empty except for machines and an empty IV stand. I found my phone and dialed.

"Tino, it's me," I said into his work's voicemail after his line rang and rang with no answer. "I just want to remind you that you have to pick up Stella this afternoon. Preschool ends at three. Aftercare ends at six. Just wanted to double-check that you had the information. Call me back when you get a chance." I was ready to press a button ending the call, then thought better of it. I put it back to my ear and spoke again.

"Oh, in case you were wondering, Ivy's doing good. The doctors have taken a lot of time with her and she's less nervous than she was last night. For the first time in a long time, I think she's not going to die."

13

"What did you bring?" I asked Veronica Garza. It was just the two of us in reception. The office on Sunday was quieter than a church pew.

For a long moment she was silent. Her eyes flicked around with something like suspicion.

I'd given Veronica my cell phone number when we'd been in the hospital on the day Strohmeyer came through and changed the course of Ivy's treatment. I rarely gave any client that kind of access to me. Too few had the boundaries necessary to handle access to someone they thought could solve all their problems. I'd done it because she had something I wanted, her daughter as name plaintiff. Her call from the lobby had been unexpected, though. Once Strohmeyer had bought her off, I hadn't ever expected to hear from her again.

I'd come to the office early to get some hours in. Casey had said she'd be in later. I could really use her help. With the arguments, especially. She was really good at seeing the big picture where I got bogged down in details that didn't move the case forward.

I was a good enough lawyer, but she was a better lawyer. Her years of struggling to get her practice off the ground, no matter how little credit she lent to them, had a great influence on her. I jiggled the change in my pants pocket and hoped this little meeting with Veronica Garza was mercifully short. Maybe Casey and I would work over a late lunch and then go back to my place.

The Strohmeyer case was challenging me on all fronts. It was costing me an arm and a leg. It was taking all the time I could be using to bill clients and keep money coming in that didn't have an interest rate. But I couldn't fail or quit or give up, no matter how much I wanted to. I owed it to Casey. I owed it to the families—forty-three now after a tiny article in the Sun Newspapers—who all had entrusted me with their children's lives.

"The arsenic thing. It's a real thing," Veronica started without preamble. I snapped back to the present. She shook some papers I hadn't noticed. "I'm not sure about what you said about mycotoxin or whatever you call it. I don't think that's the right thing, though. Even Dr. Hanson thinks that there's something to the arsenic idea."

"Come on back. Let's not talk about this in the lobby."

Ernie, the receptionist, wasn't there, of course, but I'd heard one of the other office occupants walking around somewhere in the suite. Attorney-client privilege was best protected in my office with the door closed.

I took up my usual position behind my desk. Garza pulled up one of the chairs on the other side until her knees hit the modesty panel. She was nearly breathless with anticipation. Even I had to lean forward a little and prop my elbows on the flat wood.

"I've looked into what that doctor said about the arsenic," I said to Garza. It was a little more than I'd usually share with a client, but since she'd been there when the doctor had mentioned it, this didn't feel like a violation to keep Garza apprised. "I'm going to have our experts research the two different theories. The mycotoxin *and* the arsenic."

"It's the arsenic," Garza insisted. "I can feel it in my bones."

"What was it the doctor—Hanson was it? What exactly did she say?" I asked.

"You heard her. That arsenic may be the cause. She says that Ivy's tumor matches up with some research that she's read. That long-term exposure to arsenic can cause certain kinds of cancer."

Garza shoved another group of papers over the desk. I resolved to add it to the pile of reading I needed to get done in the next few days.

"Thanks for this. I'll look everything over," I promised. "We're battling on more than one front now. Working on each of the individual cases, and working on the class certification arguments."

"Sounds good."

"How is Ivy? Strohmeyer coming in and providing insurance when they didn't have to was a nice gesture. Your husband must be important to them."

Garza shrugged. "It's still not free. There are still co-pays. There are still going to be bills."

"I think there's a way I can help you with that."

"How? I'm not asking for money or anything. You know that, right?"

"I didn't think anything like that. It's legal help."

"I thought you said that if you weren't representing me, you couldn't give me legal advice."

"That's true. This isn't legal advice, just general information. Have you heard of the Family and Medical Leave Act?"

"Maybe? Is that a new law?"

"It's about fourteen years old, so new is a relative term. That doesn't matter. What does is that it provides employees with twelve weeks of unpaid leave."

"Unpaid? I just said that I had bills."

"Look, it's not perfect. It's not even that great. It's what we have. The operative word here is 'leave.' You shouldn't have been fired for having a sick kid."

"They fired me for calling off too much."

"That's the same. It's not like you were a no-show because you wanted to sit at home watching soap operas. Your family had a legitimate medical concern. The best part is that Spasy would be required to hold your job for you and give it back after your leave period. Also they couldn't cancel your health insurance either." Garza's mouth opened. Closed. "I know, maybe you don't need that now, the insurance. But if you wanted to work there again after Ivy's recovery to earn some money to defray the medical bills, you'd at least have that option. Maybe you won't need it. At least you'd have it, though."

"What do I have to do?"

"I think you'll need to approach HR there and ask them to reconsider your termination in light of that law."

"Oh. Okay. I'll do that. That could make all of this easier. I could stop worrying about how to pay and just focus on her getting better."

I nodded, pleased that I could help her in this small way. It was the kind of low-stakes help that made a lawyer feel good without bankrupting them in the process. "How is she?"

"The surgery was Wednesday. They started at six in the morning. It took a long time, but she came out of it like a champ. She'll be home soon recovering. Then they'll come back with some more test results to decide if this is it or whether she's going to need radiation and chemotherapy too. Crossing my fingers that she doesn't. I think those would only make her sicker longer. The recovery time is already three months. She'll probably miss the first weeks of school."

It sounded like a long uphill battle no matter which way it went. I'd heard the same story from all the families. It was often one big step forward followed by two little ones back, rinse and repeat until one day it was over, either with remission or with a worse outcome—death.

"That's great. I'm happy that your family found resolution without having to sue."

I still thought that her Ivy would have been the best face to put on the case, but I had to move on. One of the other kids would be just fine. Sometimes litigating a case felt like the worst form of marketing. But tugging at the heartstrings of the judge and jury was central to making sure the plaintiffs got what they deserved.

"I...uh...really thought that Strohmeyer was going to cover everything."

"And they're not? You said that there were co-pays, but that's normal. It's true with nearly all health insurance policies."

"The reason we didn't have that insurance to begin with is that it's really expensive. The family cap is fourteen thousand. We're going to be on the hook for all that even before insurance pays its portion."

I was starting to suspect that she'd be happy to make that in a year at her spa, but probably didn't. Not to mention their regular bills, and their second daughter who had her own needs and wants.

"I'm sorry," I said. "Unfortunately, that's the system we're in. This isn't Europe for sure."

"What's going to happen in the cases? Are you really suing Strohmeyer?"

"Yes. Though I don't think they're going to offer treatment to anyone else, and those families are facing true hardships. Similar to you. Their kids are sick. One of the parents can't work. Medical bills are piling up. They need Strohmeyer to take responsibility. They need relief."

"I want to join. I want to do the thing you mentioned, for Ivy to be the face of the case."

"The name plaintiff," I clarified.

"What about your husband?" I rapidly searched my brain for his name. "How does Celestino feel? Even if the case is tangential, this is still the family he works for."

Veronica Garza's hesitation was a beat too long for comfort.

"I have the agreement. He signed it. But I left it in the car. Can I get it?"

I glanced at the clock. Casey was due, but we were done with the substantive part of our discussion.

"I'll be here for a few more hours."

"Ten minutes. I parked at a meter not too far away."

Veronica stood abruptly and nearly bolted for the door before I could tell her that it wasn't urgent for her to hand over the retainer agreement today. Before I could run, I heard another person in the hall.

Casey.

Her wavy blond head poked into my office.

"Coast is clear? I thought I saw that woman coming from your office."

"Clear for now. Come on in. I'll want you to meet her, however briefly, anyway."

"Who was that?"

"Mother of the new name plaintiff. If we consolidate, it'll be Ivelisse Garza, a minor child, versus Strohmeyer Breweries."

"I feel like you may as well call it David versus Goliath."

"A casualty of plaintiffs. That's what that group would be called."

Something like warmth spread from my belly and throughout my body at her spontaneous laughter.

"I love you for these. They're so great."

Love you too almost left my mouth involuntarily. Fortunately my brain intervened before I did something monumentally stupid.

"Okay if I come in?" The voice on the other side of the door was Garza's. I tipped my head, and Casey reached behind to fully open the door.

"I'm Casey Cort," she said in greeting. Offered her hand and swept up Garza's in it.

To relieve Veronica of her deer-in-the-headlights look, I took over.

"This is Mrs. Garza. I mentioned to you that her daughter Ivy is going to be our name plaintiff. Mrs. Garza, Casey's going to be working on this case with me. She's an excellent attorney. Graduated near the top of her class from law school. You're lucky to have such an exceptional mind helping us out."

"Here's the agreement." Garza reached across her body and pulled folded documents from the purse on her shoulder. "I signed both like you said."

I opened the two identical documents to the last page on my desk. Something about Garza's "I" statement and the fact that the two parental signatures looked as wet as a Cleveland sidewalk after the rain made me bristle. For a split second I wondered if she'd forged her husband's signature. I shook my head just the tiniest bit. Garza wouldn't do that. I added my name to one of the documents with a flourish, plucked an empty pocket folder from my desk, one emblazoned with my name and number, and inserted it.

"Good luck with the recovery. Let me know if you need anything. Otherwise I'll be in touch. I'll want you and your husband—and your daughter, if she's well enough by then—to be at the next hearing."

Garza moved swiftly, and before I knew what was happening, she was enveloping me in a hug redolent with her flowery scent. She pulled back and gave me prayer hands.

"Thank you." She turned to Casey. "And you too. Thanks for taking up my daughter's case."

After Garza showed herself out, Casey looked between me and the door. Shrugged.

"Let's work at my place," I suggested, knowing full well "work" would come second. I didn't say *that* out loud either.

Two hours later, our clothes back on, we were taking up space on the couch. It was quiet between us. I was finding that I liked silence with her. If there weren't anything pressing, that would have been enough for a long afternoon. We could work together or individually, or watch a movie, or share a Sunday paper. Shook that fantasy away. My mind's little detours into couplehoodland needed to stop.

I turned to her. Smoothed down a cowlick.

"Are you in?"

"What exactly would that mean, Justin?" Casey stopped fiddling with her clothes. She got up from the couch, disturbing Morro who'd snuck his head onto her lap when she hadn't been looking.

Casey paced around the living room a moment before walking into the kitchen. She opened a couple of cabinets before finding what she was looking for—a drinking glass. She lifted the tap on the sink and filled it.

Her intimacy with my kitchen cabinets made me nearly as uncomfortable as I'd been in the bed with her when I'd told her not to fall for me.

I turned away from the display of domesticity.

Pet the dog.

Cleared my throat.

"What that would mean," I explained, "is that we'd split any proceeds after costs. That means we'd co-chair any trial. That means we'll work on discovery together. We'd join forces."

She set the glass on the black speckled granite with a little more force than necessary. Casey turned toward me and lifted an eyebrow. I wondered if she knew she did that, slightly cocking her head and lifting her brow when she was skeptical. Maybe one of her boyfriends had told her. I pushed that thought away as soon as it had come. I didn't want to think about her myriad boyfriends and fiancés.

"You're handing me a lottery ticket," Casey said. "Nobody gives up a winning ticket."

She didn't quite trust me, yet. After all these years, and with our newfound closeness, I wanted that trust.

"It's not a blank check," I promised. "I genuinely need your help. You'll have to work hard for the money." I mimicked the lyrics of a Donna Summer song that had been popular when we were children.

"I can't help you fund this, Justin." Casey closed her eyes for a long moment, then opened them. Lasered them on me. "I hate to admit this out loud, but I'm just as broke now as I was when you met me ten years ago."

I gave her my own skeptical look. The new clothes, the boots my sister, Stacey, had said cost a lot, and that bright red car sitting outside did not exactly say broke.

I knew that Hudson had paid a lot of money—to buy our…discretion. Surely, she had some of that left over. But I didn't derail the conversation with my opinion of our former referral source, though. I'd planned to fund this case myself with loan help. I didn't need her money. Certainly hadn't planned on it.

"It's funded. Don't worry."

I could almost see the word "how" form on her lips when her eyes narrowed in a squint. But she didn't speak the obvious question aloud.

"If we finish the motion and file it," I offered, "I think we could have a hearing in as little as two weeks from Tuesday."

"How?" she asked aloud this time.

"I talked with Miriam Shively. She says that Strohmeyer and Simon Brody both want to get this over with as quickly as possible. They're willing to waive time if I waive objections. They think I'm bluffing. Think I'm going to lose."

"Not this Tuesday, but next?" she asked.

I nodded. Shively's first instinct was probably correct. I...we weren't the least bit prepared. My offer wasn't a gift. I was drowning on my own. Literally drowning. If it became a class action, I could never do it all myself.

"Is Strohmeyer pushing federal court?" she asked, her eyes had a wide-eyed look I got from most solo practitioners on our level.

"Nope. He hasn't said a thing. Common pleas."

Casey's shoulders visibly dropped in relief. I knew the feeling. Federal court was like going from JV to varsity, from bush league to big league. Neither one of us was ready for that.

"Do you have a heavy caseload?" I asked, praying that her post-Hudson time was as empty as mine had been when I'd given up the hinky adoption referrals.

Casey shook her head. "Mostly divorces, a few criminal cases where they're likely to plead out."

"Then you have time," I pronounced. I'd assumed that to be the case, but her tacit confirmation was comforting.

"Do you think Strohmeyer will settle?" she asked.

"They haven't offered anything yet. I haven't pushed for a meeting. Until I get through those documents, I won't know the strength of our case. Whether they knew they were poisoning Brighthill residents. Add that fact and we can add punitive damages. But yes, I think they'll settle."

"When? One month? Two? Six?"

If Casey dedicated time to Brighthill, the payoff if we won or settled would be huge. But like me she'd be giving up the sure thing of hourly billings in the meantime.

"I can't say. Cases like this are unpredictable."

She sat heavily on a kitchen stool. Pushed herself against the counter and spun around a couple of times before bracing herself and coming to a full stop.

"Fine. I'm in."

I sprung up from my seat on the couch. Morro wasn't pleased. I patted him once in apology, then went to Casey and enveloped her in a huge hug. Gave her a kiss that lingered more than I'd planned.

"This is good," I practically crowed.

She pulled away sooner than I'd have liked.

"Justin. You didn't let me finish. This has caveats."

"Name them." I didn't tell her I'd agree to almost anything. I needed to share this burden with someone. I wanted to share this burden with her.

"I can give you maybe four hours a day, six max. I have to work on my other cases so I can bill my clients and, you know, pay my own bills and eat."

She pointed to her hips with a disapproving frown. I didn't point out that I loved to grab at that flesh when I was inside her. Was glad it was there when I wanted to control how fast or slow either one of us was going.

"Six hours." I nodded vigorously. "Got it."

"*Four* hours, *maybe* six. Some weekends, possibly. But not every one. My social life has to fit in here, somewhere."

"Social life. Got it."

"This thing." She waved a hand between our lower bodies. "This thing we do, it can't mix with the case. That has to come first."

"No mixing sex with the law. Got that too." I gave her a jaunty salute for good measure.

"I'm not kidding, Justin."

"Neither am I. We're in total agreement. Brighthill will have to be the top priority for both of us."

"Did I forget something obvious? Something that's going to bite me in the ass?"

"We're friends, Casey. I won't screw you."

"You already have."

An unexpected burst of laughter shot out of my mouth. That's what I liked about this girl. We had a similar sense of humor.

"Wait, I have one for you," I said while brushing a curl from her forehead. Her daytime hair and bed head weren't much different. Both were equally sexy, not that I'd tell her that. Women liked to think you took them seriously at all times.

"What...one?"

"From the book of St. Albans..." I kind of liked the fact we had our own "in" jokes. Something she hadn't shared with her prosecutor boyfriends. Something she didn't share with Ron.

"Okay, I'm ready." Casey's small smile turned into a big one. She pointed her index finger in my direction. "Go."

"A tower of giraffes."

She laughed long and hard. I couldn't help but join her, put my hand on her neck, pull her in for a kiss that silenced the laughter. She gently pulled away without comment.

Nope, absolutely positively no round two today either. I'd liked it better the way it used to be before I stuck my foot in my mouth or plopped a proverbial stack of cases on her lap.

"That's the best," she said. It took me a long moment to realize she was talking about my St. Albans reference, not my kissing. "I love the British. They have the best words for things. It's like all the descriptive surnames in a Dickens novel. My favorite was Master Bates. We read Oliver Twist in tenth grade English. I think Mr. Cooper—who was a new teacher that year—realized his mistake way too late."

"Give me a second," I said. I jogged from the kitchen and opened the door and went into my tiny office where I kept my work stuff separate from the rest of my life and, more importantly, my dog's open mouth. You never knew what would attract a bored dog's appetite.

I came back from the office and handed her the stapled stack of pages I'd printed up a few weeks earlier.

Speaking of Morro, he was nestled comfortably in the spot on the couch that we'd vacated. Casey had sat back on the sofa, and his head was in her lap right where I would have liked mine to be.

"What's this?" She waved the document without reading.

"Co-counsel agreement."

"No handshake?"

"If I died, Casey, no one's paying you on a handshake."

"So now we have to add estate planning to the mix."

"Just gaming out the possibilities."

"Gotta love lawyers. Maybe we shouldn't use the word counselors, but 'worst-case-scenario prognosticators.'"

"That's a lot of words. Counselor is a lot easier. Anyway, the agreement is basic."

Casey waved the pages in the air another time. I was starting to think she disliked commitment as much as I.

Neither fiancé had turned into a husband, and it was taking a lot to get her signature on the dotted line.

"Six pages is a lot of basic," she said.

"The only change from the standard-form agreement is advancement of costs, section two. You'll be responsible for half of the costs only if we prevail, but I'll do the out-of-pocket advancement. Okay?"

"Justin, how are you affording this?" Her assessing glance around my small two-bedroom apartment was subtle, but I saw it. "Are your parents secretly rich?"

"If that were the case, you wouldn't have met me at a bar meeting all those years ago. Let's just say that I saved for a rainy day and now it's raining," I fudged.

"Speaking of, I want to get home before it starts pouring. There's rain in the forecast." For the first time in an hour, Casey looked ill at ease. I wanted to nail her down, though, before she left.

"Let's do this," I proposed. "Why don't we agree to meet on Tuesday, this Tuesday," I added for emphasis. "After lunch. Or maybe I'll order lunch in and we can plan out a strategy. How does that sound?" I was overselling it, but I couldn't help myself. I continued, "You can churn your files tomorrow on Monday, get urgent stuff out of the way and be ready to go."

Her response was slow in coming. She blinked a couple of times. Looked between me and the dog.

"Sounds perfect," was her final answer. She pushed Morro's head gently, then was up and off the couch faster than I could blink.

She turned on her heel and was out the door before I could kiss her or even turn the knob for her. Through the window, I saw her throw her jacket over her head under the first splatters of rain, then run for her cherry red car.

Morro whined a bit, and I looked down to meet his pleading brown eyes. I kind of sympathized with him. The apartment was different without her. And not in a good way.

14

Every moment between breaths, I thought Ivy was going to die.

Still.

Even now.

It was as if I'd gone back ten years. Back to when they'd let us take our first baby home from the hospital; I could barely sleep even though I was already exhausted. It didn't let up after that first night.

I'd half sit, half lie in the rocker in her room listening to her breathe. Sometimes her tiny chest would stop moving up and down. I'd count the seconds, one...two...three. Then she'd take a deep breath and shift in her swaddle, and I'd release the breath I was holding.

If I could have breathed for her, I would.

If I could have had cancer for her, I would.

"How's our patient today?" Dr. Mira Ames asked when she bustled into the cold hospital room for Ivy's first post-surgery exam. I held tight to Stella, who was squirming in my lap. She'd have run across the room and tugged at Dr. Ames' coat if she could have. My little extrovert was having a hard time not being at the center of the action. When it came to doctors and hospitals, all the focus was on Ivy. I'd had to tell Stella on more than one occasion that she would not grow up and go to the hospital one day. That hospitals weren't a phase somewhere between losing your first tooth and learning to ride a bike.

Fingers crossed.

I'd really wanted to drop my littlest one off at day care. I'd actually asked Tino, but he'd been out the door at the crack of dawn. I couldn't do two things, drop Stella off and get Ivy to the hospital on time for her first post-surgery appointment. Obviously, I'd chosen the most important. I prayed to God that Stella forgave me for putting Ivy first more often than not.

I looked between the young woman in the white lab coat and Ivy ready to jump in and respond. It was too bad Ivy didn't have half of Stella's gumption.

"Good," Ivy finally answered. She took a deep breath as if that one word had taken all her strength. Then she spoke again. "Tired."

Tired was just the tip of the iceberg. She'd been mostly sipping soup and sleeping. She'd barely stayed awake in the car ride on the way over. Dark circles lay against skin paler than I'd ever seen it. I'm not sure why I expected her to bounce back so quickly. Nothing on the reams of paper about post-surgery care had suggested a quick recovery. Every estimate was twelve weeks at best. Yet, I'd expected her to wake up and start jumping on the trampoline outside like she used to when we'd bought it for her sixth birthday as stand-in for the attention we couldn't give her with a new baby in the mix.

"That's not going to change for a while." Dr. Ames' voice was soft, careful. When she became a more senior doctor, I thought she'd be a good one. Her calm and soothing manner was so different from the others who'd worked on Ivy. "A body can work just fine with one kidney," she continued, "but it takes time for the body to adjust, because the other kidney—the healing kidney—isn't really 'online' yet, so to speak."

"How long?" I asked, though I'm sure I'd heard the answer dozens of other times.

"Three to six months. It's a long time for a kid, I know." She turned to Ivy. "I'm going to ask you a couple of questions, okay?"

"Okay."

"Have you been bloated? Cramping? Nauseous? Felt like throwing up?"

"Maybe a little. But I felt like that before for a long time."

"Mom? Has she pushed out all the gas from carbon dioxide?"

"I think so. She was gassy when we first got home, but it's been better pretty quickly," I said. I'd been so relieved she'd passed that first hurdle. Eased the worry and the fear a tiny bit.

"What have you been eating?" Dr. Ames asked.

When Ivy hesitated, I jumped in. After all, it was me who'd done the cooking. "I made some *pollo*…chicken with sofrito, but maybe it was too much? So it's mostly been just soup and, when I can get something more in her, rice and beans."

"That's good. Not too much spice. Bland is better. White foods like plain rice, toast, yogurt, maybe some simple broiled chicken and plenty of water, of course. We want to keep those kidneys functioning, but not overwhelm."

"For sure, I'll be better about that," I said, working it out in my head how I was going to make three different things for four different people on a budget that was getting tighter by the day as I waited for unemployment to kick in or Tino's supposed promotion and raise.

"Have you had problems passing gas? Diarrhea or constipation?"

Even though it felt like hundreds of people had already asked those kinds of questions before, my daughter was still shy. I wasn't. Not anymore. I think most women lost any shade of modesty once they'd given birth bottomless in a room full of near strangers. Bodily fluids used to make me squeamish. Talking about it? Even more so. Now? After hundreds of diapers and being peed on and pooped on and spit up on, I just sprayed on some oxy stain remover, washed my hands, then moved on.

I pulled a paper from my purse and put it in the doctor's hand.

"I've kept a diary of everything, actually. Food, liquids, bowel movements. I should have given this to you before. I'm sorry, I forgot."

"Mrs. Garza, this is excellent." She scanned my handwritten notes. Nodded. "Can I copy it and put it in the chart?"

"You can keep it."

Dr. Ames clipped it carefully to the board at the end of the bed that held all of Ivy's details, then turned back to my oldest daughter. I liked that about her. That she focused on the child. So many doctors ignored young patients as if children weren't walking and talking humans.

"Have you had any shoulder pain?" she asked next. I'm guessing it was on a checklist of some kind. One for everything, no doubt. Brain tumor got one. Kidney cancer another. Ivy shook her head. I sighed, relieved. When we were home, just the two of us, I wasn't sure if she was putting up a brave front or if she was truly healing.

"Exercise?"

"Yes." I nodded vigorously. I knew exercise was important. I didn't want my daughter to be an invalid, the cure of surgery worse than the disease of cancer. "First it was a block or two. Now we all go down to Rock Creek park."

"I play in the slides and stuff," Stella said very loudly. I wanted to chastise her, tell her to use her inside voice, but I let it go. I'd said no to her too many times lately. "Ivy can't play right now. She sits on the bench with Mama," my little one added.

"It's about a two-block walk," I continued after Stella was done with her contribution. "Now we walk around a little once we get there."

"Good. Good. Keep that up, but nothing harder. That'll help with any constipation as well. But I'll still recommend some fiber chews. Daily bowel movement would be best."

I looked at Ivy to make sure she heard, that she was listening. That she didn't blame me for whatever I forced her to do next. I needed her to know that everything was for her own good.

"So today, we'll get some urine and blood, then you guys will be good to go. Good job, though, so far. You'll be in tip-top shape in no time. Before I go get the lab nurse, any questions?"

"Can we speak outside? Stella, keep your sister company. Maybe you can tell her your favorite parts of *Akeelah and the Bee* again."

For some reason, Stella idolized that little black girl's moxie. With both girls occupied for at least three or four minutes, I stepped out of the room and moved to the side of the wide door.

"You have great daughters," Dr. Ames said. "That little one must be a ton of fun."

"Stella? She is a lot of fun. I wish she had more of it. I wanted to ask you a question about the cancer. Do you think it could be caused by arsenic?"

"Arsenic?" Dr. Ames' brow furrowed and her face creased in a frown of non- understanding. "I'm sorry. The cause? We rarely know the cause of cancer outside of lung cancer or something like what people who are exposed to industrial pollutants get."

"That's exactly it, though. There's a lawyer suing Strohmeyer who's saying that dumping arsenic into the water may be the cause of kids, like my Ivy, getting cancer in Brighthill."

Dr. Ames' face cleared, but the sigh that accompanied her change in expression wasn't one of relief.

"Without any research or studies or other information, I can't answer that question for you, Mrs. Garza. Let me say this, though. I was reading an article from Harvard's school of public health. There are two concomitant issues that come up when we as doctors and scientists look at cancer. The first is whether it can be prevented. The second is what successful treatments can we do that save or prolong the life of the person."

"I hear all that, but I need to know if what Strohmeyer did was the thing that hurt Ivy. I don't want to upset my husband and maybe hurt my marriage and family if it's stupid. I mean, it's not that I don't wish all people could be spared from cancer or that all people could be cured. I just want to know if the kids in Brighthill should have been spared."

"Again, I hear you. I deeply sympathize with your pain of being a parent of a child with cancer, but it's not that easy."

"Do you think Ivy shouldn't be a part of the lawsuit, then?"

"I'm not saying that either. What I guess I'm saying is that this is not as easy as lung cancer, where I tell you to quit to lower your chances. This is an unfortunate thing that happens to some children in some families. There are trillions of cells in the human body. We're not perfect. Our bodies make mistakes when replicating our cells. Whether those mistakes are an inside job or an outside job is something that I can't make any pronouncements about. You'll have to do what's best for your family and what your conscience can live with. There are no easy answers, and for that I'm truly sorry."

The doctor nodded her goodbye, then walked away, her heavy clogs slapping against the spotless floor. I took a very deep breath, then pushed my way back into the hospital room, passing the nurse as she left, rolling a cart in front of her.

"Where'd you go, Mama?" Ivy's voice rose in a panic. "Is there something wrong you're not telling me?"

I quickly changed my face to be as straight as possible. My mother had always said it revealed too much.

"No, honey. No, of course not. I wouldn't keep anything from you. You're too old for that. I think you can understand what's going on. Need to understand so that you can best care for yourself."

Ivy shifted on the small bed so that she was sitting up higher than a moment before. Her sudden intolerance of hospitals was something new.

"Can we go soon? They're all done—"

"They took blood from her arm," Stella interrupted. "A lot of blood. Then she had to pee in a cup, Mama. They took that too. I touched it. It was warm. Why was it warm? In the toilet it's cold."

I tried not to let disgust show on my face. Of course she'd stuck her little hand in the toilet. Stella was my inquisitive one.

"Everything in your body is warm. Probably ninety-eight degrees like when they take your temperature here. The water that fills the toilet is cold. The bowl is made of china, and that's cold too. All that cold makes the pee cool too."

"Oh." I could see Stella thinking. Taking in the new knowledge. Scary smart my youngest was. In a different family she'd probably get the stimulation she needed. In this one, she was lucky to get three meals a day.

As soon as Ivy was better, then I could focus on the younger one. Hopefully she wouldn't be too behind without daily flash cards or classical music playing in her ears all day like all the other moms from day care were doing.

"Here you go," Dr. Ames said, handing me another stack of care instructions. I did my best to fold them together and shove them back into my bag.

The oncological urologist had followed in her wake.

"There you are, Ivy," the urologist started. "Dr. Ames tells me that your recovery is going great. I'll see you in a week or so for another checkup, okay? Then we'll make some decisions about what comes next. I'm super hopeful, though, that this will be it. That the cancer will be gone. You won't need chemo or radiation. Then there will be nothing more to do than heal and live life like every other kid."

I looked between the two doctors and my two daughters and sent up a not-so-silent prayer.

"From your lips, to God's ears."

15

"How is she?"

It was the second or maybe even third time Tino had asked the question. This time he was standing in front of the huge flat-screen plasma TV that had busted our Christmas budget.

With his hands on his hips, I couldn't see to the right or left of him. I lifted the remote from the couch next to me and pressed the button that quieted the voices coming from the screen.

It looked like I wasn't going to see how the home makeover was going to turn out. Too bad, I wanted to see how the family was going to create a multipurpose living room for parents and kids alike. I toed at the half-naked Barbie doll on the floor. Maybe I'd figure out how to have a picture-perfect home where tiny plastic dolls weren't constantly under my feet. I looked up again. When Tino stayed as still as a brick house, I finally answered.

"Sleeping."

His already wide chest expanded with his sigh.

"I can see that," he replied.

"Where have *you* been?" I could hear my voice rising but couldn't help it. "Your daughter had cancer surgery, had one of her body parts—a vital organ—carved up like a ham, but somehow you were too busy to come home."

He folded his bulky arms across his chest. I tried not to be reminded of how much I'd liked those arms when we'd first gone out. Arms that had gotten big and strong from hefting around sacks of grain and kegs of beer. I tried to push the memory of him hugging me tight and whispering promises of a fantastic future together if we went to Cleveland and struck out on our own.

"There was a crisis at work, Veronica," he huffed.

I didn't point out that Strohmeyer leapt from one crisis to the next like an Olympic hurdle runner.

For beer.

Not lifesaving cancer treatment or vaccines or anything important—just alcohol.

"There was a crisis at home." I jabbed my finger into the space between us.

"But I fixed that. Do you know how hard it was for me to beg them for help?"

"Beg them?" I pleaded. "Beg them? It's work-provided health insurance, not charity. We still have to pay the expensive premiums we couldn't afford before. Plus all of the co-pays. They were careful to explain that to me when we went to the office to arrange the hospital transfer. I appreciate that your work insurance covered most of this surgery. I really am grateful that my daughter got the best care money could buy. But we didn't have that insurance because we could never afford it. Still can't."

I knew my frustration probably wasn't fair, but it's not as if Strohmeyer had come in and waved a magic wand. They'd provided something that they'd have provided anyway, if we'd been able to sign up for it before. I didn't want to have to grovel and get on my knees every time we talked about this.

"Is this about Stella?" he huffed.

Ivy had been right on the money. The preschool had called fifteen minutes before Tino had, to say that she needed to be picked up. Fifteen minutes and forty-five dollars in late fees later, I'd gotten my crying child who'd thought we'd forgotten all about her. I didn't know if there was a sufficient amount of reassurance that would ever fix that, not if Ivy on the brink of surgery remembered the time her father had forgotten *her* as well.

"Is this about Stella?" I repeated, and shook my head. There weren't enough words for me to explain this to him in either English or Spanish. "This is about Stella. This is about Ivelisse. This is about your commitment to your family. The Strohmeyers are not your family. I am. Stella is. Ivy is. You seem not to be able to remember who you're related to."

"I know—" His eyes darted away hiding the guilt I knew I'd see there if he could muster up the *cojones* to face me.

"Do I need to draw you a diagram or one of those family tree ancestry things everyone's into right now? I'm happy to get some pen and paper. Maybe then you'll understand."

"You're not supporting me." He uncrossed his arms. Held his palms up to the sky. "I need that right now. I'm at a critical time in my job."

"You've been in a critical time since the moment we moved here. You're always on the verge of some damned promotion."

"I've gotten most of them, Veronica. I bought us this house you're all living in. The car you're driving."

"I didn't ask for all of that. Any of that. That doesn't even matter now. Our daughter has cancer. Had surgery to remove part of her damned kidney."

We were both quiet for a second. Around the side of my husband, I watched the TV designer arrange beautiful turquoise baskets that fit perfectly inside a sparkling white cabinet made for just that purpose. The TV designer slid one out and all of that girl's Barbie dolls were arranged in little trays. Those dolls were all dressed up in their perfect tiny outfits with tiny Barbie shoes still on. I reached down to pick up Stella's doll, shoe-less and without pants or panties, hair half braided and half matted. I smoothed the hair as best I could. Wondered how I could get her dressed, but I didn't see any tiny clothes in my own living room among the mess of toys and other kid stuff.

"I'm here now." Tino's arms came down. He bowed his head, then looked at me. Met my eyes for once. "What do you need? I can check up on her."

"For the love of God, don't go in there waking her up."

"You always do this, you know. You say you need help with the kids, but don't let me help."

I bit my lip hard. I'd needed him to pick up his other daughter when Ivy was recovering from surgery. That's the help I'd needed. If he didn't do the one thing that could have been a massive help to our family, then how in the hell could I trust him on anything else?

"What was the crisis at work, anyway?" I asked. Not because I cared, but because he cared that I cared. That was *his* loyalty test.

"The DOJ is on our backs," he sighed. I could tell, though, he was happy the conversation had turned back on him. He seemed to think that whatever he was doing was more important than anything else. I probably should have pushed back on that years ago, but now wasn't the time to take a stand. I pressed the off button on the remote, turning the screen to black. Now that he had my full attention, Tino sat next to me on the couch. Took my hand in his. A wave of affection went to war with a wave of anger. I pushed both down, scooted to a far corner of the cushion.

"DOJ?"

"Department of Justice."

"Did the Strohmeyers do something illegal?" I tried to keep the panic out of my voice. Was the health insurance a payoff for my husband not blowing a whistle? "You've got to protect yourself, Tino. Rich people can do whatever they want and get away with it. People like us...we...we...can't."

"I'll be fine. Strohmeyer is facing about eight million in fines, not jail time, at least not now."

"What did they do?"

"Probably nothing. But when the Feds came sniffing, everyone up the food chain started panicking."

I was panicking and there were no cops anywhere close to my door.

"What's this nothing?"

"They're saying that water from the plant wasn't disposed of properly."

"I thought the waste was the opposite of anything toxic or bad. Just like the water after I soak the rice for *arroz con habichuelas*." I was parroting back the thing he'd said to me countless times. But that was competing with the facts that Justin McPhee had laid out. What Dr. Hanson was suggesting. That maybe the disposal of water from Strohmeyer and that water ending up in our drinking water *was* a problem.

"It's true," he said. But there was something in his voice. Something that wavered just the tiniest bit. If I hadn't been married to him, known him for more than a dozen years, I'd never have heard it. "It has to be true, otherwise people all across Europe would have been poisoned and dying for centuries."

"This makes no sense. What are they saying?" I was prodding, gathering evidence that maybe could help Ivy. Because if I had to be honest, I'd do anything for my kids. Die for my kids. After Ivy'd been born, she'd replaced Tino as the most important person in my life. After Stella, he'd been demoted to number three.

"We filter the water we get from the city."

"I thought you used well water. Isn't that what they advertise?"

I knew those ads like the back of my hand. Tino made sure to slow down and point to every Strohmeyer billboard that featured a beer he brewed personally. And with the constant downtown sports promotion, there was practically a microbrew ad on every corner.

"For some brews, sure. That's how they started. But if they made every variety with well water, we'd bleed the wells dry. That's not being a good corporate citizen, so for the biggest seller, Coop, they just use plain water."

Strohmeyer's best seller, Cooperhouse—Coop for short—was as much of a household word as Budweiser. Coop's brown-and-red labels were as familiar as my own name. I let out a breath. Tino was exclusively in the craft brew side of things. I relaxed my shoulders and patted the space next to me on the couch.

Silent truce reached, my husband uncrossed his arms and moved next to me so that we were touching from shoulder to knee. I slipped my fingers into his thick hair. Massaged the back of his neck and scalp. He leaned into me like a happy cat.

"No matter where we get the water from, we can't just add it to the grains like you would in the kitchen. Who knows what's in that? So we use some super high-end RO filters."

"RO?"

"Reverse osmosis. Complicated term, I know. It just means that we can take out everything—chemicals...minerals. For water, we just need to remove stuff like heavy metals, mercury and the like, and arsenic."

"Sounds normal." I'd seen a sink filter in almost everyone else's house. I'd never thought it important. All those water quality reports that came in the mail with smiling cartoon water drops were very reassuring. "What's the problem with all that?"

"They're saying that we didn't properly dispose of the stuff we filtered out."

"But isn't that the city's problem? They leave all that stuff in the water to begin with."

"I wish. But in the water supply, it's just parts per billion. When we filter it out, it's parts per million. So we use these filters made from sand, nothing complicated, just your average ordinary sand. When the filters get dirty, then we just use water and hydroxide to clean the filters. Then we pour that water into a lined pool on the brewery's property. Now the justice department is saying that those pools contaminated the drinking water for Clearwater Park." He caught my eye. "Not Brighthill or anything."

I flashed on Justin McPhee's statement, that water didn't follow city borders. Tucked that one away for later.

"What does that mean for you? What's the emergency?" I asked Tino.

"They think an indictment's coming down for us."

"An indictment...like, criminal? People are the only ones who go to jail. Companies don't go to prison. You're not facing jail time or anything like that, Tino? You said fines, but is that the whole truth?"

"No, nothing like that. No one's going to jail. Just money, like I said. But the possible eight-million-dollar fine is a lot."

"You're not on the hook, though, for any part of that money?"

I could just see a company like Strohmeyer divvying up the debt and dividing it among employees like they were shareholders or company owners and not just workers subject to decisions from higher-ups.

"No, no. Of course not," Tino insisted. My tension was eased a tiny bit with that worry taken off my shoulders. "I just need to make sure that our documentation doesn't make us look guilty."

"What do you mean? Did Strohmeyer do that? Leave pools of arsenic in the ground?" Just like that my worry ratcheted back up. Following the corporate lead was one thing. Altering documentation seemed like the kind of thing that could lead directly to jail time for the doer. And getting some mid-level person to do the dirty work had bad corporate behavior written all over it.

"It's not as bad as it sounds. There's already arsenic in the ground. It's like saying pouring water into the ground that already has stuff in it doubles the amount of toxins. If that were true, we wouldn't be able to use tap water for plants or farms. Toxic in, toxic out. If it's not toxic, then there's nothing wrong."

"Arsenic pools..."

"Just business stuff." Tino ended the discussion when he stood. "I think I've got it handled. If everyone's asleep, I'm going to go upstairs, pack it in."

Ten years ago, I'd have begged him to stay downstairs with me. Instead, I hit the power and volume buttons the minute he left the room. But not to hear more about how light ceilings can make a room look taller, but so I could make a call to Justin McPhee without Tino overhearing.

If I had to choose between my daughter and my husband, Ivy came first. Jobs could come and go, but I only had one sick daughter, and she was much more important than any rich family ever would be.

16

"Your Honor, Justin McPhee. I'm representing the plaintiffs in this consolidated matter against Strohmeyer Breweries."

Justin was standing up at the podium in one of the thirty-four nearly identical wood-paneled courtrooms on the fifteenth floor of the Justice Center. Once he'd cleared his throat a few times, then gripped the sides of the lectern until his knuckles had turned a blinding white, his voice had gone from quavering to butter smooth.

I let out a breath. I was so nervous for him, for myself. He may have had more experience than me, but neither one of us knew what in the hell we were doing with this case, in handling a class action. The moment I'd started seriously perusing the blizzard of papers from Morrell Gates, I knew we were out of our depth. My clients always said they wanted a Johnnie Cochran, and would have hired him if they could have afforded it. I'd always been deeply offended. *Now* I got it. For our team, *I* wanted Jan Schlichtmann, famous for his big cancer cluster settlements in Woburn, Massachusetts, and Tom's River, New Jersey.

When Judge Patrick Brody started speaking, I finally pulled my eyes from Justin's smooth suit-clad back and trained them on Judge Brody.

"You were here before," Brody intoned. "Something to do with that prostitution ring. Ms. Cort, you're like a bad penny. Enlighten me. Tell me why Mr. McPhee seems so familiar."

Justin looked over his shoulder, confirming it was my turn. I hadn't planned to speak, but stood, smoothed down my gray silk skirt, tried to feel around as surreptitiously as possible to make sure my blue blouse was tucked. Patrick Brody used to like me when I was his soon-to-be daughter-in-law, when I was the underdog lawyer. Maybe not so much after my erstwhile former client had taken down his son. The judge's "bad penny" reference left a bitter, coppery taste in my mouth.

"One of the coconspirators, Derek Waters, in the State of Ohio versus Jarrod Carter, et al, needed his own defense, so I referred him to Mr. McPhee."

"Right. He's the one who tipped the whole thing. Got arrested with a so-called burner phone he shouldn't have kept. It's always one stupid criminal that unravels the conspiracy."

There weren't any questions in that last bit, so I didn't say another word. I smoothed my skirt under my butt and sat down as quietly as I could so that Judge Brody could pick a fight with someone else more equipped to do battle. The judge turned toward the defense table.

"Ms. Shively, you have more people on your side of the aisle than a good baseball coach has in the dugout. Are these all your pinch hitters?"

"Your Honor, Morrell Gates is representing the wrongly accused Strohmeyer. We are putting our best on this case to save this local family business from ruin by the plaintiffs' spurious claims."

"Your Honor." I stood, unable to keep myself in my seat. "If Ms. Shively keeps this up, we're going to need an ophthalmologist on call to save all of us from eye injury."

"Your Honor," Shively protested, her voice nearing a whine. Had she been like that when I'd been a summer associate? I'd looked up to Miriam Shively. Thought she'd be one of those strong women who'd have my back while we hammered at the glass ceiling side by side. One word from the Strohmeyer family and my name had been mud, and our nascent alliance had been broken.

Brody swatted in the air as if we were all pesky flies.

"I should have recused myself, but I think that I won't need to. Looks like you're all going to be out of here faster than a northeastern Ohio weather front."

"Recuse?" Justin asked.

He glanced back at me. I did a subtle head tilt toward the defense side. It hadn't gone unnoticed by me that my ex-fiancé, my *first* ex-fiancé, was in the so-called defense dugout. Not to mention my fellow summer associates I'd come up with, and Ted Strohmeyer who was now a partner. Talk about bad pennies.

"Now that my son is with Morrell, I will no longer hear any cases from them. All of the cases currently assigned to me where Morrell Gates is on either side of the aisle will be reassigned to other judges."

"Even if we're willing to waive like everyone did in the Carter case?" Justin asked. He'd said more than once that Judge Brody could be our ace in the hole. Looked like we were going to be the ones left holding all the cards.

"Even if, Mr. McPhee. The appearance of impropriety is to be avoided at all costs. The Code of Judicial Conduct tells us...let me quote, 'A judge shall uphold and promote the independence, integrity, and impartiality of the judiciary, and shall avoid impropriety and the appearance of impropriety.' That phrase, 'appearance of impropriety,' appears eight different times in the code. *Eight*. Tells me it's something important."

There was nothing to do after all that proprietary judicial posturing but nod. Justin couldn't see me, but we'd bobbed our heads in unison.

"Yes, Your Honor."

"I'm actually surprised that you're here. It seems that the numerous defense counsel over here has filed a 'Notice to Adverse Parties and State Court.' According to section fourteen forty-six of the United States Code, I have no authority here, not until the big boys around the corner rule on this motion for removal attached here as a courtesy."

"Removal?"

Shively stood. "Your Honor, the agreement that we executed with Counselor McPhee here whereby we waived time on our responses so we could get in front of you as soon as possible. The flip side to that was that Mr. McPhee here"—Shively said "McPhee" as if she were referring to a child—"waived any objection to us filing defenses. The single motion we filed was for removal."

I hated being blindsided. I knew it was going to happen. That's how firms practiced law. But I thought it would be later or at least not today. From the posture of Justin's back, I couldn't read him.

Judge Brody lifted and dropped some papers on the wood.

"Service looks good."

"But, Your Honor...we're here ready and prepared to argue our motion for class certification pursuant to Civil Procedure rule twenty-three," Justin insisted as if our readiness was going to persuade Judge Brody to ignore the black letter law. In light of all the recent controversy surrounding Tom's departure from the prosecutor's office, and the little speech on judicial conduct we'd all just heard, bending law or procedure in our favor was the least likely scenario.

I'd said as much to him a few hours earlier when we'd been getting ready at his apartment. He'd convinced me we could work better at his place, get a good night's sleep, and get ready to go this morning. We'd worked some, but eating and sex had taken up more time than I thought it should.

"Mr. McPhee. Ms. Cort. I sympathize with you. I do. I was more than ready to rule on your class action motion today. But we all know how this works.

"Federal supremacy always trumps. The District Court for the Northern District of Ohio will decide if you can come back over to our little old common pleas court. Counselors, I wouldn't hold my breath on that one. But if they do, you'll get a new judge out of the stack. As presiding judge, I'll make sure of that. For now, I'm suspending the forty-one cases enumerated in the class action certification pending a ruling from federal court."

Judge Brody stood. Nodded curtly. Turned and walked through the door behind the bench, because there was only one thing a judge loved more than absolute power in their courtroom: a smaller docket.

17

"I made reservations at Sergio's for seven. Is that too early? Will you be able to make it?" Ron asked. The way he framed the invitation made it seem like he really wanted me to say yes.

It was nice to be wanted.

I looked at my watch. It was two thirty. One hearing plus possible forced settlement negotiations times how many lawyers equaled a late day. Factored in the fact that it was Friday and Jacobs Field would be busy.

"What time is the baseball game tonight?" I asked a passing guard. I was in the federal courthouse. This call, Ron's voice on the line, was the only thing keeping me from falling down and curling into a ball of fear and dread. My new self, my pseudo big-firm lawyer self, the me that was going to take on the world, wanted to shove that promise into a closet and pull it out tomorrow. But the court had set up a hearing for today. Like I'd done for the last ten years, I was going to have to learn on the job.

"Seven. Night game. Indians are playing the Rangers."

I turned away from the guard. Kept my knee-jerk reaction to push back at the reference to Native Americans to myself.

"No problem. I'll be there. Looking forward to it." That last had been the truth. Ron had done exactly what he said he'd wanted to do over the last few weeks. He'd moved from the casual dating zone to the boyfriend zone. Not only was he my regular date, he was my regular date with plans. I liked it, a lot, being pursued as if I were a prize to be won.

"Are you done?" Justin stood in front of me, shifting from one foot to another, looking at his watch, and generally acting impatient. I looked at my phone. The federal courthouse was intimidating the crap out of me. He was probably feeling the same. I'd taken the call from Ron just to have a sense of myself. To have a part of my life I could control. When I was in court, it sometimes felt like anything could happen, despite all the rules, regulations, procedures, and laws that covered it.

"I was just talking to Ron," I said. Then waited for what I knew had to come next.

"That mean you're busy this weekend?"

Yup. Justin McPhee didn't disappoint. He didn't want to date me but was far too concerned about my weekend plans nonetheless.

"Tonight at least," I answered. "We're going to Sergio's."

"Good Italian," he proclaimed. "Went on a date a few weeks ago."

I ignored the twinge of jealousy in my belly. I dated Ron. Justin dated other women. We were just colleagues with a sexual relationship on the side, kind of like creamed spinach at a steakhouse, unnecessary but oh-so-good.

"She stick?" The thing about our *other* relationship is I had no idea when it would end. It was more a when than an if. At least I was old enough to know that. Maybe I'd be the one to pull the trigger if things became more serious with Ron. I liked the idea of controlling that part of my life as well. Maybe it was time to stop letting my choices blow with the shifting winds.

A federal officer came out into the hall and signaled toward us with a half salute.

"That's our cue."

I looked up and down the quiet hallway. Federal court was a world away from state court. Every department in common pleas was filled with litigants, parents in juvenile court, married people wishing they weren't in domestic relations, and remorseful defendants in criminal. This hallway was whisper quiet. Somehow the entire Morrell Gates team didn't make a sound. I tried not to breathe too loudly and ruin the ambience.

"Where's Ivy Garza's mom?" I asked under my breath. Judges would deny it to their dying breath, but they could be swayed by a sympathetic face, and I figured that this Veronica Garza probably had one.

"She said she'll be here." The clip, clip of heels sounded on the stone floor. Justin turned toward the sound. "There she is."

And there she was. I'm not sure what I expected of Veronica Garza, mom of a cancer patient. But the person coming toward us wasn't it. I guess I hadn't really been paying attention the first time we'd met in Justin's office.

She was pretty. Really pretty. Petite and what men would call stacked. Big boobs, big ass. Curves in a much more attractive configuration than my own. A mop of curly hair on top of tawny skin. All that wrapped in a bone-colored sheath dress that complemented her skin but would be more at home in a club than a courthouse. That kind of dress would make me look ruddy and my hair even more colorless than normal.

"Sorry. Sorry." Her eyes were the very picture of apology. "Ivy was more tired than usual. Took her a long time to get back from the park. By then Stella was hungry. Then I had to pick up Señora Ramos. So much traffic." A couple passed in Indians jerseys. Her eyes followed them while she took a breath between words. "Are people already getting ready for the game?"

"Take another breath. We're just going in now. Courts are not always on time. This is Casey Cort, by the way. You guys met in my office."

I shook her hand while I was enveloped in a cloud of perfume. It was almost too much, but not quite. She pulled her purse closer, then walked ahead of us toward the courtroom with confidence even I didn't have. When she was out of earshot, I turned to Justin.

"What's up with that outfit? Didn't you tell her it was federal court, not a dance club?"

"Too much you think?" He shrugged it off and kept walking, pulling open the courtroom's heavy wooden doors for Veronica Garza. It nearly closed behind them until I stuck my foot in just enough to catch it.

I didn't say a thing about how much his eyes had popped out of his head the moment she'd walked up. I tried to tuck away the weird twinge in my stomach when Justin put his hand against the small of her back and steered her into the courtroom, putting her in the third seat at plaintiff's table.

When Justin took the first chair position, I had no choice but to take the seat in between them. It felt less like a seating position and more like a statement. She smiled and turned the full force of that on me. I could see how Justin and probably her husband were dazzled by it. I blinked, then arranged my own face in something less than a scowl.

"Justin McPhee is an amazing lawyer, isn't he? Are you excited to be working with someone like him? You'll probably learn a lot," she said. "I can't thank you enough for fighting hard for my Ivy and kids like her."

Something about the way Garza said Justin's name made me want to shift my chair a little bit father from her. I shook my head clear of whatever was buzzing inside.

"You're welcome. Where's your husband?" I asked as I gestured toward the other parents who populated the gallery. All but one were in pairs.

"I didn't tell him about today's hearing. It's too much with Ivy and everything. He's worried enough about losing his job without adding more absences to his record."

Lose his job? I wanted to lean over and probe that with Justin, but just then the courtroom deputy appeared by the bench.

"All rise! Magistrate Judge Carol Wheeler presiding."

The magistrate judge was a tiny elfin creature. I wondered if she'd had to special order her robes because they weren't like clothes. Probably didn't come in kids' sizes.

"Morning, folks. Sit." She used her tiny hands to gesture downward. "Please sit. Looks like we're here on a removal matter. Who's here for the plaintiffs?"

"Justin McPhee with McPhee and Associates. I'm here with Casey Cort."

The magistrate looked between Garza and myself. "In the white dress?"

I shifted in my seat and tried not to feel insulted. Like any lawyer worth her salt would show up dressed like she was auditioning for *Dancing with the Stars*.

"Representative plaintiff, Your Honor," Justin corrected. "Mother of Ivelisse Garza. Ivy's a ten-year-old with kidney cancer from Clearwater Park."

"Your Honor." Miriam Shively stood, indicating her objection to what, I had no idea.

"You'll get your turn, counselor. Surely you're not objecting to the fact that the child has cancer or is from Clearwater Park."

Miriam's sigh was nothing short of dramatic.

"No, Your Honor."

"Since you feel the need to speak in my courtroom when it's not your turn, why don't you tell me who's here for the moving party, the defendant, Strohmeyer Breweries."

"Miriam Shively, Your Honor. We were on the Ohio Bar's Banking and Commercial Committee together. In 2004."

Magistrate Judge Wheeler pinched at the top of her nose as if the memory weren't particularly strong and squeezing hard enough would somehow bring it back. "Were you the asbestos lawyer?"

I was sure if I looked up disdain in the dictionary, Wheeler's current facial expression would have been exhibit one.

"Among other aspects of my practice." Miriam's voice was defensive. Now that one I'd heard before.

"Right." Wheeler's voice was clipped. "Who else?"

Ted Strohmeyer stood, buttoned his suit jacket. Paused like a crown prince.

"Ted Strohmeyer—"

"You here as the client?" Wheeler interrupted.

Ted shifted in his visibly expensive clothes as if a woman speaking to him made things chafe a little.

"No, Your Honor. I'm a partner at Morrell Gates."

"Is there going to be a conflict here?" Clients rarely if ever got to speak on their own behalf, and certainly not at a hearing that was purely on a legal motion. Ted being a major shareholder in the company being sued put Morrell Gates in an awkward position of having someone with a stake weighing in on things. Ted Strohmeyer's goals and Morrell's goals were not perfectly aligned.

"No, Your Honor." Shively's voice, speaking for Ted, had gone a bit quiet. He was a partner. He was the client contact. If Morrell didn't play nice with him, they'd lose millions of dollars in yearly fees and someone's head would be on the chopping block. Shively didn't want it to be hers. It didn't matter if there were a conflict, this was the kind of thing everyone was going to go along with.

Money talked.

Ethics walked.

It had talked when I'd gone up against the Strohmeyers. That fundamental fact of American economics hadn't changed in a decade.

"It's practically a baseball team, let's get on with it."

Wheeler's pale hands waved again. She was a hand talker. I was going to have to get used to watching for them to come out of her robes. Though our case was assigned to a "real" federal judge, we'd probably never see him.

The United States Courts had become so clogged that a new layer of so-called magistrate judges had been added. They had neither the scrutiny of having to be confirmed by the United States Senate, nor the security of a lifetime appointment.

All that aside, they could preside over nearly everything a regular federal district court judge could, except felony trials. We were nowhere near that exception, so it was very likely we were stuck with the mini-magistrate. I didn't yet know if that was going to be a good thing or a bad one.

"In the interests of time," Shively said, "I'll do the rest. We have Tom Brody, David Cummings, and Patricia Ritchey here from the firm on behalf of Strohmeyer. Last at the end of the row is Simon Brody. He's the client representative."

"Brody? Are you two of Patrick's boys?"

Tom and Simon nodded. Two handsome dark blond bobbing heads.

"Where are we on talks?"

"Talks?" Shively said.

"I'll spell it out for you," Wheeler condescended. I tried to imagine what Shively had said or done at some bar meeting to offend the magistrate. I chalked it up as an advantage for our side. The judge continued, "By talks, I mean settlement negotiations. The plaintiffs have a demand. You make a reasonable offer. They take it back to their clients. We can possibly save the citizens of this great nation some money."

"We're not at that stage, Judge Wheeler," Shively answered. Her tone wasn't convincing. Like me, she knew that judges would throw opposing parties in a room, like gladiators in an arena, at the drop of a hat.

"Any case is *always* at that stage. Two lawyers per side in chambers in two minutes. No client reps. Tom not Ted if it comes to that."

I stood, ready to follow the bailiff. I looked back and Justin was leaning his head toward Garza, ostensibly explaining what all had just happened. I knew Justin wasn't going to kiss her, because why would he? But still their heads were a little too close for comfort. Or I was experiencing irrational jealousy. I shook my head and turned back toward the bailiff to the magistrate's chambers. They were not as plush or nice as my former client Claire had described Judge Grant's chambers. No working fireplace here.

Magistrate Judge Wheeler did not remove her robes. Instead, she opened a plastic bottle of water, swigged, then sat in her chair and rolled forward until her chest was nearly to the edge of her desk. She looked between all of us. Me, Justin, Miriam, and Tom Brody. I liked it a lot better when Tom and I didn't see each other. All this togetherness was breeding contempt.

"What are the issues?"

"Your Honor, Justin McPhee for the plaintiffs," he announced.

"I didn't forget your name in the last five minutes," Wheeler snapped. Fortunately, Justin didn't appear put off. He continued.

"Strohmeyer's brewing practices have polluted the groundwater. Children from Brighthill and Clearwater Park have been the unfortunate casualties. We have a bona fide cancer cluster right here in Cuyahoga County."

"Ms. Shively? I assume you're the one speaking here."

Shively nodded. She'd been studying some papers in her hands. Shifted in her chair. Took off her reading glasses, folded them, set them on her lap.

"Causation? We haven't seen any evidence of that to begin with. Second, we challenge the idea that these cases have enough in common to be joined in a class action."

"What do you have to say about that, Mr. McPhee? Last time I checked, Strohmeyer wasn't the only business in Clearwater Park. Before the burners were turned off, Acel Steel was operating there. Even before that, it was mercury when Messing was turning out plumbing fixtures. Manufacturing has been the backbone of not just this city, but this county for generations."

"Furthermore," Shively continued as if the magistrate hadn't just asked for Justin's response. She slipped her cheaters on her nose. "That mycotoxin theory my opposing counsel is floating has been refuted in many different jurisdictions—Middle District of Alabama, Southern District of Florida, Eastern District of Kentucky, Eastern and Western District to Michigan just to list a few."

Shively took down her reading glasses and rattled her stack of papers for effect.

"Mr. McPhee." When my co-counsel nodded, Judge Wheeler smirked. "Look at that memory of mine. Is that your theory of causation, this well-refuted mycotoxin hypothesis?"

"No, Your Honor."

I'm pretty sure my eyes widened as much as Shively's did. I closed them as soon as I realized that Tom had caught wind of my expression. It sucked having my ex-fiancé on the other side of this case. While I still stuck with the belief that he'd never loved me, had used me as a very convenient dupe, not once, but twice, I still knew that he could probably read me as easily as a toddler's board book.

Judge Wheeler waved her hand, wrist limp, motioning for Justin to get on with it.

"The criminal enforcement section of the Environmental Protection Agency is investigating Strohmeyer for the improper disposal of wastewater."

"That sounds like mycotoxin," Shively said.

Justin glanced my way. I knew what he was asking, but he'd already gone rogue. I couldn't do any more than give the tiniest of shrugs.

"More like arsenic."

"Agatha Christie's favorite poison?" Wheeler asked. For the first time that afternoon, she looked something more than disinterested.

"That very one," Justin said.

"Ms. Shively, what light can you shed on this matter?"

"Such an investigation hasn't been brought to our attention. We'd have to confer with in-house counsel to answer this specific allegation."

"Your Honor, there have been successful prosecutions of this theory." Justin glanced at me meaningfully.

I picked up the paper Justin had handed to me earlier without comment and read my own list.

"In the District of Oregon, District of South Dakota, Western District of Tennessee, and so on," I said.

"Touché," Judge Wheeler said. "Mr. McPhee, Ms. Cort—are you the same Ms. Cort from the container girls case?"

"Yes, Your Honor."

"Welcome to federal civil practice. You're not doing too bad here. Maybe it's time to step your game up."

I wanted to interject but stayed mute.

"What's your demand?"

I channeled every women's magazine article that said women are too timid when numbers get big, swallowed, then spoke. "Thirty million."

Judge Wheeler didn't blink. "That include specials?"

"Compensatory and general, Your Honor. Special damages are limited. They're all in primary or secondary school, so there's no income to lose. Punitive if it comes to that could be added."

"What are you authorized to pay?" Magistrate Wheeler turned sharply on Shively and Brody.

"We have no authorization, Your Honor," Shively responded. "Our client maintains complete innocence."

"Might have bought that if the EPA..." Wheeler looked at Justin. "That Ohio or federal?"

"Both," he answered.

"You have two government departments that have nothing but time and taxpayer dollars. If there's smoke..."

"Again, Your Honor, we have zero authorization on this case. As far as counsel was concerned, we were here to argue for removal, and oppose class certification. We're only at the preliminary stages of discovery."

"Get Strohmeyer's counsel in here, the other Brody," Judge Wheeler said to her desk intercom.

"Your Honor." Shively stood as if she could end the meeting by walking out. That move only worked in her own office was my guess. That wasn't a show she could or should take on the road.

"Sit," Wheeler said when Simon Brody came into the room. She looked directly at him, unblinking. "Plaintiffs' demand is thirty million. They have a solid theory of causation. What's your response? Ms. Shively and the other

Mr. Brody here suggest you've given them zero authorization."

"Half million, plus costs. That's what we pay for nuisance suits. Each of you—" He looked right at me and then Justin. "—gets eighty-three thousand seven hundred fifty. Your clients each get a little walking-around money. They can add decks or buy new cars or whatever."

"Mr. McPhee? Ms. Cort? You want to weigh in here."

"Of course we'll take this number back to our clients, but I can almost guarantee you, they're not taking this. We're talking about kids with cancer, Your Honor. Kids who've been sick. School that they can't ever make up. They have lower life expectancies. They're more susceptible to getting adult cancers. Eight thousand one hundred seventy of so-called walking-around money doesn't even begin to compensate for that."

"Ms. Shively, have a gander at this. It looks here like we have a negotiation. I'm going to table these motions until Tuesday. If you reach a settlement before then, let my clerk know and we'll take you all off the docket. If not, see you Tuesday."

When *Wheeler* stood, the meeting was over. I filed out after everyone else and went to collect my stuff from counsel table.

"What happened? Why didn't the judge talk from up there?" Garza asked. Ready to defer, I looked around, but Justin was talking to Shively and the Brodys.

"She's moved the hearing until Tuesday."

"Why?"

"She wants us to negotiate, try to reach a settlement."

"She's not interested in hearing about Ivy? What it's been like having a child with cancer? How can she make a decision until she's heard all the facts?"

Justin was still talking. We'd had, I thought, a de facto agreement that he'd do this kind of hand-holding. No matter how many times I explained it, clients always had the same thought perpetuated by too many legal shows. That somehow everyone was interested in their personal tale of woe. That worked to squeeze tears from a television audience. The real legal system didn't care a whit.

"Judges always pressure the parties into settlement," I said. "You'll get to tell your story soon enough in depositions or even before the judge and jury, but not today. Even with the hearing adjourned, it wouldn't have been today. This was just a motion to join all of the parents' cases together into one big case."

Garza nodded. I looked over at Justin, now speaking to the group of collected families. No doubt he was giving a version of the same speech I'd just done for Garza.

Justin waved us over. I gave Garza a meaningful glance, and she followed me to the gallery. I looked over, but all of the Morrell Gates attorneys and errant Strohmeyers and Brodys were gone.

"Ohio law requires that I notify you of any offers from the defendant."

"They're already willing to pay?" one parent questioned.

"It's just a token offer," Justin answered. "The judge pressured them to offer something. They'd started at zero today. I want you to remember that we're seeking thirty million. Which would leave each family with half million. Strohmeyer's offer is about eight thousand per family."

One of the parents actually gasped. The timing of that response couldn't have been more perfect. In a millisecond, the families descended into outrage. Justin was smooth, I had to give him that. When he broke down the numbers that way, it wasn't quite so obvious that we'd make out much better than the families with a half million settlement. We'd each net a mid-five-figure payday.

"That's what they want to pay for kids...with cancer? Our kids?" a parent asked, her voice and expression the very picture of dumbfounded.

"They called it offering you some walking-around money," I added to the outrage. "They suggested you could use the money to add a deck."

"I already have a deck. I want money to get my daughter the best care, not county care, but Clinic care."

"We get that. We really do," Justin soothed. "But we're required by law to let you know of any offer."

"Are you saying we should take this...this insult. That this 'walking-around money' is all our kids are worth?" This parent, a father, crossed his meaty arms across a broad chest, his face set in a frown so dark I never wanted to be on his bad side.

Justin and I locked eyes. Nodded in near unison.

"We think it's outrageous," Justin said. "We'd never expect you to accept anything like this. Like I said, though, we have to tell you about any offers of money. Let you come to a decision."

"Can I say no for all of us?" a third parent asked. There was nothing but murmurs of agreement. Not a dissenter in the bunch.

"Good. Good that we're on the same page. We're going to be in negotiations this week. We'll keep you all posted. Please let my secretary know if your numbers or addresses are changed so we can be sure to be able to reach you. Sometimes cases move very slow. Sometimes fast. Either way, these are always your decisions to make."

The parents, suitably incensed, filed out of the courtroom, their conversations at a dull roar. The only one remaining was Garza. She'd maneuvered between the two of us.

"So I can go home?" she asked Justin. He patted her on the back, leaving a hand at her waist as he steered us out of the courtroom's gallery.

I answered when he didn't.

"Yes, please. Go be with Ivy and the rest of your family. I'm sure Justin will call you if we have any updates."

I'd have stayed to do more hand-holding, but Justin appeared to have that under control. When I peeled away to make sure I wasn't late for my date with Ron, he and Garza had their heads together as if they were planning a bank heist. I turned away from the uneasy feeling and toward my future. That lay with Ron and a classic Italian dinner.

I was calculating whether I had time to get home or if I was going to spend dinner trying to keep sauce from my suit, when I felt a hand grasp me above the elbow.

"Let's talk." I nearly fell from the shock of the touch. The voice sounded familiar, and I turned my head. It was whom I'd imagined, Simon Brody.

"About what?" I asked. I was wary. I wasn't in the mood for a lecture on how *I* had somehow ruined an already corrupt family.

"Not here," he said, his grip on my arm firm. I let him steer me to a small room with a modular oak table and four matching chairs that would have been at home in any Ikea showroom.

"What Justin said in there is true. It's the arsenic."

My eyes and head felt like they were spinning.

"What are you telling me…why are you telling me this? Did you go to medical school?" Diarrhea of the mouth wasn't attractive. Sometimes I talked when I needed to listen. Like now.

"I'm not saying arsenic causes cancer. Only God knows that. What I'm saying is that Strohmeyer knew the arsenic pools were dangerous, knew they were seeping into the groundwater, and did nothing about it."

"If the EPA, federal, and state are investigating, won't this come out? Won't it come out in discovery?"

"Not likely."

"Simon?"

"I've always liked you, Casey. You have gumption."

I held back my retort about this starting to feel like a 1950s black and white with a suitably plucky heroine.

Brody continued, "Tom is an idiot. He should have either married you or left you alone."

"I used to think marriage would have been a cure too. Now I know that it would have been a disaster. I wish he'd left me alone in law school or that crappy time right after."

"I've worked for Strohmeyer for nearly as long as you've practiced law. There are things they do that are good. They employ nearly ten thousand people. But they cut corners. They need to pay for this one. That's all I have to say."

"Simon, you offered half million. Called us a nuisance. I'm very confused." That was the most honest thing I could have admitted. I scrutinized his handsome face. I wasn't sure if this was a gift horse or a Trojan one.

"They're like a pack of wolves. Sometimes they need a culling."

"Why are you there? You could work for the government in any number of jobs or a firm, or you could even be a judge."

"John eight seven, Casey. Matthew seven fifteen."

Biblical quotes. Had he found God or something like it?

"I majored in poly sci, not religious studies."

"Every man is guilty of all the good he did not do. That's not the bible, but Voltaire."

He opened the door and stepped through it, turning back with a jaunty mock salute. The whoosh of air and noise from the hall made this half twilight zone waking dream I'd just entered disappear. I blinked slow and hard, clearing my eyes and mind. When I looked right and left, the hall was full, but I didn't recognize a single face. One glance at my watch let me know that if I hurried, I'd have time to get home, change, and get to my date with Ron on time.

While on the tram, I parsed out his biblical references. The first about he who is without sin casting the first stone. The second about a wolf in sheep's clothing. A pack of wolves. A flock of sheep. Justin would have laughed.

Justin.

The moment I was off the tram but before I got home, I picked one of the dozens of benches on the square, facing no one. Justin was number four on my speed dial. Number one was reserved for the most important person in my life. It was currently empty. I fingered the button, wondering if Ron was going to fill that slot, then moved down one. Pressed the correct sequence to get my co-counsel on the line.

"What's up?" His question was hesitant. He was getting ready for a date, I was sure. Was afraid I was going to intrude somehow. I wanted to scream that I knew the rules.

No real dating. No falling in love. Check. Check and check. Instead, I let him off the hook softly.

"I'm getting ready for dinner with Ron." He must have pulled the phone away, because all of a sudden there was silence where his breathing had been, but I could still hear his sigh of relief. It was like a soft poke in the gut. I continued, "I think I need to share something with you."

"Listening." I could also hear him zipping and brushing.

"I encountered the strangest animal of all this afternoon—a Brody with a conscience."

18

I was ready to lift my bum off my chair, stand, and show Garza the door, but she settled a little more into her chair ready to keep talking. Better boundaries would have been good right then. I just had to hope that Casey would be here in a few minutes, so her arrival cut this impromptu meeting short.

All the time I was on my date last night, with some acquaintance of my sister, two women dominated my thoughts, and neither of them was the pretty woman who'd been across from me in the restaurant. I'd wanted to apologize but ended the date early instead.

Both women who'd distracted me from my date were going to be in my office today. There was a whole lot wrong with that, I knew. In any other situation, I'd have avoided both until they'd stopped contacting me. But I couldn't ghost my co-counsel or the mother of my name plaintiff. I was too deep into this.

The kids' ghostly faces in their pictures.... Representing the families from my Brighthill and Clearwater Park files were the greater good, the bigger picture. For them, for justice, I was willing to sacrifice emotional discomfort.

Last night when I'd said goodbye to the date that hadn't gone past the first prosecco, instead of getting in my car, I'd taken a brisk walk to my office.

With all the lights blazing, I'd torn through every single file. Any discovery I'd received. There hadn't been a single reference to arsenic. Not a single one. If Simon Brody had said as much to Casey, he must think we had some way to access the information. Two cups of coffee told me that the link had to be Garza. Either her or Tino. Her call was a happy coincidence. I just couldn't figure out how to ask for what we'd need to put this case on the fast track to settlement.

Garza wrung her hands. More was going on here than a chat about my co-counsel, the pretext for this meeting.

I got more physically comfortable in my chair. Looked at Garza in the eye. It was my cue for her to speak. She didn't hesitate.

"You have that Casey Cort helping you? Is she good?"

"She's better than good. She has a special kind of...I don't know the right word...relationship with the people on this case."

"Relationship?" Garza's eyes drew so close together that a deep crease formed on her forehead.

"It's something that makes her hungry," I tried to explain.

I could see Garza trying to work out what I was saying without saying it, but she was struggling. Then her face cleared, and her eyes widened in wonder.

"Wait...is she the lawyer who represented that man who kept young girls in that container? That's what the judge was talking about, wasn't it?"

Sometimes I forgot about Casey's infamy. Knew her long before she represented the headline making runaway federal judge and racist cop, then the sex trafficker. I nodded.

"One in the same."

"Has she ever done *this*?" Her fingers pointed to the papers she'd dropped on my blotter. "A case about pollution and cancer and all that?"

"No." My answer was both blunt and truthful.

"But then..." The wrinkle between Garza's brows was back.

"Let me tell you a story. Then I think you'll get it. You'll hear me out?"

Garza popped up out of the chair. Paced for a good twenty seconds.

"Can I sit on the couch?" she asked.

"If you don't mind, I'll sit next to you. I want to talk to you person to person for a minute. Not lawyer to client."

"That would be good. Can I call you Justin? You can call me Veronica."

I lifted my bum for real this time and took one end of the couch while Garza settled in on the other. Shifting forward, I placed my elbows on my knees so I was hunched over. Earnestly, I began the story.

"When I met Casey, she was at this huge low point in her life. She'd thought she was going to be an associate at Morrell Gates."

Garza's eyebrows shot up under her curly bangs as the name recognition worked its way through her brain.

"Isn't that the firm who is on the brewery's side? Strohmeyer's side?"

"Yes. She used to work there."

"Why doesn't she work there anymore? Are you worried that she's loyal to them and not us?"

I liked the way she said *us*.

"About ten years ago when Casey was in law school, she discovered that a student had completely plagiarized an article he'd turned in for publication."

I didn't think Garza's eyebrows could go up any higher, but they did. I whispered *wait for it* in my own head.

"That student is Ted Strohmeyer," I revealed in a whispered rush.

"He was allowed to become a lawyer?" she asked.

"Everyone circled the wagons to protect him, not her. He was one of the lawyers in the gallery," I explained. "He was the one Shively asked whether he was a lawyer or a client."

The way she nodded, I knew that she remembered. That she saw how unfair things had been for Casey. And now how unfair they could be for the sick kids in Brighthill and Clearwater Park.

"Typical, I guess. So, they picked him over her, right? That's why she's not at that Gates firm." She shook her head in resignation.

"That about covers it. The partner who's leading the case, Miriam Shively, was Casey's mentor, and one of the lawyers on the defense side, Tom Brody, used to be her ex-fiancé."

"Wow."

"Small town, Cleveland." I shrugged. I was well used to the constant intersection of men and women in the legal community. "I think it's safe to say that Casey's on our side."

"I guess so. Can I say something?" What was coming next was going to be the reason she didn't leave. She'd had to vet me first, though. Make sure that Casey and I were trustworthy enough for what was coming next. "I think we can get more documents about the arsenic."

It was my turn for my eyebrows to shoot up. Though I'd been waiting for a break, I didn't think it would come this way. I'd been thinking I was going to have to work up to asking her husband to do a document hunt for us. I'd been wavering because I *still* wasn't sure her husband was on board. Sure, I had his *signature* on the retainer agreement. I had Veronica Garza's say-so, but other than the single time we'd met at the hospital, I had zero idea where Celestino Garza stood on not only his daughter's case, but the whole proposed class action in general. Not to mention I'd never seen his reaction to his daughter possibly being the name plaintiff. It was a lot, all of that. The permutations. The possibilities were staggering. I started with a simple question.

"More documents?"

"Strohmeyer's hiding more than they're letting anyone know about."

"Did your husband, Tino, say something?" I asked. When I'd found out that my client's husband worked for the company I was suing, my first thought was that my name plaintiff would disappear like smoke. My second thought was hope for a Deep Throat whistleblower-type situation. The first was far more likely than the second, which was essentially a fantasy. Veronica confirmed my wishful thinking with her next words.

"It's what he didn't say...Justin. He normally tells me everything. I know more about hops and fresh fruit versus fruit juice in craft brews than any person outside of a brew room has a right to. I know when he thinks Strohmeyer is cutting corners. I know when he thinks they're doing false advertising. When I asked him about the arsenic, though, after he first mentioned how overwhelmed they were by the EPA investigation...nothing. Nada. *No más. No más.* He may as well have been Roberto Durán protesting after the fight with Sugar Ray Leonard."

I was losing my poker face. I knew it had slipped when I felt my fingers massaging the spot between my brows. Clients hired you as an expert, then spent too much time trying to investigate their own case. Except for criminal defendants. The people who actually needed to be the most involved were the most checked out. Incarceration was as little of a motivator as it was a deterrent.

My hope that Garza had the answers was just that— irrational, wishful thinking. Simon was probably throwing out a red herring. A pure third-dimensional chess move. Casey and I needed to put our heads together to even figure out if this angle was worth pursuing. For that to happen, I needed Garza to go home to her daughter.

"What do you think he knows but isn't saying?" I asked. I wasn't listening for the answer. Instead, I was planning Garza's eviction or my own escape. I glanced surreptitiously at my watch. It was too early to suggest a lunch break. Though after having Chinese with her, I'd already crossed that line, and she may well invite herself. I turned my ear toward the door, hoping like heck Casey was early for some reason. That she hadn't done brunch with her neighbors or Ron. Sometimes our Sundays were like that—starting early, especially when they were extensions of Saturday night.

"I can't guess like that," Veronica was saying when I tuned back in. "Maybe I could, but I've been too worried about Ivy. I...I...I shouldn't say this. If what they say on legal shows is true, I could get into trouble..."

"Just say it," I blurted out. I hope my impatience didn't show. There were about one thousand ways this case or cases could go sideways. I wasn't interested in frolicking and taking detours.

"I know where Tino keeps the important papers in his office. He has them in a file cabinet. He doesn't even have a lock, because he's so far down on the totem pole, that no one thinks he has access to anything important—corporate secrets or anything like that."

"I can't condone anything illegal." There was no wink and no nudge. I couldn't imagine a low-level brewery worker had access to bet the company documents. If a smoking gun existed, it was in the hundred or so boxes in the conference room down the hall. I'd have to have missed it the first time around. Casey and I would just have to burn the midnight oil until we found it.

"I know. I know." Garza nodded. I nearly stood a second time ready to go find that needle in a haystack. The documents that would give us the leverage for an eight-figure settlement. Then her next words surprised me. "I'm going to go over there, though, to Strohmeyer."

"On a Saturday? Why do you think they'd let you in?" Those weren't the real questions I had, about breaking and entering and felony arrests not working so kindly in our favor. But my questions gave her a wide exit door from crime land.

"Hi, my husband—" Garza's voice was unusually high, accented. "—he left something in his office. If he doesn't have it, he'll be fired."

That she did in an accent stereotypical of Hispanics, the kind you'd hear on a semi-offensive late-night comedy show. I wanted to be horrified, but it wasn't half bad. I could see her getting anything she asked for if she spoke that way, because she'd be forgettable and non-threatening.

"You'd be better off saying your husband left something for your kid, but the kid's at a game and you need it before she goes to bed." I found myself giving her advice on breaking the law before I thought better of it.

"You don't have kids..." I confirmed her supposition with a quick shake of the head. "You're good...that's good."

"I can't ask you this because I'm required to report a client's future crimes. But hypothetically, if you were going to do this, were you planning to do this today?"

"As soon as I leave here. Tino would ask too many questions if I don't come home soon or if I came home but went back out. With him working so many hours and Ivy at home recovering, there aren't many other days where this would be an option."

"Veronica, the case is just beginning. We're not desperate," I said. Though I wasn't sure if that were true or that someday in the not too far future, I wouldn't be. "Just because the magistrate is pushing us toward settlement, and that first offer was bottom basement low, doesn't mean that we're close to losing the case." Gentle dissuasion worked on the majority of rogue clients. I sat back and waited for her capitulation.

"It's not that." Garza shook her head. "I watch TV news magazines and sometimes even documentaries, and I know that companies destroy papers. Tino says they're facing criminal charges. I'm not sure if that means they'll go to jail for real like regular people, or just lose money. Either thing, I think, can make men do desperate things."

A desperate thing was the very definition of what *she* was thinking. I didn't point out the irony. Instead, I made a split-second decision, one which I knew right then I was likely to regret later.

"Let's go, then." I stood.

"What?" Her face said I was as crazy as I'd thought her a moment ago. This was, no doubt, how criminal conspiracies started.

"I'm going with you."

"You can't do that. If I get caught, I'm just a crazy Latina mom. If you get caught…"

"If I get caught, I'm just a white lawyer who assumed I had permission from my crazy Latina clients," I retorted. Two could play at that game. I'm sure everyone from every different background had put some serious thought into what their get-out-of-jail-free card looked like.

"Are you serious?"

I pulled a sport coat from the hanger on the back of my door. It was something I saved for unplanned court appearances or rogue weekend corporate fishing expeditions.

"Let's go before I change my mind."

While in the elevator, I texted Casey to let her know that I'd stepped out. She had her own key, but I wanted her to wait for me.

During the twenty-minute drive to Strohmeyer, I went back and forth a million times. This was either the best idea ever or the worst—one that would end my career. Seemed a lot more like a Casey type of move. She always appeared to be skirting the edge of ethical behavior from what I could see. That kind of existential danger did not excite me, I liked to walk a middle path.

I had to come to terms with myself while I was driving to Clearwater Park that I wanted to win at all costs, but I didn't believe in cheating to get there. It would be a huge victory, set me up financially, and get compensation for families who could otherwise go on victimized without adequate recompense. Those weren't the real reasons I was pulling into the football field–sized lot that surrounded the brewery, though. I settled where I started. My job today was protecting my client from herself, and if she came up-on a smoking gun while at it, bonus.

"Let's just park in front. There's no supervision on the weekends," Veronica said after I'd pulled into the back of the vast employee lot. Following her directions, I wove through the nearly empty lot until I was close to the front door.

The parking spots right in front had permanent plac-ards. Strohmeyers had three of the spots, their names up top, titles in smaller lettering underneath. Simon Brody's was there as well with a Mercedes parked in it. General Counsel under his. The rest of the names were unfamiliar, but all of those spaces except for one other, the CFO, were empty. As a fuck-you move, I chose one of the Strohmey-ers' spots, then turned off my car.

"I can see you thinking," Veronica said after I'd turned the key in the ignition. "Stop and let me do the talking."

I nodded in agreement, then got out and opened her door. Once she was out, I closed and locked my car. If I were better, I'd have unscrewed the license plates so my car couldn't be easily identified. That oversight I couldn't fix, but I did duck my head as we made our way to the door. At least I wouldn't be full frontal on camera. I'd wit-nessed too many clients go down that way.

"Hi, can I help you guys?" a guard said the minute we stepped inside the front door. It had been locked, but he'd opened it when Veronica had waved him over.

"Hi, this is my boss." She spoke quickly in the accent she'd tried out on me. Her head was lowered just a frac-tion, her manner obsequious. Veronica stuck a thumb over her shoulder directed at me. "He just drove me over. My husband works here, and I need to pick up something from his office. He's home with the kids...he left my daughter's birthday present here and her party is tonight."

It wasn't half bad. I had to wonder how long she'd worked on that story. Ten minutes, twenty. Had she come to my office already planning a heist and I'd become her unwitting patsy?

The guard frowned as he tried to puzzle out the odd couple we probably made.

"Why didn't he come?" When Veronica cocked her head in question, the guard continued, "Your husband? The one who works here?"

"Oh…it's a surprise party. My boss here is letting me use his backyard and I've been setting up when Tino called me. Celestino Garza. That's my husband."

"Tino!" At the mention of Veronica's husband, the guard's face relaxed. "Man, you're Veronica. You're his lady." The guard extended his hand. "Nice to meet you. You're even prettier than he described."

She smiled like she was cheesing for the camera. It felt fake to me, but the guard didn't seem to notice. A goofy smile took over his face. He nodded as if he'd decided something.

"Can I go back? I know my way." Veronica pressed on with pleasantries.

"Sure, no problem." The guard waved us past the empty reception desk. "The offices should be open. They're doing a deep cleaning of the carpets today. Be careful—it may be wet or have that chemical smell. I'm staying up here for now until it goes away. They always swear everything is nontoxic until there's a lawsuit. Smoking was safe when I was a kid for Christ's sake."

"Can't be too careful nowadays, huh," I tossed in as casually as I could muster. "At least a brewery isn't a chemical plant…"

"Right." He mock saluted us. "I gotta do a sweep around the building. The door locks behind you automatically if I don't see you. Have a great party. How old will your daughter be?"

"Four. She'll be four. Cute as a button. But I gotta get a tent set up in case of rain. Let me get her present."

I followed Veronica to another door that we were buzzed through. It wasn't much different than visiting a jail with all of its doors behind doors behind doors.

The guard's last words, "Have a great weekend," were muffled by layers of glass. I nodded thanks.

With another half salute, the guard was off and we were in.

"That accent was a little much," I said as I followed Veronica down through a brewing floor filled with ten-foot-tall stainless containers, tubes, and temperature dials on bottom and top. Then up a set of metal stairs to an open hall of office doors. There were five blue doors on the side. All of them were propped open with metal garbage cans. The chemical smell the guard had warned us about was in a single word—overpowering. I lifted my sport coat lapel and put it in front of my nose. "Did you bring wrapping paper? How are you going to explain coming back without a present?"

Veronica placed a hand squarely in the middle of her chest. Crossed her eyes a little bit sillily. "My mistake." She was accent-heavy again.

I tried not to laugh, but didn't make it. Taking in too much cleaning fluid odor caused me to cough, which looked better than the easy camaraderie of thieves.

"Can I help you guys?" A petite man in a blue rubber apron and paper face mask asked.

"Nope. Just need one thing. We're good, thanks," I answered this time. He looked like the kind of guy who would respond to a man much better than he'd respond to a woman. I think I called it right, as he turned and went back to doing something to one of the huge stainless-steel tanks that dominated the room.

We found the right office, walked in and closed the door marked Celestino Garza, Brewer.

"He wants that to read Brewmaster." Veronica pointed to the part of the door where the name plaque hung on the other side. She shrugged. "Anytime now, maybe."

Even with the door shut tight, I felt exposed. To minimize the time we were there, I turned meaningfully toward the single four-drawer-high file cabinet and pointed to get Veronica on task.

"What are we looking for?" I asked.

"You tell me," she responded. I had to turn away for a second to hide my face. I'm sure it was showing—my frustration. I'm not sure why I'd been so damned confident she had something in mind beyond the breaking and entering part. Now I understood why she'd roped me in.

Veronica had the balls, the gravitas to do something as bold as commit a felony. But she didn't have the faintest idea of what she needed or what the case needed. That's where I'd come in like a stooge. It wasn't lost on me that at least one Strohmeyer was in the building. From the outside, the whole compound looked like one huge single-story brick structure. I had no idea where the executive offices were, but didn't want to take a chance on anyone who could end my legal career wandering down here.

"Okay." My next words were hushed, rushed. "Let's look in the file cabinet first. Maybe the desk next."

When I didn't move, she tilted her head. Then I think she got it when I held up my hands. I did not have any OJ Simpson–style leather gloves. If push came to shove, I needed some kind of plausible deniability. If the gloves don't fit, you must acquit wasn't going to work for me here.

I watched her pull open the second drawer from the top. Then I came closer and craned my head to see the contents. It was filled with various OSHA regulation manuals. One each year for the last five. I shook my head.

The middle drawer was filled with human resource type materials. I resisted the urge to pull those. They would tell me a lot about how Strohmeyer was run. But that was something I could get in an hour-long deposition. Caught with those in hand, I'd look desperate.

"The top?"

She stood on her tiptoes and pulled at that handle.

I craned my neck, and from what I could see, they were recipes and other chemical formulas on what I guessed had to be beer making. When she thumbed through documents, I could see that there were lists of procedures and temperatures and what was permitted and what wasn't. When Veronica looked my way, I shook my head.

"The desk, then."

She pulled at the big drawer on the right. It didn't budge.

"Locked."

My heart sped up. I could feel the sweat prickle in my armpits. Locked was the line between trespassing, a misdemeanor, and breaking and entering—a fifth-degree felony. This was disbarment territory.

I looked down at my hand on the desk and lifted it. I should have used some OJ gloves. I wasn't any good at this. Hopefully this little heist wouldn't come to dusting for prints.

One of the first things I'd had to do before I was admitted to the bar was get my fingerprints done. I have no idea why anyone in Columbus had needed them, but I had no doubt Cleveland police would be able to match them up in a heartbeat. Speaking of heartbeats, mine was rivaling a Stewart Copeland solo.

From her pocketbook, Veronica produced three tiny keys.

"Borrowed them from Tino's ring," she said. My heart sped up even more when someone came to the door and pulled it open.

"You gotta leave this open," he said. "The rugs need to dry. Okay?"

Veronica said something to him in rapid Spanish. The guy laughed, said something back to her, but left us alone.

The first two keys yielded nothing. The third key turned easily in the lock. The EPA's blue and green flower and water symbol on the top page let me know we'd hit pay dirt.

"Is there a copier?" I asked. It wouldn't be stealing if we left the documents here, I rationalized. No one called the police for disheveled paper.

"Of course. Somewhere. I'll go scout it out while you figure out what needs to be copied."

I tried not to let panic set in at the thought of being alone in enemy territory. Though I could see and feel my hands shaking in the way the papers rattled. I took everything from the drawer that featured the Ohio EPA logo with its distinctive green leaf and anything else that looked like it was state or federal related.

I relaxed when I heard brisk footsteps.

"Thank—" Any other words died on my lips. The unmistakable profile of Simon Brody graced the head and body of the one man directing the defense of these forty-odd cases.

He stopped for a moment, shoved his hands in the pocket of his slacks, and barely turned his head. "Working on a Saturday. Great work ethic you got there. It'll take you far here at Strohmeyer. Have a good weekend."

He said all of that, but didn't once look me in the eye. Then hands thrust deep in his chino pockets, he shuffled away. I was just another lowly employee to be encouraged with a patronizing pat on the head. Nothing more. I was offended and relieved in equal measure. Veronica came back, stopping at the threshold.

"Sorry," she offered. "Saw one of the bigwigs on his way to the executive dining room. Tino said the chef will come in on the weekend especially for them. Imagine a whole employee, a whole man coming to work to make lunch for another grown man."

I wasn't interested in a conversation on the inequities of America or even of executives versus rank and file employees. Especially not now when there was a target on my back if I didn't get the hell out of here.

"The copier?"

She lifted a hand and waved me into a bigger room at the end of the hall in the opposite direction of where Brody had gone. It was a combo of break room and copy room.

The copier was humming as it warmed up. One of those one-cup coffee machines sat idle with a rack of multicolor pods nearby. A fridge joined the hum. I had to believe Veronica's observation that Brody's lunch and beverage would be had in entirely different surroundings.

"It says it's ready," Veronica prompted.

I jammed the papers in the feeder face side down like it appeared the little raised plastic icon was indicating. Veronica pressed the copy button and the sound of paper being fed through various rollers started.

The smell of warm ink combined with rug cleaner made a truly toxic scent. I ignored the carcinogenic combo in favor of pulling papers from the done end. All of a sudden, the stupidity of this became obvious, and I was ready to get going.

The rollers made that grinding, rubbery sound that I'd dreaded every time I'd ever approached a copier.

"Jammed?" I tried to keep exasperation out of my tone. Nothing that happened was Garza's fault. We were in this stupid effing caper together.

"Just out of paper." Veronica quickly sourced a ream, tore open the wrapper, then jammed five hundred sheets between two big metal spring plates. It beeped, seemingly in protest, as she pressed at buttons.

"Does it work?" I demanded, impatient to get back into the safety of my Honda.

"Don't talk. You're making me nervous. I'll get it running. We had a copier at Spasy. Just do something to look busy."

I opened the fridge and peered in. Was a bit surprised to find that there weren't beers in there, though. I closed that, then took a paper towel from a dispenser and tried to look busy wiping down already clean counters.

"Okay. We're done."

I took the originals back from the printer feeder and shoved them under my arm as unobtrusively as possible. I stayed close to Garza while she carried a neater stack of warm copies down the hall.

Back in Tino's office, I gave Garza the signal again to open the desk drawer. She did, and I placed the papers as near as I could to how I thought they'd looked before we'd disturbed them.

"Let's get back to the office. *My office*," I said once the drawer was closed and locked. "We can discuss stuff there. Okay?"

We were both quiet on the drive back downtown, and in the slow elevator ride up to my office. Before she took up her place on the couch once again, she dropped the stack of photocopied documents on top of my blotter.

"Can you believe it?" Veronica's voice was full of "we got away with it" exhilaration. I couldn't say that I didn't share the feeling.

"That's got to go in the vault," she continued when I didn't reply.

"The vault?" I asked, somehow thinking there'd been a second break-in I'd missed while my knees had rattled when she'd left me alone in her husband's office.

"Stuff that you take to your grave," Garza clarified.

"If I'm going to start taking stuff to my grave," I responded, "then I'm going to add this to the list."

Unconsciously I'd gone back to my earlier position, having taken a seat next to her on my couch. In a flash of realization, I could see that I was much too close. A moment later, Garza leaned closer to me, her eyes drooping to half-mast.

I knew where she was heading. I could see it in her half-closed eyes. I opened my mouth just enough to try to push out the word no. That little two-letter word didn't make it past my brain.

Instead, I felt the soft lips of my client meet mine. I almost gasped at the surprise. She tasted like licorice. Spicy black licorice. The kind my grandparents mistook for candy when my cousins and I asked for treats.

The surprise feeling of arousal coupled with that sense memory from childhood deafened me to the sound of my office door banging against the doorstop. When my brain cleared of the kiss-induced fog and finally processed all of the sounds and sensations of the last half minute, it was too late.

"I didn't mean to interrupt." I didn't need to open my eyes to know it was Casey's voice.

Garza and I both pulled back, caught doing something we shouldn't.

"I'm sorry. I don't know—" Garza's suddenly startled face filled my vision. She scooted back even farther, then darted from the couch like a scared rabbit. "I should go," she panted breathlessly.

"Wait," I called when Garza had her hand on the door.

Both women looked at me like I'd lost my mind. I fished in my pants pocket and extracted three tiny keys. I put them in Garza's outstretched palm.

She curled her hand around them. I could see the gratefulness in her eyes. She would already have enough to explain come Monday. Missing keys would only make her look more guilty. She pocketed the keys, grabbed her purse, and slammed the office door before I could think of saying goodbye.

Casey stood stock-still. She had a coffee in one hand. A bag that probably had two fresh pastries in another, and her beat-up brown leather messenger bag nearly sliding from her shoulder.

I took the coffee and pastries and put them squarely on my desk before there was an accident, or I got hot coffee on my face and shirt. I could see from Casey's shocked expression that there were many places a hot beverage could end up. I wanted to avoid all of them.

Her messenger bag dropped to the carpet. The only spill, though, was of papers and pens. Casey made no attempt to retrieve her bag's contents. She simply stood.

Blinked slowly.

Blinked once again.

"What. Just. Happened?"

"Nothing," I answered like a guilty toddler, as if closing my eyes could make the immediate past disappear. I was nearly tempted to try it. I'd seen determined two-year-olds almost make it work.

"If that's nothing, I'd hate to see what you consider full-on sexual intercourse."

My mind wasn't working. The brain that had gotten me through college and law school and had passed the bar was overwhelmed and intimidated by this simple, logical question. Casey looked like she was getting angrier by the minute, so I started talking before I could form a coherent thought.

"One. I think you already know the answer to that. Two, it was just...nothing...something that happened. I can't really explain it."

"Let's skip past explanation and get on to what I'm going to testify to at your disbarment hearing."

"No need to be that dramatic."

"Really? Am I the only person who scans those weekly decisions in the little green OSBA bulletin that arrive in the mailbox every Saturday like clockwork? They always read like some kind of soap opera.

"Last week it was permanent suspension for a lawyer and client conspiring in some painkiller pill scheme. I haven't seen one about a lawyer sleeping with a client, but if I can borrow your computer, I'm sure I could research it for you. See what you'd be facing."

Those nerves that had me shaking an hour ago came right back. The adrenaline-fueled adventure was not quite over.

"She kissed me. It won't happen again. She's having problems with her husband. Her daughter is recovering from surgery, but they're not sure of the final prognosis. For just a moment, I'm sure, I looked like the solution to her problems."

For a long moment, Casey stood there. I could practically see the gears turning in her head. I needed to distract her. Stop her from asking any more questions. When it looked like she was ready to strike, I went on the offensive.

"What do you care, anyway? You have a boyfriend."

I knew I sounded like an asshole, an ethically challenged asshole, but I wasn't ready to back down. Not now.

"This is not about whether or not I have a boyfriend. This is whether or not you've engaged in client misconduct."

She was so right, but I wasn't ready to concede. Whether it was because I was embarrassed, mortified, or because my ego had been bruised this whole time, I couldn't say. I just pushed everything back on her so I didn't have to deal with it.

"You sound like Judge Brody," I sneered.

"He wasn't wrong about the appearance of impropriety," she said. I didn't want to point out that being a Miss

Goody Two-Shoes had landed her in common pleas, broke like the rest of us.

"He very much missed the irony of a Brody making that statement."

"Why?"

"Are you being deliberately obtuse? When there's money involved suddenly everyone turns a blind eye. The Brodys have to be one of the most crooked families that ever graced Ohio government."

"None of that matters, Justin. Not one bit. The Brodys can do whatever the hell they want. You and I? We can't. Keep the coffee. The apple turnovers are your favorite. I think I need to go home now."

"We have a ton of discovery to review. Arguments to prepare for Tuesday." What I was saying was true. I very much needed her. From her face, I could see that I'd have to fly solo.

"I think there's been enough work here today."

19

Veronica
August 4, 2007

I'd been tense from the moment I got home from Justin McPhee's office, but Tino was none the wiser. He hadn't said anyone from Strohmeyer Breweries had called. The other...the kiss...that one I'd take to my grave. That was two today. My final resting place was going to be so full of lies that there'd hardly be space for flowers or...me.

Once I'd checked on Ivy who looked like she'd probably been camped out in front of the television the entire time I'd been gone, then unwrapped Stella's little arms from my calves, I'd gone into the kitchen and had gotten started on dinner.

Guilt had made me stop by the store and pick up the ingredients for Tino's favorite dish, *frituras de batata y queso*. I loved Puerto Rican food. Missed it most days. Tried to cook healthier, steaming vegetables and baking chicken breasts. Tino wasn't too happy with the stateside menu, but didn't complain most days. He was one of those guys who could lose five pounds by just thinking about it.

I'd stopped cooking a lot of that stuff because the potato and cheese fritters went straight to my butt. But I wasn't squeezing back into my Spasy uniform anytime soon and I needed him to be feeling kindly toward me when I finally told him about today.

Lying wasn't an option.

I wasn't sure when I was going to do it tonight, but I couldn't risk the hit his ego would take if that guard told him before I could. Macho didn't even begin to cover Tino's feelings.

Betrayal was his Achilles' heel in love. He nearly divorced me during our first year of marriage when he'd caught me kissing another man. I'd been foolish and drunk. Tino had forgiven me, but that forgiveness had been grudging and hard won. He'd only believed my devotion when I agreed to move up here.

I did promise after that honesty would be my policy. That didn't mean it wouldn't be a very hard conversation to have or that he wouldn't be very, very angry. I tried to get myself in the mood for the sex afterwards that would hopefully smooth things over.

While I was peeling the potatoes, I tried to push Justin McPhee out of my thoughts, because he was the first person who came to mind when I thought about kissing and what usually came after. I had to shake my head when I was throwing away the peels. Shake it again when I heated up the lard in the frying pan. When I put out the paper towels, I heard Ivy cough.

"You okay, *mija*?" I called over my shoulder.

"Yeah. Water just went down the wrong way," she responded as she walked into the room, her favorite Country Bear Jamboree mug in hand. Reminded me of a time when whether to spend fifteen dollars on a souvenir for a five-year-old had been my idea of a big decision.

"That's bottled water, right?" I eyed the brown bears suspiciously. It was still hard to take in that something as innocent and simple as plain water could be the reason my daughter lost half a kidney.

She nodded. "Daddy poured it for me from this one." She pointed to the shiny new dispenser that sat in the corner of the kitchen, with its five-gallon bottle upside down, the occasional glug sounding when a large air bubble rose to the top.

"I'm making one of your daddy's favorite meals tonight." I turned back to the stove, lowered the heat a little before the lard started smoking.

"You don't fry stuff much."

"Everyone says it's unhealthy, so I'm trying to do better. Your dad works hard for all of us, though. I think he deserves something special every once in a while."

"Can I watch TV in your room?" she asked.

"Just until dinner, okay?" I silently added not-so-great parenting to my ever-growing list of sins. "How are you feeling?"

"Tired, Mama. Not as much as before, though. Don't worry. I'll get better. I'm getting better. It's going to be okay. They took all of the cancer out. Next year when I'm in fifth grade, I'll be just like all the other kids. Running. Jumping. Playing and getting good grades, of course."

I stepped back away from the frying fritters and patted my child on the head. Smoothed down her frizzy hair. She was like that, trying to make other people feel good when it should have gone the other way—me making everything better. A big weight of guilt lifted. If going behind Tino's back got justice for her and for the other kids, then what had happened that afternoon, everything, was what needed to.

"I can't wait," I said. That was true. I couldn't wait until she was just like the other kids again and not child cancer patient Ivy Garza.

Two hours later, after I'd cleaned up the kitchen and all the grease splatter, I slowly made it up the stairs and sat on the bed, on top of the covers. I pulled off my house shoes and rubbed at my feet. I'd been on them a long time today. Not working at Spasy had made me soft, I realized. There I'd be on my feet for ten hours straight. Three hours in my own house shouldn't be so exhausting.

My stomach squeezed when Tino came in. I tried to shake it off.

"Stella asleep?" I asked. He'd volunteered to do the bath and bed routine. It was a rare offer, so I took him up on it.

"What did you get from my office?" he asked.

My heartbeat immediately went right off the charts. If I'd been like Ivy in the hospital, the rapid beeps from the heart rate monitor would have alerted the nurses' station. They'd have rushed in with a crash cart ready for action. I tried to breathe normally, didn't say a word.

"I can't remember asking you to take my keys and bat your eyelashes at the Strohmeyer guard." His questions sounded like an interrogation.

"Um." My mind had gone completely blank. "I...uh...Justin..."

"Is that the name of the guy who was with you? The attorney? Can't he lose his job for this? Watergate was just breaking and entering and look how that turned out."

"Jesus Christ, Tino, Strohmeyer isn't whoever was being targeted by that scandal. This isn't brewery-gate."

"President Nixon ordered a break-in to the Democratic national headquarters," he explained like he was talking to Stella.

I wanted to clap back that every school year always ended before any history teachers ever got past the Second World War. Vietnam and anything after that wasn't something I knew about. I shook my head vehemently.

"This isn't about history. It's about Ivy. That's just stupid politics, Tino. We're talking life and death here. Kids with cancer."

He looked uncomfortable like he did every single time the C word was mentioned.

"Ivy doesn't have cancer. She's…what do they call it in all those pink ribbon rallies? A survivor."

His words were like a punch in the gut. Like all the years she'd been sick had somehow been pretend.

"She *did* have cancer just a few weeks ago. She's still recovering. If she's lucky, school is all she can do in a day. She's sleeping the rest. That's no way for a child to have to live."

"But that's just it, Veronica, our daughter is alive. She'll live. In a few months, she'll be good and we can put all of this behind us."

"I don't want to put it behind us. We can't drink the water here. Now that the case is getting press in the papers, we'd never be able to sell this house. I don't want to live in a place where every other kid is dying of cancer."

"That's a lot of hysterical talk, Veronica. This is a nice house in a good school district. And that company you're treating like the big bad wolf is putting food on the table, not to mention they got the health care that saved her damned life. That lawyer can't wave a three-piece suit around and do that for sure."

"Mama! MAMA!" I was off the bed and down the hall in a shot. I knew that cry. It was never good.

Ivy was off the bed and on the floor clutching at her middle. I looked from her to the bed. The covers were thrown back and a large wet spot darkened the middle of the white sheets. For the briefest moment, relief shot through my veins. It was going to be okay. She'd just peed the bed. The kidney was working, just not conveniently.

"What happened?"

"It hurts. My stomach hurts."

I regretted the fried food immediately. I grabbed a towel from the bathroom, set it onto the little kid chair in her room that was supposed to mimic an adult recliner. I pulled Ivy up and set her on it and eased her back. I went over to strip the bed, then realized the sheets were tinged with pink. That meant blood. Dr. Ames had given me a list of possible reactions to the surgery and all the pills Ivy had to take. None of them was this.

"Tino! Call 911."

20

I knocked on the door, with a lot of hesitation. I loved my neighbors, but their potential adoption being botched by Hudson, the agency I'd referred them to, weighed heavily on me.

They'd chosen me above everyone else to help them in their journey to parenthood. All I'd done was have a single consultation before pulling the rug out from under them.

Gay parent adoption was hard enough without me having stuck my foot into the situation and all but killing their chances to start a family. I almost turned back and walked the three steps across the hall to my own door, but I heard the locks turn before I could pivot. I didn't want to add prankster to my list of crimes.

After Jason Corry pulled open the door, a big smile took over his face. I let him envelop me in a big hug. My fears were eased almost immediately when I stepped into the smell of something good on the stove permeating their apartment and a warm hug from his partner, Greg Salazar.

Every single time I was at their place I marveled at how they could make their apartment—a mirror image of mine—into something warm and cozy while I still lived no different than a graduate student on a shoestring budget. Albeit with some newly purchased Arhaus furniture. But my walls were still white, my carpet still industrial, and my accessories still collegiate.

"What's in your hand?" Jason asked. I was grateful to be distracted from my feelings of inadequacy.

"Rosé?" I lifted the bottle by the neck to his eye level, rotating the label for him to read. "The guy at the wine store said it was the most versatile for pairing."

I was too old, I thought, to keep showing up with whatever was on the discount shelf at the grocery store. Now I stopped by Shaker Wines whenever I was on the far east side of town and bought exactly what was recommended, no more guessing on my part.

"He may have been right," Greg said, removing it from my hand. "Can we pour you a glass?"

"I feel a little guilty...I wasn't exactly invited," I stammered.

The three of us had been friends from the time we'd all moved into our small six-unit building more than a decade before. Over the years, we'd more or less had an open-door policy. They'd supported me when things went badly. I loved their warmth and hospitality.

It's just that I'd kind of felt our relationship could be one-sided. An occasional offer of a pan of my German mother's strudel wasn't enough to make up for all they'd done.

When they'd been ready to adopt from Hudson, I'd thought helping them find a child and start their family would be the ultimate recompense. Make everything more than even between us.

Then Justin's hints had turned to flashing warning signals that the Hudson agency may not have been on the up-and-up, and I'd felt compelled to let Greg and Jason know any baby or child they may receive may not be truly free to adopt. Once again my honesty and candor had brought someone's dreams to a crashing halt.

"Casey, you're always welcome," Jason said stepping back from the door. Immediately, I took off my shoes and let my toes feel the cool wood under them. For the thousandth time, I vowed to pull up my own industrial Berber, getting me one step closer to something approximating the warmth and coziness I'd always loved in their home.

"How's it going?" I questioned. I was really asking about their new resolve to become parents through the county's foster-to-adopt program rather than the private route. But I'd take any answer they gave even if it was about the current Shaker Square redevelopment plan.

"It's going...slowly, I guess," Greg said. He didn't pretend to misunderstand me. "Becoming a foster parent is bureaucracy at its finest. Sometimes when we're sitting there in a class or during yet *another* home visit, it's hard to imagine that abusers would bother with all of this. It feels like such a thorough vetting process that pedophiles wouldn't have the patience."

"And yet..." I shook my head. "I don't really know either." I'd wondered the same things when I was in that GAL training at Justin's suggestion. All the vetting and classes and time seemed like it should weed the worst out of the system. "But it happens all too often."

I didn't point out that it wasn't always the person who took the class, but the husband, father, boyfriend...some man with a penchant for pedophilia and cruelty who up-ended the cart.

"Horrible," was all I could conclude.

Olivia Grant flashed through my mind as she always did when this topic popped up. In her case it had been another kid in foster care who'd violated her, not the parents who'd passed all the background checks.

I pushed those thoughts out of my head before I did a long lonely walk down woulda, coulda, shoulda lane. I'd lost hours of sleep and days of work in a guilt spiral over how ineffective I'd been in that case and others.

"I'm glad that you're doing it," I continued. That much was true. "The county needs great foster parents. You'll be such a good example for the kids."

"We're about halfway through the home study, I think," Jason said. "The social worker says we should be approved by the end of the summer."

The county and state were blatant in their discrimination against gay couples. If Greg and Jason wanted to adopt, only one of them could be the "parent," but both of them had to go to the required classes before a child could be placed in their home.

"After that, a kid may be placed with us as early as October," Greg said. He'd moved back into their kitchen and I followed. Once I was in the small room with him, the smells nearly made me weak in the knees. The only other person who could do that was my mother and her hearty German meals.

"What in the heck are you making? That smells amazing." I tried to think why spending my Sundays with Justin had won out over ethnic cuisine of the month at my neighbor's house. I didn't probe that thought too far. Instead, I watched, mesmerized as Greg, an occasional professional chef, patted some kind of dumplings between his hands.

"*Papas rellenas de carne.*" At my raised eyebrows, he explained it was Peruvian. "Meat, hard boiled eggs, onions, garlic, raisins, and cilantro stuffed into mashed potatoes and deep fried."

Forget sex with Justin or dinners with Ron, *this*, this is what I really needed.

Food and community.

After Greg demonstrated how to make more of the dumplings, I washed my hands, borrowed an apron, and got to work like I'd done thousands of times alongside my mother.

"Foster or foster to adopt?" I asked, returning to the original conversation, my hands wrist deep in the stuffing.

"Both." Greg shrugged. "It's hard sitting in that room during those classes and looking at those kids' pictures on the wall and thinking that they're not worthy because they're not newborns."

"That's…" I ducked, focusing on the food in my hand, swallowing down the emotions that bubbled up. Those posters were only one of the reasons I avoided the Jane Edna Hunter building.

It wasn't much different than the way I'd sometimes felt at the animal shelter when I'd found Simba. It forced me to think of the hard questions—like how it was that newborns and purebreds were worthy and young children and mutts weren't.

I kept my head down in case tears welled up.

"Thank you," I whispered. "You're doing God's work as my parents would say."

We worked in companionable silence until all the potato balls were done. Jason came into the small kitchen eyeing what we'd accomplished. Instead of asking when dinner would be ready, he had a different question.

"Where have you been on Sundays?"

For a moment, my heart sped up like my parents had caught me kissing a boy in my teenage bedroom. The moment I realized they couldn't read my mind, my breathing returned to normal. I went for half of the truth.

"I've been working on this case that has the potential to be huge. Like a big payday. It's the kind of thing that could set me up so that I can finally choose the kinds of cases I want."

"You're pulling all-nighters?"

I ducked my head for the second time. They wouldn't have known about the overnights if I hadn't needed to ask them to feed my cat Simba—dinner *and* breakfast.

Guilt and anger fought a war inside. Guilt for ignoring my friends and my cat. They'd all been there for me during the hard times, and I'd abandoned them for the attention from a cute boy. I sighed, resigned to telling the whole truth and nothing but the truth.

I took off the apron I'd donned and moved to the dining room, picking up the glass of rosé they'd poured earlier. I sunk into one of the plush chairs and pulled my bare foot onto the cushion. Jason and Greg followed, pulling up their own chairs.

"You remember how hard it was during that first year after law school...I met Justin...Justin McPhee back then. He's the one who got me started in juvenile court."

"Should we curse him?" Greg asked without humor or irony. "Juvenile court was hell on you, not to mention your finances."

"It was well intentioned," I defended. "I mean, I was able to make a living. Support myself and my cat." That much was true. I did often wonder if I'd been more successful without the crutch of two-hundred-fifty-dollar-a-pop cases. Would I have been more ambitious and have gone for the bigger and better cases right out of the gate instead of just, *just* realizing now the ways I'd stymied myself?

I'd never know.

"What does Justin have to do with Sunday nights?" Jason probed. He'd leaned forward, wiping condensation from the side of his goblet with a single finger. I'd always marveled at how clean his doctor hands were.

"He was the lawyer that referred Hudson as well," I doled out like breadcrumbs.

"Better and better. But you're avoiding the question. Don't forget we've had a mini-crash course in child psychology. Distraction and deflection apparently work with the kindergarten set. We're not five," Greg said.

"We've been...hooking up, I guess." That I said *sotto voce*. "But we really *are* working on a case together," I amended.

"So many questions..." Greg said. He poured himself another very full glass of wine and got comfortable in a dining room chair. I leaned back in my chair for a better angle into the kitchen and eyed the Fry Daddy on the counter. Didn't look like either one of them was too eager to fill my belly. At least not until I answered some questions. Free food had strings.

"I'll ask them, if you don't," Jason said with a nod toward his partner.

"Go ahead." Greg did a hand flourish turning the floor over to Jason.

"What about Ron?" Jason asked.

"What about Ron?" I parroted.

"Casey..."

I looked between the longtime partners, momentarily jealous of how settled they were with each other. Envious that they'd long left the dating life behind.

"He wants something serious." I paused. A long sigh left my lips. My shoulders slumped. All of a sudden, enthusiasm felt hard to muster. "I want that too, so that's what we're working toward."

"Damn, girl, you make dating sound like a job," Greg said.

"Maybe it would be better to approach it like a job. The way I was doing it before wasn't working for sure." I'd gone with my heart time and again and that had so far yielded two broken engagements, and even worse, two broken hearts—both mine.

Using my head was looking like a much better option going forward. It didn't seem romantic or sweet or like any of the rom-coms I might secretly love, but I'd graduated from college with honors and law school near the top of my class and had passed the bar. I needed to use the brain in my head for more than education.

"So Justin..." Greg prompted.

"It's just a casual thing. We like spending time together. It kind of takes care of certain needs and lets me not be too crazy when I'm with Ron."

"What's the case?" Jason asked. "Another headline maker?"

I was grateful that they'd left Justin and Ron and my mess of a love life alone. Maybe I'd have good news the next time we were together. Another engagement to announce or maybe just a commitment from a man who loved me for me.

My mind shifted to thoughts about the scope of the potential class action and my head nearly exploded. In a few months I could be debt-free as well as engaged for the third and final time. It was time for a shift in my life.

"No...well, I hope not, but maybe. It's been mentioned in a couple of the *Sun* newspapers, nothing major. Actually, I'd like to pick your brains if I can. Just a little bit. We...Justin and I are representing a bunch of families suing Strohmeyer."

"*You'll be a high flyer if you drink...*" They started to sing in unison. That damned jingle. Maybe I'd have some bagpipe players do it at my wedding. It was the theme of my life.

"*Strohmeyer beer,*" I finished for them.

"What's the case?" Jason asked. As a doctor, he understood the kinds of professional pressures I faced. He'd been a great sounding board over the years.

"Obviously, I can only tell you what's public."

"Of course." Jason nodded somberly. As a physician he was well acquainted with privilege and the secrets required of confidentiality.

"We're representing about forty families who are suing because their children have cancer.'"

"A cancer cluster?" Jason's brows rose to his hairline. "Here in northeast Ohio?"

I nodded, somberly. No one wanted to think that our little patch of earth could be contaminated. Pollution always seemed like a distant thing that happened in places like New Jersey. "Looking that way."

"What's the cause?" Jason got up and poured himself more wine. Cancer did that—unsettled people. Even doctors.

"That's the rub, of course. We have a couple of theories. But bottom line there are far too many cancers for the size of the towns."

"Where are we talking about?" Greg and Jason looked around as if there were going to be poison sprouting from the ground here in Shaker Square.

"Clearwater Park and Brighthill so far."

"The air. The water. Contamination of some sort," Jason surmised.

"Are those the first questions that any expert would ask?"

"Should be. At least that's what I learned in school. There's always a cause. Some are obvious. Some are not. But the younger a person is, sometimes the more obvious the cause. I mean, by seventy, a person has been exposed to everything chemical and all the carcinogens known to modern man. In the US, there aren't even any laws regulating that companies even tell us what they are. Children under ten, under five...they've only had a handful of exposures."

"Makes a lot of sense," Greg agreed.

"Have you read about Woburn or Tom's River?" Jason asked. Those two towns were probably the most famous cancer clusters. Lawyer Jan Schlichtmann had become famous from representing families in both places. I nodded vigorously. One morning this week had been my library day. I'd been in the architecturally beautiful downtown building skimming *A Civil Action*.

"A bit. I've been overwhelmed with trying to get my hands around the cases themselves. We're trying to get a class action going. There's a hearing on our cases this Tuesday."

"What was your question, then?" Jason asked. I'd emailed him earlier this week to seek out his advice. After food prep and wine and pleasantries, now we were down to it.

"This is the confidential part," I started. "We're kind of chasing two theories. The first is that the water was contaminated with mycotoxin. The second is that the problem could be arsenic."

"What kinds of cancers?"

"Kidney for one. One little girl had the cancerous part of her kidney removed and is only operating on one now."

"Wow." Jason put his wine on the table, sat far back in his chair. "I mean, that sounds like a good medical decision, but still a hard one for a parent to make. Just crossing their fingers nothing goes wrong with the remaining kidney tissue or even the remaining kidney."

"Fingers crossed." I sent a prayer up to a god I wasn't sure existed. "Does that make sense to you, the theories?"

Justin and I needed to present a strong front, a united front to the clients, opposing counsel, the Strohmeyers, the court. In theory, any lawyer could argue multiple causations. In reality, we needed a single path to follow. One unified story to tell, to sell to not only a judge and jury, but to opposing counsel as well.

When I took more than a shallow dive into the files, though, I had doubts. Big doubts. Before I went to Justin or even talked to the experts he'd retained in the last days, I wanted to put together my own theory. Get some facts and my own ideas in place so I knew what questions to ask, not only of any expert or any parent, but of myself.

Questions I should have asked before I signed on the dotted line of that co-counsel agreement.

"Those theories could hold water.... I mean we know that either of those, mycotoxin or arsenic, in large enough quantities can have deleterious effects on the human organism or be carcinogenic."

"What does your gut say?" I wanted to know what his first feeling was. My gut was always right even though I ignored it more than I should.

Jason closed his eyes a long moment. Opened them. Looked directly at me, no levity.

"Arsenic."

"Okay." I took that in. Wondered how the shift from one theory to another would affect proving our case. "Thanks for that. The court has pushed us to try to settle, so we'll see about all of this after the conference."

"Settle? This early in the case? How could you know what those kids deserve?"

"We'll be fine. Plaintiffs always start with a big demand. As far as the court is concerned? One less case on the docket is all they're thinking. The facts? The plaintiffs? None of that matters. Right now, these kids with cancer are no more than just a burden on the already overloaded federal court system."

"You sound cynical," Greg added.

"Justice is a business."

"Enough court talk. How are you going to balance your friend with benefits and your soon-to-be boyfriend?" Greg asked.

"Has it been too much?" I swallowed down the rising guilt. "Asking you to feed Simba?" I demurred. I'd had a sense that I'd skated by too easily earlier.

"That is never a bother." Greg patted my hand. "Your cat is cute. It's like being an animal owner by proxy. This isn't about the cat. You're avoiding or maybe evading the question."

"I think Justin and I need to cool things off."

"Did one of you catch feelings?"

"No, nothing like that." I heard my denial, knew it had almost been too swift. "I walked in on him kissing someone else."

"Whoa, that's awkward."

I nodded, but didn't add anything. I didn't add that Justin and I had no hold on each other. That we only talked about other people as part of our safe-sex discussion, not one on fidelity. That the woman he'd been kissing was not only married, but the parent of a client. I thanked God my stomach announced itself at that moment with an impolite rumble.

"Are we going to fry the Peruvian potato dumplings?" I asked. "You guys know my parents are German and Polish immigrants. Hearty food is my jam. I love a good potato dumpling. Gotta see how these Peruvians do it."

Greg checked his watch.

"Probably enough time chilling. I'll get the fryer hot, but we're not done here. We'll have all of dinner to grill you."

"I…"

"Casey, we love you. But we also want you to be happy. We want you to make the right decision this time. One that not only makes you delighted to wake up every day, but a decision that puts you with a guy who deserves you." Greg's face was unusually solemn.

I nodded. I wanted to hear everything they said. Take it all in. For now, though, just for this moment I wanted to eat and drink and laugh and not think about men or the case that I'd signed up for having once again forsaken one thing for another. I wanted a Sunday like those I'd had before Justin had taken over my weekends.

21

Veronica
August 4, 2007

"What happened?" someone in a white coat asked. I didn't get his name, nor did I ask him to repeat it.

"My daughter, she had surgery on her kidney. She woke up in pain. I think I saw blood in her pee. They said if anything happened we needed to come here."

"Who was her doctor?"

"Ames. Mira Ames."

"We'll do a work-up and I'll page her."

"Do you think the cancer came back?"

"We're not going to be able to give you any answers right away, ma'am. Mrs. Garza, did you say?"

"Yes, Veronica Garza."

"Did you bring someone here with you?"

"My husband is coming. He had to get my little daughter dressed. We came in an ambulance."

"Please wait for him in the waiting area. We're going to get your daughter Ive…"

"Ivy. Just call her Ivy."

"We're going to get her queued up for a CAT scan. Someone will come to get you from the waiting room when we have more information. Don't worry. It steals joy from today. You're at a great hospital. We'll give her the best care we know how."

I didn't want to admit I was surprised to see Tino in the waiting room. So often I'd felt like I was on this journey alone. My youngest daughter had her head on his shoulder.

"She asleep?"

"Didn't really wake up. I just put her princess blanket around her and tucked her in the car."

I didn't want to ask if he'd used her car seat. Didn't matter. She was here. Safe and sound. At least one of my kids was okay.

"They're taking Ivy for some scans. Paging the doctor she had before. They asked me to wait out here."

Tino fingered the gadget in his hand. "Just got an email from Strohmeyer."

"On a Saturday night?"

"They had news that couldn't wait."

His face was unreadable. It often was before bad news was about to come my way. I braced myself for the worst, that my stupidness from today had been unearthed. That Tino was going to be fired. I looked at the emergency room doors. There were no police officers, hands on guns, waiting to arrest me. I was safe, at least for the moment.

"What is it?"

"The promotion to craft brewmaster. I'd oversee nine brands and the new brewpub they're planning to open in eighteen months."

"*Dios mio!* Oh my God. Finally." I put my hand in front of my mouth. Lowered my voice when Stella stirred. In a lower voice, I continued, "Congratulations. This is everything you've ever wanted. I'm so proud of you. Why aren't you smiling?"

"There are just two conditions attached to the offer."

"Please say it's not moving. They wouldn't want you to move, right? That other brewery they opened in North Carolina...you said it was just low-level staff there making a product, not creating it."

"That wasn't it, Veronica."

I hated when he used my full name. It meant he thought I was to blame for something. I tried to imagine what I was to blame for now, today.

"What is it, Tino? I'm too worried about Ivy right now. I don't have it in my brain to play guessing games."

"The first condition is easy, that I keep away from any EPA investigators. They want to leave any and all of that to the engineers and corporate and legal folks involved."

"Fair enough. They don't pay you to get them out of trouble. I said this in the beginning. It's best that the people who did the crime pay for it. You don't need to go to jail behind some corporate mess."

"I heard you the first ten times you said it, Veronica. Low-level guys like me need to mind their own business."

"I wasn't saying you were low level. I was saying this company is wholly owned by a rich family. They can do whatever they want, which isn't fair, but it is what it is. What I was saying is that if they do the dirt, then they need to pay for it."

"The new job does come with shares."

"Shares don't make you an owner."

"They kind of do."

"We could talk around this forever. What's the second thing?"

"They want us to drop the suit against Strohmeyer. A surprising request, because not only did I not know that we were suing my boss, I didn't know that Ivelisse was going to be the face of the case."

"About that…"

"About that. When were you planning to tell me? When her face showed up on the front page of the *Plain Dealer*?"

"I can do that as her parent. Sign on to the case to get what she deserves from these people. And also on the parents' behalf, because we're the ones who are responsible for her medical payments."

"Did you forge my signature? Did that lawyer put you up to this?"

"I may have signed your name, Tino. I do it every day for taxes…for anything that we need to do. You know that. You're never around when important stuff comes up."

"I'm not okay with this. Yes, that happened a few times, like April fifteenth or when we were getting a new roof, but not this. Not something big like this. Did you even think how this could affect my job?"

"Your job? Tino, our daughter has cancer. We're here in the emergency room because our daughter has cancer. Justin McPhee is pretty sure it's because of the run-off from Strohmeyer. You said yourself all the agencies are investigating. Strohmeyer is just a job. Ivelisse is your daughter, your flesh and blood. Beers come and go. They come in singles and sixes and twelves and cases and kegs. There's only one Ivy. I don't care if I'm homeless. I'll do anything to help her, defend her, save her from all in this world."

"Homeless is what we'll be if you don't drop it."

"When do you have to give them an answer?"

"They gave me a week to think about it."

"Then I'll take the week as well. It's not that I don't love you and appreciate what you do for our family. It's that I don't want to have to make a choice between a daughter I have now and know and love, and your potential future with a company with shaky morals and a loose relationship with the truth."

Tino looked like he wanted to say more, to argue more, but he stopped when someone shouted, "Garza family."

I turned from him to see Dr. Ames coming toward us. I never thought I'd be so relieved to see someone outside of my family. I wanted to run and hug her. Standing and shaking her hand had to be enough.

"Let me start by saying, she's okay. There's no cancer recurrence that we can see."

"What's wrong? What happened?"

"Looks like kidney stones have started a minor infection. We've given her a dose of intravenous antibiotics. We'll follow up with another in a few hours. I don't think we'll need to send her home with anything more than the meds we've already prescribed."

"Oh my God. Thank you. Thank you. I was so worried. What happened?"

"Not enough water. Her body's making a big adjustment in how it's filtering waste. Keeping her filled with water, and if she's not drinking that, then even juice will help. Cranberry if you can swing it."

"Of course. We'll go to the store right now. Can we take her home?"

"We want to keep her overnight. We'll keep her on an IV and keep pushing liquids."

"I'm so sorry. I'll do better. I'll make sure she drinks the bottled water. That she keeps hydrated. I'm so, so sorry."

"Don't blame yourself. Recovery is hard. It's hard for people to drink when they're sleeping and resting so much. It's not a new malignant growth. Let's rejoice in that small victory, okay? Take your little one home and rest. Ivelisse is already asleep. You can see her in the morning. She'll be rested, and we'll talk again when it's time for discharge."

When there was nothing left but the flutter of air from Dr. Ames' white coat. I just wanted to fall down. All the exhaustion and stress I'd kept at bay came upon me all at once.

It was almost too much. A child with cancer. A lawsuit to fix that same. A husband who wasn't supportive. I'd call Justin McPhee first thing. If the case were somehow close to settling, I'd lie to Tino for as long as it took for my Ivy to get justice.

22

Casey
August 7, 2007

Tuesday was here way faster than I wanted it to be. Not only that, but I wasn't the least bit prepared for what I was about to walk into.

I couldn't see one scrap of the fabric of my butter yellow duvet, one of the gifts I'd given myself after Hudson. My bed was heaped with discarded clothes, and I wasn't even getting ready for a date. *That* was much easier than *this*.

This was getting ready to come face-to-face with my rivals. And my ex-fiancé *and* Justin.

I'd hardly slept for two nights as I'd played and replayed in my mind the kiss I'd walked in on. Justin and Veronica Garza, their lips pressed together like they were boyfriend and girlfriend, not lawyer and client.

There were so many issues, but I had no idea how to talk to Justin about any one of them. Instead of going to his place on Sunday like I'd done for enough weeks for it to become a routine, I'd come here to my apartment. But not before I'd popped into a Buckeye bakery and helped myself to a Napoleon and a panini. Normally, I'd have gone to Arabica, but that had been squeezed out of Cleveland by Starbucks and Caribou.

Then I'd laid fried potato dumplings and a lot of rosé on top of it. Not my proudest moment. I'd promised myself that I'd stop doing it. Using food to cope with feelings. Yesterday had tasted like failure.

I looked at the clothes again, thanking God that all the food I'd eaten last night wouldn't go to my hips immediately. I picked the most boring outfit I could find: a Theory stretch wool pantsuit. The suit looked good on me. I could see the difference money could make. But it wasn't that feminine.

Magistrate Wheeler didn't seem like the type to hold it against me that I wasn't wearing a skirt or that it wasn't some soft pastel color like pink or peach. From her interactions with Miriam Shively, professionalism was the magistrate's top priority. This outfit said that.

I went to the bathroom and hung the suit on a hook that I used during showers to steam out any wrinkles I didn't catch. On the way back into to my room to get dressed, I pulled a mint green mock turtleneck from my dresser drawer. It was my pastel backup.

Even youngish woman judges could be just the tiniest bit sexist. No reason to alienate Wheeler even if the double standard annoyed the hell out of me. Funny how pleasing irrational judges for the sake of clients wasn't on the bar exam.

Three hours later I was at the courthouse suited up and ready to go, anticipating our class certification hearing. I was the first person there, so I checked in with the courtroom deputy, then took myself to the hallway to wait.

"What happened to you yesterday?" That was from Justin. Before he'd approached, I'd seen him walking down the hallway at a brisk pace headed straight for me. For long moments as his stride ate up the distance, I wanted to be anywhere but where I was.

"I checked in." I lifted my butt and stood so I could look him in the eye. "I'm the first here. I haven't seen anyone from Morrell." My tone was all business. I put away friendly, cool-girl Casey. That girl had been a pushover and stupid to boot. Lawyer Casey was smarter.

"Let's talk." Justin gestured toward one of the attorney rooms along the hall. I shifted in my low-heeled shoes, but didn't move toward the open door.

"About what?" That one came through gritted teeth. I was angrier than I thought. I turned my head away so I could gather myself. So I could be in the right frame of mind when I walked into the courtroom. My vibe needed to be right. Judges hated contentiousness. I'd accepted the irony of that years ago.

"Casey." Justin lowered his voice. "Please don't be like this."

"Like how. What is *this*?" I shrugged like I had no idea what he was talking about.

Ted Strohmeyer was coming down the hall. I didn't have to tilt my head far to see that Tom Brody and Miriam Shively were bringing up the rear.

"We can't do this here," he stage whispered. "We can't do this now."

I lifted my messenger bag as if it were the heaviest weight in the world and followed Justin. He picked one of the small private rooms and twisted the knob.

"Thanks for talking to me in here," Justin said. He closed the door behind himself. All the noise from the hall disappeared. It was just him and me in this tiny room together. No clients or pacing opposing counsel to come between us.

"The ethical rules. No, the *legal* rules require that I talk to you out of earshot of opposing counsel. Attorney-client privilege and all that."

I hoped my facial expression conveyed that I believed he had no interest in upholding the oath he'd taken in Columbus. It was nearly impossible to believe this was the same attorney who'd warned me against Hudson's gray areas. Justin ignored my obvious dig.

"I called you," he said. He dropped his briefcase and lifted his hands to face the ceiling. "Left you a voicemail. Emailed you. Sent you a text."

"Maybe you should have tried a carrier pigeon."

Justin laid his briefcase down on the table and flipped the latches. He lifted the lid and hefted out a large sheaf of papers.

"This is what I was going to show you yesterday, if you'd answered any of my messages."

"When? *Before* or *after* you were done with your make-out session with Mrs. Garza?"

Justin placed the stack on the table. He gently pushed down the briefcase lid. His stare was direct and uncomfortable.

"I thought that may have been it." He sighed as if I'd caught him with his hand in a cookie jar and not with his tongue down a client's throat. "That you'd misunderstood what was happening."

"Misunderstood?" I ran a hand about two inches through my hair, then almost immediately regretted it. It would turn into a rat's nest without the least bit of provocation. I met Justin's eyes and forgot my hair. It was the least of my problems. "No. I completely understood."

"It was just adrenaline. A reaction to what I wanted to tell you."

I braced myself. My life had needed a lot of bracing. That hadn't changed despite my best efforts. That was part of the change that needed to happen. May not happen right now. I closed my eyes. Opened them. Ready, I thrust my open hand toward him.

"Go ahead."

"We went to Strohmeyer to collect some papers that were in Tino Garza's office."

My thoughts pinged from one place to another. I couldn't make sense of anything he was saying or anything that had happened in the last three days. I started with what was right in front of me.

"Collect papers? Why didn't Garza's husband...Tino...just give them to you?"

It was the first time I'd ever seen Justin's face tinge with pink.

"He...um...he didn't know."

"So that ethical violation wasn't your biggest problem. A felony was. Jesus fucking Christ." My hands went to my face before I could think better of it. I pulled them away hoping my face wasn't a nightmare of sticking-up hair and smudged eye makeup. "You know, Justin, my career hasn't been stellar. Hasn't been nearly perfect. I left Hudson at your say-so, because you said they weren't on the up-and-up. So, I have to say that I very much didn't expect this from you. What do I do now? If I look at whatever you show me, am I going to be tainted by this?" My mind flashed forward to my own disbarment hearing. Didn't like that picture.

I backed away from Justin in case I got a glimpse of the incriminating documents. I needed plausible deniability.

"You know what? I can't see this now. This conversation never happened."

I picked up my bag and left Justin to himself in the little room. While I stood there wondering what in the hell I'd gotten myself into, I flashed back to the last moral dilemma I'd had. That time, that time I'd ratted out the bad guy, Ted Strohmeyer. It wasn't like I didn't see the irony of the situation. Same family. Different case. I'd learned my lesson, though.

Tattling did no one any good.

The hall felt too big, so I went toward the first ladies' room that I could find and pushed the door open. I could not be happier that there was a new courthouse. Years ago, I'd have had to sequester myself in a bathroom with industrial marble that smelled like the hundred years it had been in use.

This one was beige and almost clinical. I tucked myself into the farthest stall, lowered the toiled lid, and sat down to think. I tried not to cry, but tears leaked out nonetheless. How had I cursed God so badly that I kept ending up in the stupidest situations.

Wrong guy.

Stolen documents.

Ethical breaches.

If the definition of crazy was doing the same thing and expecting something different, then I had to really wonder what in the heck was wrong in my life. I kept doing different things, but ending up with the same result.

Even through the sound of someone coming in the door, opening a stall and urinating, I didn't move. Instead I took three deep breaths. That was supposed to calm me. I'd read it in some magazine. Wasn't quite working. But maybe a courthouse public restroom was the wrong environment for a mini meditation.

I only had to do one thing, and that was get through today's hearing. I could make a new decision tomorrow about this case and about Justin.

Because I didn't want anyone to think I was gross, I flushed and came out to wash my hands.

"Casey, long time no see."

I'd been so blinded by my sadness that I hadn't seen Miriam Shively at the other bathroom sink.

"Miriam." My mind blanked for a good long moment. I didn't have a script prepared for this one.

"You're doing class actions now. Seems like you jump around. Last week it was defending a sex trafficker. The week before you were representing that cop. Before that juvenile. And now the big leagues, federal. You ready?"

I knew the speech was meant to unsettle me. To intimidate.

"Big league? Miriam, your approach is bush league. You can't forget that my first job *was* at Morrell Gates. I remember the meetings when you talked about undermining common pleas lawyers with big-firm intimidation tactics. I'm not so easily bullied."

"Do you think this case has legs?" If I wasn't so easily influenced, she wasn't so easily swayed from her intimidation strategy.

"Not only legs, but arms, a torso, and a head. Strohmeyer is poisoning kids in Brighthill. Kids in Clearwater Park too. Don't forget my first defeat was at the hands of this family. I know how the Strohmeyers work. There's evidence of this. All we have to do is find it."

Miriam shook her head like I'd flunked kindergarten.

"You don't have causation? We should be here on a motion to dismiss and not defending this baseless class action claim."

I wasn't going to take the bait. I'd learned a little something in the last decade. Instead of dodging and feinting when she thrust, I parried.

"How is it that you're in bed with the Strohmeyers? You saw how they threw me under the bus."

It was only the slight widening of her eyes, but I could tell that Miriam did not like my characterization. I wanted to tell her tough titties, you lie down with dogs and get up with fleas. Kept my mouth shut though because I knew that she probably wouldn't appreciate my pointed clichés.

"Threw you under the bus? What are you talking about?" she shot back. It caught me off guard that she could forget the reason I never got a chance to work at Morrell full-time.

"Law review?"

"Casey. My God, that was ten years ago. Is that what this case is really about? Some grudge from law school?"

"No, it's about a cancer cluster downstream from a brewery."

"Casey, you were born and raised here. You know better than this. It's beer. That's the cleanest industry there is."

Even though I knew the reason for what she was doing, I couldn't say it wasn't getting to me. Justin's actions had put everything I believed about him and the righteousness of this case on shaky ground.

"It's nearly eleven," I glanced at my wrist meaningfully. "I need to get in there and confer with Justin before the hearing."

Miriam's face was so full of pity I wanted to cry and scream at the same time. I'd felt sorry for myself for so long, and I was tired of it. I didn't want anyone to pity me. I wanted that part of my life to be done.

"I know that it's probably hard for you, but you know better than this. You don't belong on that side of the table. You belong in a place like Morrell Gates. It's where honors graduates and law review editors work. Now that I'm a partner, I'd certainly be willing to recommend that you come on as an associate or even of counsel given your decade of experience."

I didn't know which shocked me more: the backhanded job offer or the sound of my phone vibrating. I fished the little black gadget from the open back pocket of my leather bag. I read the brief message from Justin. As a courtesy I shared the substance with Shively.

"Magistrate wants counsel in chambers." I turned my back, but it didn't silence her.

"Think about my offer," Shively said. "You can do the white shoe thing, Casey. It's where you belong."

23

Casey

August 7, 2007

"Mr. McPhee, good morning," Magistrate Judge Carol Wheeler said. We were in her chambers, pre-hearing. The courtroom wasn't busy. Gathering us in here was a move to make us uncomfortable. The magistrate did not want us thinking we could take up space on her docket for too long.

I tried to think cool thoughts, not to sweat. There were too many lawyers for the small space. The magistrate sat alone on her side of her desk. The rest of us—me, Justin, and Shively—all crowded on the other. I was grateful neither Tom nor Ted were in here as well. That would have been too close for comfort. "What did your clients make of the offer from Strohmeyer?" the magistrate asked.

"They've chosen not to accept it, Your Honor," Justin replied.

Judge Wheeler turned sharply toward Miriam Shively.

"Is that your last, best, and final, Ms. Shively?"

"Yes, for now, Your Honor," she said. "We'd like to argue the motion."

"Mr. McPhee, Ms. Shively, are you going to speak for your respective sides?"

"Yes, Your Honor," they said in unison.

"If you're ready, then let's get this over with." Judge Wheeler stood. That was the signal. We'd been dismissed.

Garza had still been seated at counsel table when we came in from the conversation with Shively.

"What's going to happen now?" she whispered. I hadn't looked at her. I couldn't look her in the eye. Now, I swallowed, turned my head, then did my best acting.

"Justin's going to argue for class action certification. Ms. Shively will argue against it. The judge will ask them questions. Then she'll make a decision."

"Right now?"

"Possibly now from the bench. Or by written decision. Or both," I shortcut. I didn't tell her that no matter what happened, there'd be a written decision because class action certifications were such a huge deal. The more money riding on a judgement, the more words a court gave it. I didn't tell her that the Sixth Circuit could allow an interlocutory appeal fourteen days after a decision, and possibly reverse the decision of the trial court. Not one word of that. Instead, I turned to the bench.

Magistrate Judge Carol Wheeler straightened her robes, opened a leather portfolio, turned the barrel of a gold pen, then cleared her throat.

"Mr. McPhee?"

"May it please the court, I'm Justin McPhee, attorney for the plaintiff families of the cities Clearwater Park and

Brighthill, both in Cuyahoga County. Our firm, McPhee and Associates, have filed forty claims for relief."

I'd heard it all before. Justin's preparation had included him practicing the argument we'd worked on together. I'd played the opposing counsel making every counter argument I could throw at him. I'd impersonated the judge and had done the same from her perspective. We may not have met this weekend like we'd planned, but he was more than prepared. Or maybe as prepared as he could be.

"I thought you had forty-one," Wheeler interrupted.

"One family has pulled out, Your Honor. Their child is on life support and they couldn't take the additional stress of litigation."

"I'm sorry to hear that." She swallowed a sip of water from the glass on the bench. "Please proceed."

Justin was doing a pretty good job, so far. His voice was calm, even. I did my best not to show how nervous I was for him.

"I want to be clear, you have forty?" Wheeler pressed. It was obvious that numerosity was one of her main concerns. I wish we'd beat the bushes for more kids. The experts' early estimates based on statistical modeling was that there were at least one hundred families affected. Unfortunately, it was also likely that most of them didn't yet know why their children were sick or even that there was a cancer eating away at their child's chances of surviving into or past their teens.

"Yes, Your Honor. Forty. The list of cases and numbers are included in the latest amendment."

"They are all children with cancer? That's unusual for Cuyahoga County, no?"

"Unusual cancers, Your Honor. Not unusual for cancer, but unusual for children. These are the kinds of cancers that seventy-year-olds, eighty-year-olds get. That's extreme carcinogenic exposure, Your Honor."

"What do your clients want?"

It was the softest of softball questions. I sat a little bit forward in my seat as if my grip on the table could influence the way Justin answered. I could feel Garza tense up, but I couldn't soothe her.

"Justice, Your Honor." He took a deep breath. Wasn't sure if it was for show or to calm his own nerves. "More specifically, they want compensatory damages, reimbursement for medical treatment. Many have reached their cap and some have even lost their health insurance. Those families where the parents are self-employed, they can't get new insurance because of these kids' preexisting conditions. Some families are out thousands. Others are hundreds of thousands in debt. Facing a bankruptcy that will solve one issue but make them further ineligible for future treatment. Furthermore, there are single issues of law and fact." Justin paused. The magistrate followed his cue as if she were another actor in the play.

"Can you fairly and adequately represent the class?" She was giving him the pillars. All Justin had to do was rest the case on them.

"Yes, Your Honor. These cases are not at all like the cases we hear about in Texas and California where the lawyers get millions and the individual members of the class get pennies. While we endeavor to be compensated for work, there's no likelihood that our attorney interests will conflict with those of the clients. We're here to make sure that our clients get justice, are able to pay their bills, hopefully treat or even cure their children, and hold Strohmeyer Breweries responsible."

"Thank you, Mr. McPhee."

From the corner of my eye, I saw Garza move. She'd almost put her hands together as if to clap in response to Justin's performance. My left hand caught her right like a hungry hippo catching a marble—swiftly and completely.

"Ms. Shively, can you please tell me why I shouldn't certify this class?"

Justin and Shively traded places at the podium. I trained my eyes forward not wanting to look at the people on either side of me, not until I was ready to fully confront what I'd seen between them on Sunday in Justin's office.

"Your Honor, let's start with issues of law and fact. The fundamental pillars of the case aren't there. When in negotiations with Ms. Cort, she admitted that causation wasn't there."

I hoped my gasp was inaudible. Not only was that a mischaracterization of what I'd said, but I was dying to know when bathroom chat had transformed into negotiations.

Justin's gaze felt like a burning hot poker that was coming through the side of my head. Resisting the urge to turn and disavow anything she'd said, I turned my own hot poker gaze toward Shively's back. I could only hope that she felt the burn.

"Ms. Shively, let me familiarize you with the standard. What I need to decide today is whether the, now forty, cases before me in this motion share common issues of law and fact and whether or not aggregation or combination would lend itself to court efficiency and the best representation of the class. Would you like to address *that*?"

Shively opened her own portfolio and began the argument she'd obviously prepared. For five long minutes, she listed all the ways in which we and our case were—inadequate.

"You have a removal motion here as well, I see." Wheeler took a page from the stack of papers on the bench in front of her.

"Yes, Your Honor. The Northern District of Ohio is a better forum for adjudication of this matter."

"But you'd rather have me hear forty different cases instead of one case."

"The cases are so different, Your Honor, that yes, that's best for the administration of justice my opposing counsel speaks of so reverently."

"Yes, it's the right move that I hear them, I agree. A federal forum is best, but if it's here, then I'm going to certify this as a class. I'm only going to do this once."

"Your Honor." It wasn't a whine exactly, more like a plaintive wail of defense attorney annoyance.

"You know what, Ms. Shively, I'll give you a choice. Either the case is heard in federal court as a class action or in state court, where it could be heard as a class action as well. Do you want to talk to your clients, or would you be able to make a decision now?"

This was the first time since that summer when Shively had been worried about whether she'd ever make partner that I saw her appear unsure.

"I'll need a second, Your Honor."

Shively strode back to counsel table where Tom and Ted and Simon joined her. The brief discussion was heated but held in near silence nonetheless. The defendants were between a legal rock and a hard place, and from their body language, they were having a hard time deciding which alternative was better.

After another moment, Shively cut her hand to end the discussion and came back to the podium.

"We'll remain in federal court, Your Honor."

"Then pursuant to rule twenty-six of the Rules of Civil Procedure," Wheeler intoned, "I hereby grant plaintiffs' motion for class certification. I'll enter a judgement entry so noting this decision. In five minutes, please come into my chambers so we can hammer out a discover and pre-trial order."

Magistrate Judge Carol Wheeler stood and very deliberately stepped from the courtroom.

"So we won?" was Veronica Garza's first question when the door closed behind the judge's robes.

"Yes," I said. I took my own pad and pen and stuffed them in my bag for something to do. A reason to avoid looking at Garza. "The court is going to hear all the cases as one."

"Thanks for all you do. I have to go."

I was surprised that Garza wasn't going to stay to bat her eyes at my co-counsel. "Go?"

"Ivy's in the hospital. Something happened this week-end and she got very sick all of a sudden. They think it may be her other kidney."

All my bad feelings about Garza gave way to compassion—empathy for a mother of a daughter with cancer.

"Oh my gosh. I'm so sorry," I said, suddenly sorry for this morning's cold shoulder. "You didn't have to come."

"But I did." Her brown eyes pleaded with me. "I need everyone over there to know that being poisoned has a face."

24

Justin
August 23, 2007

"You wanted me to come with my suit on. Here I am. Tell me what you couldn't on the phone earlier. I just pissed off Judge Miller by bailing early. You know how she loves to talk about herself and her federal court aspirations as if any of us have a direct line to the president or the Senate judiciary committee.

"She was about to launch into some kind of juicy story on the Sheila Harrison Grant divorce. I had no idea she was the judge on that one. Or maybe I knew. I must have seen the documents when there was a putative father determination…"

Casey wound down of her own accord, having burned through the nervous energy lots of lawyers get when they had a court appearance. Admittedly, it was hard to go from on to off like a light switch.

"Settlement conference at Morrell Gates at one o'clock."

"It's eleven thirty now. Settlement? Why? What's going on?" Her eyes narrowed with well-deserved suspicion.

"Simon Brody called."

"Out of the blue?"

"Not exactly..."

"Is this about the thing I can't know about?"

Slowly and deliberately, I lifted my wallet from the inside pocket of my suit jacket. Opened the slim black leather billfold, extracted the only bill I had, a crisp fifty straight from the bank teller's drawer, handed it to Casey.

"Retainer fee."

"Justin! This is not television. This is not a criminal retainer."

"Yes, yes, it is."

Casey snatched the money from my hand. Stuffed it in her bra. I tried not to be wholly distracted by that.

"Fine. What did you do?"

"Broke into Tino Garza's office at Strohmeyer."

"I know that."

"I just wanted to make sure it was clear *that* preliminary communication was now covered by attorney-client privilege."

My actions needed to protect us both.

Casey cocked her head, then seeming to understand, pushed on.

"What made you think he had anything of value?"

"After what Simon Brody said to you and what Veronica Garza said to me, her husband became an obvious nexus."

"For what?"

"For this." I lifted the stack I'd carefully reviewed not only by myself, but with the two experts I'd finally put on retainer. Very expensive retainers.

"What's this?" She eyed the documents like they were nuclear waste that were going to poison her with radiation.

"To start, Strohmeyer's under criminal investigation by the Ohio Environmental Protection Agency and the federal EPA as well."

"Criminal?"

"The agencies are alleging that they cleaned their on-site water filters and left pools of arsenic on the grounds to soak into the earth, I guess. That arsenic tainted the groundwater."

"Moved downslope to the houses in Clearwater Park and Brighthill that are on wells. The babies drank it in their formula. The kids drank it in their Kool-Aid and here we are. Kids poisoned with a high concentration of a known carcinogen and cancer."

"Yes, that's it. That's the bottom line there. The criminal part is that Strohmeyer knowingly did this. Were warned to stop, find some alternative dumping methods or amelioration. They hired Roscommon General Services."

Casey's face screwed up as I knew it would. "Why does that sound familiar...?"

"Roscommon is a county in Ireland..." I wanted to lead her down the same path I'd tread earlier.

She snapped her fingers. "Right. I remember. Tom's family is from there. We were going to go there on our bar trip. So, an Irish family owns or runs this company. What does that have to do with the price of tea? Irish families are a dime a dozen in America. You, Mr. McPhee, should know this."

"Not just any Irish family. The Brody family."

"They—no. Nope. This is starting to sound crazy conspiracy."

"No conspiracy. Strohmeyer hired Roscommon to remove the tainted water."

"Drop the shoe."

"The contract was fake. There was never any waste removal. The whole deal was there to give the appearance that they were handling the problem. But they never planned to handle it. The filtered water waste remained exactly where it had always been...on Strohmeyer's campus."

"And Simon knew this. Not because he's in-house counsel. Because telling me that would be a violation of his fiduciary duty to his client. And because he was a Brody. That's just family business. So you're saying that all that's in these documents? That pile looks pretty small."

"Two memos. That's all it takes to establish a conspiracy."

"Why did Tino have these? Seems like the kind of thing that should only have been talked about. And if it was written down, then with an IBM Selectric at best, no carbon copies."

"He was, Tino Garza, de facto in charge of brewery waste. They had to tell him something, otherwise he'd have perpetrated the truth or the wrong lie to investigators."

"And this...neither one of these memos is anywhere to be found in those forty or forty-one-odd bankers boxes in the conference room?"

"I looked thrice. Probably more than that. I went through everything with a fine-toothed comb."

"Damn. So how are we at settlement?"

"I called Simon. Told him what we had. He named a place and time."

"Is this even ethical? Using stolen documents to essentially blackmail a defendant into paying out the plaintiffs?"

"Isn't this the exact definition of the end justifying the means? It's the greater good, Casey. It's what could save these families from the endless heartache of that awful double whammy of a sick child on one hand and medical bills ruining them on the other. A few hundred thousand dollars each could be the buffer between healing and financial ruin."

"I need time, Justin. Time to research. Time to consider."

"Not to sound like Jake Bauer, but there is no time." I quoted the most oft-repeated line from the high-stakes TV drama *24*. "We have an hour. Half of that will be getting through building security. The other half will be making sure we pee before we leave."

"Jeez, Justin."

"I'm nervous, Casey. This is the biggest case I've ever handled. I don't want to let the families down. I don't want to let you down. I don't want to let myself down. I know that what I did wasn't right. It was a heat-of-the-moment decision that I may not do again. I can't say that I wouldn't..."

"Stop. That was just the tip of the iceberg, Justin. We haven't even talked about the other."

"She..."

"No. Nope. Not she. You're an adult. You're an independent actor. Any sentence about that needs to start with I. And now the time has dwindled even more. So if we're going to do this, then we're going to do this. I'm not happy about the documents. About Veronica. But I'm with you on the families front. I don't want any more people suffering at the hands of Cleveland's rich families. Not anymore."

25

Casey

August 23, 2007

Maybe the paint was refreshed or the art work was different. The wood and brass plaques from Best Lawyers and Superlawyers were new. The ones from Martindale-Hubbell were not. I wanted to laugh and cry and run away all at the same time. Instead, I took a deep breath and walked further into the belly of the beast. Further into the reception area of the place I'd called home for a brief period before that rug was pulled.

"Do you know who's going to be in the meeting?" I asked Justin after we'd announced ourselves to reception, flashing our stick-on visitor's badges received from security downstairs.

The look he gave me was a close cousin to pity. It didn't at all make me want to laugh. I wasn't going to cry. Not today. Not now. If I wanted to be the successful lawyer I knew I could be—one with my own plaques touting my abilities and the respect and admiration of my peers, I needed to stare down my past.

Part of the mystery was solved when Shively appeared in reception.

"Mr. McPhee, Ms. Cort, so good to see you. Let me take you back to the conference room. Actually, I need to speak with the girl in reception for a minute. It's the Huron conference room. I'm sure you remember the way, Casey."

I wanted to say that I'd long forgotten. But that wouldn't have been the truth.

"Down the hall. Third door on the left. It overlooks the stadium."

Shively nodded in confirmation. "There's coffee. Tea. Some bagels and muffins. Make yourselves comfortable. We'll all be right in."

I tried to do what she said, get comfortable. I took a chair near the head of the table, laid my bag at the side. Took out a yellow pad, my Cross pen. Justin mimicked me, but with more. Stacks of documents in manila folders. We'd agreed on the labels affixed to the front: Contamination read one. Damages read another. It was to give the impression, not wholly untrue, that we had lots of evidence pointing to Strohmeyer's culpability. And also to elicit if not sympathy, then fear of reports of dozens of sick children appearing all over the news linking their rare cancers to one of the city's most beloved employers, one with a reputation for clean operations.

I heard them before I saw them. The muted sounds of feet on carpet. One by one they entered. First Shively, then Ted Strohmeyer. Tom Brody was next followed by his brother, Simon Brody, who closed the door behind all of them. It was only Simon's presence that was unusual. Like the Garzas, Simon Brody was the client. For a long list of reasons, starting with their inability to often be rational, clients were generally excluded from settlement negotiations. This was the first hint that somehow this was going to be different. My stomach bottomed out, nerves nearly made me shake. I swallowed. When that offered no relief, I got up and procured two bottles of water.

Shively opened the meeting before I could get back to my seat. If I hadn't been in danger of losing my lunch, I'd have been offended. I needed the movement to keep me from jumping out of my own skin. I had to work overtime at keeping my hands steady while untwisting the cap and pouring water.

"I'm not sure any introductions are necessary," Shively said with a crooked grin. "I believe everyone here knows everyone else. Some more intimately than others."

At Shively's use of the word intimately, my hand jerked and some liquid did spill on the wood. For a long moment no one moved. We all watched the water bead move a millimeter at a time toward Justin's documents stack. Finally, as if a spell had somehow been broken, Simon Brody got up, retrieved a few napkins, then wiped up the mess.

I gave him grateful eyes, then sat heavily in the fabric-covered chair, careful to control the rolling action by planting my feet firmly on the carpet.

Justin sat up straighter in his chair. "We're here at your request." It was a strong negotiating start. We'd agreed in the elevator that we didn't want to look like we'd come hat in hand willing to accept whatever crumbs were doled out. Though it didn't look like it, we were in a strong position. While we may have only a few dozen plaintiffs and not hundreds, and while causation was and may forever be an issue, the fact that they'd called a meeting meant their discomfort with this case may be greater than ours. Whether it was the EPA investigation or what the documents Justin and Garza had stolen revealed, there was a reason Simon Brody had summoned us here. Before we laid even the first card on the table, we needed to know what that was.

"Right, yes," Shively said. She glanced at my ex-fiancé, his brother and Strohmeyer's in-house counsel, then to my law school nemesis, the man who'd caved in my life without so much as a backward glance. Then she peered between the two of us as if there were some unseen third person. "What are you looking for in this case?"

"Our demand is thirty million," I declared. There was no reason to start anywhere but at the top. I didn't know if Strohmeyer would be footing the bill, or if it would be an insurance company or somewhere in between. Though it was a private company, the publicly available documents told they could afford to make this right, to make us go away.

"Is that something your clients are willing to accept?"

"Yes. Preliminarily. Of course we'd have to meet with them, but I can say that yes, it's within the ballpark."

"What kind of authorization do you have?"

A class action had a lot of moving parts. We'd need the approval of the court. Because corralling individual plaintiffs could be a nightmare. That meant that Justin and I ultimately had the decision-making power today. We'd decide how much each family would receive. The court would determine what the attorneys got. If we got the thirty million we'd demanded, that didn't mean we'd get the thirty-three percent or nine million dollars. The upside of a class action was a bigger settlement. The downside, no court was going to hand over that amount of money for the work we'd done. We had to build in something for our-selves, and it was going to be a lot, but not one-third for sure.

"Just court authorization, of course."

"What are the families' expectations?"

"To be fairly compensated, Miriam," I interjected. I didn't need to have all this preliminary stuff. I just wanted to get down to it before it went off the rails. Sure, I had familiarity with everyone here. But most of that was bad.

"How are you, Casey?" Tom asked. "Been a couple of months."

"Glad to see that you landed on your feet," I said.

"Brodys always do. Don't you worry. The prosecutor's office will be okay without me."

"I wasn't worried, Tom."

"Interesting to see you here in the big leagues."

"Does that mean that you guys have a reasonable offer? Or am I wasting my time in the 'big leagues'?"

Simon Brody scooted his chair forward. "I know it's unusual that I'm here, but I want to cut to the chase. I don't want everyone to be here for a million phone calls back and forth. Strohmeyer is interested in doing what's right. Ted here heard about Ivelisse's problem with her other insurance. It's the reason we came forward and helped her to get the kind of care she needed at the Clinic. The idea that there are other children suffering a similar fate leaves a bad taste in our mouth."

"So does your beer," I said *sotto voce*.

Justin's foot nudged mine. I nudged back acknowledg-ing my less than professional behavior.

"Why isn't thirty million enough to compensate fami-lies with children suffering from cancer?" Shively said un-doing the goodwill that Simon had just put forth.

I pulled one of the manila files toward me. Slowly, deliberately, I flipped open the outside. From there I pulled out a stack of glossy photos. They were blown-up shots of the plaintiffs. Most were in the hospital or at home. I slid one across the table for opposing counsel to view.

"This is Ciara Mullins—acute lymphocytic leukemia. This is Denise Lowery—neuroblastoma. This is Peter Bealls—lung cancer. This is Fermin Serrano—bladder cancer. And this is Rene Poulin. His parents relocated here from southern France to follow their dream of opening a little bakery. They've had to close it to care for their son. Rene has skin cancer. And of course, Ivelisse Garza, renal cancer. Her lifesaving surgery at the Clinic that Strohmeyer provided insurance for has left the family thousands in debt with co-pays. Last week she had a new cancer scare. It turned out to be a false alarm, just stones that caused an infection. That visit, though, with all the top-of-the-line scans given her earlier condition will put the family in the poorhouse. All for something that wasn't their fault."

It's the kind of presentation I'd have given to a jury. It was the kind of thing I'd have hired someone to blow up on a big screen to show everyone in the court who we were talking about. Before we got to carcinogens and causation and clusters, I'd want them to know the case was about sick children. Because more than anything else, these children deserved justice.

"Cancer is bad. It's not mesothelioma. It's not like the fire bricks."

"There's a bigger world of carcinogens out there than asbestos."

"Why should we settle? The jury may be swayed by your little performance here, but we're not your standard Cuyahoga County jury. You still don't have causation."

"Miriam, you're right. This will be the usual battle of the experts. My guys will say you're pouring poison into the well water. Your guys will say that breweries are the cleanest industry there ever was. It could, honestly, at that point go either way. Then we'll call Simon Brody to the stand."

"In-house counsel? You were a better lawyer than that. Everything he does is privileged. His job to represent the corporation is the very definition of privilege."

Tom's eye caught mine, and I gave him the slightest nod. He'd been on the receiving end of one truth bomb. I didn't think anyone in his family wanted to be on another.

"I'd, of course, anticipate this and hand over to the magistrate judge my brief on exceptions to privilege, which in this case would include communications with non-lawyers and those outside the corporation. In this case, that would be Roscommon. I'd happily produce these memos between Strohmeyer and Roscommon about disposal of a known carcinogen and the cover-up regarding the fact that it was never disposed of, as was presented to the EPA, but dumped on the Strohmeyer campus. Then I'll point out that even if there's any argument about privilege remaining, there's a strong conflict of interest with Simon Brody being a major shareholder in Roscommon. Not to mention the crime-fraud exception."

"That's a lot of posturing." This came from Ted Strohmeyer. He nearly knocked me off my stride. For someone who'd changed my life so dramatically, I couldn't think of the last time I'd heard his voice, the last time we'd even been in a room together. It probably would have been this room with the same catered food, only that would have been some kind of case strategy session during my one summer.

"The posturing would lead to us handing over a memo, once the privilege exceptions were done for. The memo showing that Strohmeyer knew leeching arsenic into the water table was likely to cause some kind of injury, if not cancer. The memo showing that finding dumping sites was extremely costly and cut deeply into the bottom line. That the main worry in ceasing use of the filters was worry about a possible false advertising claim. Marketing was more important than children's lives. That would be the first line of my closing argument. That's what I'd present to the jury. That's why I imagine we're here for settlement."

"You have such a memo? Let me see a copy."

Prepared for this, I handed over a copy to each whose hand was out. One for Tom Brody. One for Ted Strohmeyer. One for Miriam Shively. Simon Brody was looking out the window. He'd left the conference room table. I wondered what his expression was. He'd led me down this path, and I still couldn't figure out why. I'd thought it was his conscience. But once I'd read what Justin had illegally procured, I saw how Simon Brody was implicated and tossed out that rationale. If he'd had a conscience, the time to have used it would have been when Strohmeyer was covering up arsenic dumping.

"Where did you get this? This was not part of discovery," Shively demanded. Tom was the next to turn his back and have a look out of the floor-to-ceiling windows. Simon Brody was guilty. Tom Brody had no illusions as to my new ruthlessness.

"In television shows and movies, there's always an envelope that comes under the door. In my last case it was a video tape." I saw Tom flinch at that. "This time it was this. Some well-meaning person or people decided justice was more important than money."

I didn't flinch in my half honesty. I'd have excelled as a big-firm lawyer.

"This could be faked. This could be forged. There are hundreds of objections to this. It will never come in front of a judge or jury."

"A nun once told me a secret is never a secret unless a single person knows it and can take it to their grave. If it doesn't come out in court, then it will come out later. I think we're here because Simon Brody's interested in damage control."

"Any settlement will quiet things. We'll make notifications to those others who may be in the class. The period will end, the case will go away quietly, and that will be all."

"Done and dusted," I said. "So all we're here to talk about is money."

Simon Brody turned then, took out a tri-folded single sheet of paper. Laid it on the table. Pushed it toward Justin and me. Miriam's hand lifted as if to look at it before it came to us, but one cutting look from Simon Brody and her hand was back on the table in front of her. If it hadn't been my very real life, I'd have thought it was a movie.

Justin looked at me and I him. I laid my own hand on the sheet and slid it toward us. The light scratching of paper upon wood was the only sound in the room. I laid down the pen I hadn't realized I was clutching like a lifeline, and unfolded first the top, then the bottom. There were only two lines. The first read, class fund to be established. Each class member to receive $525,000. The next line was what the defendant was willing to pay for legal fees separate from the award which would, I knew, eliminate either a high percentage or a lodestar check from the court. That sum was three million for fees and expenses. That would be split between the two of us.

I did a quick calculation in my mind. It was a twenty- to twenty-five-million-dollar settlement offer. Up until this moment, the most I'd earned on a case had been in the low five figures, and that was after more hours put in than I'd been paid fairly for.

Justin and I looked at each other again. There was nothing to object to. At a percentage of fifteen or well under, the court would approve it with ease. It was a win for everyone. I wish I could have said why the win felt almost hollow.

"Deal," I said. We all stood then. Everyone shook as if it were a wedding receiving line. They scurried out of the conference room like rats leaving a sinking ship. Someone's secretary stood at the door. Presumably to escort us to the elevator and make sure we didn't take any silver on the way out. Once she pressed the down button and gave us a curt nod, Justin and I were alone. My smile seemed inappropriate, but I couldn't help myself.

"The kids…"

"The kids got what they deserved. It's all I'd wanted from the beginning."

"Now what?" My question was not about the legal procedure. Filing a settlement. Making a request for fees. Sending a notice to the plaintiffs and those who could be putative plaintiffs. The approval of the court. My question was about us as much as it was about our respective futures.

When the call button darkened and a soft chime sounded, we stepped on the elevator. Our steps silent on the carpet were noisy on the stone floor. When the door closed, I turned my smile full force.

"You did it."

"No, Casey, you did it. Or maybe we did it. Your class action idea saved this case from piecemeal settlement. From some families getting more while others got less."

Quietly, I nodded and accepted his accolade. Then I lifted my lashes and took in my co-counsel.

Even after expenses, I was looking into the eyes of another newly minted millionaire.

26

Veronica
August 25, 2007

I hung up the phone not knowing at all how to feel. It was like the first time I'd been on an airplane. In the beginning, there was the elation of taking flight, defying gravity. That had been quickly followed by being scared shitless not knowing what would happen. Whether the big metal bird would fall from the sky, killing us all.

"Who was that?" Tino asked. He wiped his mouth. Tossed his paper napkin, orange with grease, onto his empty plate. He was eating at the table alone as usual, one hand on his fork, the other on his Blackberry. He'd worked long hours today even though it was a Saturday.

Dinner with the kids had been rice with pigeon peas and pork. Tino had just finished an adult-sized portion with a beer on the side. All the exhaustion I felt over being cooped up alone on a rainy day with two kids had vanished in an instant after I'd heard the words come through the receiver.

I moved from the counter where I'd been putting away dishes and wiping down the counter. I took Tino's plate, bussed the table. Without looking at him, so my eyes didn't betray my complicated feelings, I answered.

"Justin McPhee."

"That lawyer." Tino shook his head as if I'd just hung up from speaking with the devil himself. "I thought we'd talked about this. I thought you'd agreed to pull out of the case. I told the higher-ups that we were out. That we were all done except for the paperwork. I can't bite the hand that feeds me. Feeds us. Not now that Strohmeyer's finally come through with my promotion."

I bit my lip—hard. He talked about that promotion as if he'd been given the holy grail *and* been coronated on the same day, instead of a large raise and the obligation to do more work.

"Do you want to know what he said?" I asked. Most life-changing news that came through a phone was bad— death, illness, destruction from the latest hurricane back home. It was the first time something good had come across the wires.

"Is it about when he's delivering the paperwork?" Tino demanded. "That whole thing has been slower than a Cleveland bus in the snow."

Every time Tino asked about us all being out of the case, I deflected. It was the first time I'd been grateful he hadn't been home. The fewer questions asked, the fewer lies I had to tell.

"We won." With anyone else, my voice would have been light with joy. Instead it was heavy with fear and dread, because I knew our marriage would come out bruised and bloodied on the other end of this conversation.

I didn't want to have it—the hard conversation. I'd have loved to have run upstairs, run away, hide. There was no hiding from the truth any longer. I'd laid down my life for my daughter and I'd risen victorious.

"We won what, Veronica?" Tino's voice was deadly quiet. I had to swallow hard to keep my own rice dinner in my stomach. "You can't win if you don't play," he hissed through his teeth, "and we weren't playing."

"I didn't pull out," I whispered. "I never told Justin...Mr. McPhee...the lawyer we were out."

Tino seemed to grow three times his original size. His face was dark with anger like I'd never seen. It was almost purple.

"But...we...we won," I pressed on. I was sure once he realized that I'd made the right choice, played the odds and won, that his anger would go away. That after he stopped being more macho than immature, he'd turn back into the loveable bear of a man I'd married all those years ago. I took a breath, got the stutter out of my voice. "Strohmeyer agreed to settle. They knew we had them dead to rights."

"Because you stole papers from my office." The whites of his eyes were red with anger. "Would they have been so quick to settle if they knew how you'd gotten the papers? Papers I know you must have fed to that lawyer. What does he have on you, this lawyer? Why are you so quick to do whatever he asks but never did what *we* agreed upon? Are you fucking him?"

It was my turn for my face to warm, turn dark.

"No...no..." I stuttered out the very truthful answer.

"Are you sure?"

"Yes, I'm sure, Tino. I know how to stay faithful."

"Faithful...*fidelidad*...is not your middle name. I remember a certain Jorge Diaz."

One kiss. One time and he acted like I was the whore of Babylon.

"When are you going to stop punishing me for that? It was one kiss, maybe two. I stopped seeing him. Killed a years-long friendship. Blocked him on Facebook when he tried to friend me. I moved up here without complaint. I've been nothing but faithful ever since. Not that you've given me much to be faithful to."

"I'll treat you like a lady, when you stop flaunting your stuff in front of any man that can do you a favor."

"Flaunting?"

"I saw how you were dressed. How that lawyer looked at you. How you looked at him."

"That lawyer...as you call him. That *abogado* just got us five hundred twenty-five thousand dollars for Ivy's cancer. That's more than half a million dollars. Even with your raise, it would take you—" I did a quick calculation in my head. "—more than six years to earn that. The Clinic, the doctors, the labs. No one is waiting that long to get their hands on what they're owed. With that, Tino, we could pay off the house. Pay off all the bills, the medical, the car, the credit cards. The rest we could put away for college for both Ivy *and* Stella. We could do right by our girls."

"I was planning to do right by them, Veronica. I have been doing right by them as long as I've been their father. There's not a day that I didn't get up, go to work. Swallow my pride and do what I had to do to finally get where I always wanted to. Now you want me to give that up for a onetime payday."

"I hate the way you said that. It's a payment for causing her cancer, not winning the lottery. She's owed this."

"I told you from the beginning we were not the kind of people who sued. Between me and God, we got this. We don't have to go out hat in hand begging for scraps. If I violate the promise to quit this case, then where does that leave me? Us? The kids you claim I don't love will be homeless without food in their hungry mouths."

I looked at the remains left in the beer bottle sweating on the wood tabletop. Was there some kind of drug in there, in that bottle that made him more loyal to Strohmeyer than to me?

"You could get a job somewhere else," I said. My voice was deadly calm, reasonable. "Why would you want to stay here? Stay in a place where your bosses poison the people around them. Stay in a place where the water is contaminated. We'll never be able to drink it. This settlement will be confidential, the lawyer said. We could sell the house. Find somewhere else to live. Maybe go back to Puerto Rico."

"You want me to throw away everything I've ever worked for?"

"Strohmeyer isn't the only brewery in the country. Even if it's not Puerto Rico, it could be one of the big ones. The one in Colorado or Milwaukee or even Columbus, here in Ohio. I did some research. The other breweries are as big as Strohmeyer. They're all getting into or already are into the craft market."

Tino was quiet for so long, I thought he was making his own list of other breweries that could hire him. I was ready to see where else I'd probably have to move when he dropped a bomb disguised as a choice.

"It's him or me, Veronica."

"What are you saying?"

"I'm saying that if you take that money, you're on your own with the girls."

"You'd divorce me...over this? Over doing what's best for our daughter? Our daughter who's healing from cancer surgery? This is crazy, Tino. You can't mean it. Let's go to bed. We can talk about this in the morning. Maybe we need to go to Mass first, pray for our sins. Maybe talk to the priest."

"I've never been more serious. It's me or the money. What's your decision?"

I looked out the window. Through the glass of the back door. Pleaded with God for time or fairness or a discussion without an ultimatum.

I felt trapped, like a cat on the wrong side of any door. I looked at the man in front of me. The man I married. The man I followed from Puerto Rico to Ohio. The man who is the father of my children. I realized then I was not only looking into the eyes of my daughters' father, but a man who'd become a stranger.

I laughed softly at the irony of all of it.

He could stay in this house with its poisoned well. He could stay with Strohmeyer Breweries. Maybe they could keep him warm on the nights the arctic breezes blew across the lake. There was something in the way that Justin McPhee had touched me. Something that told me there was more out there. A man who would love me more than his job. A future for my daughters away from this place.

"I'm going home, Tino. I'll pack my bags and those of the girls. I'll call my mother to come and help me move. Then, Tino, I'm going home."

I'd made my choice. I'd chosen myself, my daughters, and my family.

It was the only choice to make.

27

I shuffled to the door in my super soft, comfy Old Navy pajamas and Uggs. I was about fifty percent sure I'd heard a knock. Maybe my neighbors Greg and Jason needed something, though truthfully those requests usually went the other way. My fridge was the opposite of stocked.

After I twisted the dead bolt, I pulled the door open. One day I'd get a peephole. I was very surprised to see my best friend, Lulu, on the other side. She hefted a bottle of red wine in one hand and a paper drugstore bag in the other. I couldn't put those two things together in my mind as having any reason for going together. Instead, I focused on the time. I'd been watching reruns of Law and Order in bed.

"It's past ten. What are you doing here?"

I didn't mean to sound ungrateful or mean-spirited or rude, but I was dog tired. Had been for a couple of weeks. Another case had beat me into submission. I wanted to be elated. Winning, getting that settlement money when the court ultimately approved it was going to change my life. Even if after all the calculations and taxes I'd end up with something closer to eight hundred thousand. I didn't yet know how I was going to move forward. Since that meeting at Morrell, I'd been existing in a kind of limbo. Figuring out how I saw my life from this point on had left me in a brain fog. I couldn't even decide if I wanted to continue to practice law.

There had to be an easier job out there. I just didn't know what it was. Or whether I was even qualified to do something else. Why hadn't I gone to medical school? That was a service job just like mine, but with a whole lot fewer moral and ethical dilemmas that I could see.

"I think I'm pregnant." Lulu cut right to the chase. All thoughts of relaxation from my incessant worry about the future and our semi-estrangement over the last months fled from my head in an instant. My nighttime pity party was over.

"Is Richard Sinclair the father?" I asked. He was the reason we hadn't spoken as often as we used to. She insisted he was good for her. I insisted that his fundamental character flaws, abandoning me when I most needed it, and—you know—being still *married* and formerly her boss made him unsuitable. We'd come to an impasse that hadn't been bridged by conversations over Chinese food.

"Who else, Casey?" Lulu's sigh was full of exasperation.

"Aren't you using birth control?" I asked. "We're old enough to know better, aren't we?" I'd been strict with insisting that Justin and Ron wear a condom any and every time we'd had sex. "I have condoms if you need them."

After that left my mouth, I stepped back from my door and lifted my hand in invitation. None of my neighbors needed that kind of detail about my or Lulu's sex life.

"I have a calendar," she said as she set down the bottle and package on my coffee table.

"The rhythm method?" I could feel my eyebrows nearly kiss my hairline. "What is it—1952 up in here? You have heard of the pill, right? It's revolutionized women's sex lives."

Though I wasn't on it myself. I kept waiting for a regular partner before I picked a set-it-and-forget-it birth control method. It wasn't the smartest plan, but *I* wasn't the one who thought I was pregnant.

Lulu's normally smiling, happy face was anything but.

"That's not helping."

"I'm sorry. Honestly, I'm not in the greatest mood right now. What do you need me to do?"

She leaned forward and slipped a lone cardboard box from the white paper bag. It had the unmistakable hot pink and pastel blue swirl of colors all those boxes shared. They hadn't changed much since I'd bought one in college during my own pregnancy scare.

"I need you to hold my hand." Lulu's face was starting to crumple in on itself.

"Aren't these supposed to be best in the morning?" I said, picking up the box and scanning the back for instructions.

"It's been at least two, maybe three weeks since my period was supposed to start."

I felt my own eyes widen. A missed period was the first sign, but not the only one. I reached into the bag of ideas women trotted out whenever one of us was late.

"Maybe you're stressed. Sometimes that changes your cycle."

"Stress?" Lulu looked a little wild-eyed. "What fucking stress—the changing weather in Cleveland?"

Obviously pulling theories from that big bag of ideas wasn't helping.

"Okay. Sorry. Tired. I was dozing off when you knocked."

"You didn't answer your phone."

"Sorry again." I didn't have anything else. For her, this was more stressful than anything else in Cleveland right now. I shoved the box back in her direction. She took it in hand and stood.

"Can I use your bathroom?"

"Sure. Whatever. I'm very much alone. Come on." I started down the hall toward my one bathroom that was at the back of the apartment near my bedroom.

"No Ron? No Justin?" She craned her neck as if a grown man was going to pop out of my linen closet like Athena sprung from the head of Zeus fully formed.

"Don't even say their names out loud." I shook my head. I'd been in bed using dark television drama to drown out the thinking I didn't want to do. "I have a lot of decisions to make, and I'm having a hard time making them."

"What's the issue?" Lulu asked while she ripped open the box, then tore the plastic packaging around one of the test sticks. "Last time I checked, Ron wanted to marry you and Justin did not. That choice seems very easy."

She set the test on my hamper and untied the cord at the waist of her Juicy sweats.

"Only issue is that Ron hasn't proposed anything more than us getting to know each other better." Until then, I was having a hell of a hard time giving up Justin.

"He laid out his intentions. That's more than I can say for the rest of the people you got engaged to."

"It's not *people*. You can count them on two fingers."

"Sorry," Lulu apologized. We were doing a lot of that today with both of us on edge. The test stick fell to the floor with a clatter.

"Your hands are shaking. It's no wonder you dropped that. What gives?"

"I'm not ready to have a baby." She turned her worried gaze on me.

"Fortunately, you have options." Reproductive freedom was still an uphill battle some thirty-plus years after *Roe v. Wade*, but last time I'd checked, women still had the right to choose not to have a baby.

"That's why I'm here. I think if Sinclair were to find out I'm pregnant, I'd have fewer options."

I tried not to shiver.

That scared me.

"Don't you have the same two options every woman has? Have the baby or don't have it." I pressed for details with all the subtlety of a hammer.

"He's been hinting that he would like to start again. Have another family."

That one didn't surprise me. I think he'd do anything to tie her down like a Christmas tree on the roof of a car.

Sinclair was no spring chicken, though. He'd been a law professor at our school before he'd come in as a partner at Lulu's law firm. I did the math in my head.

"He'd be close to seventy when your kid graduated from high school," I blurted.

"Casey. You're not telling me anything I haven't already considered. I love him. It's hard *not* to think about a future with him and all that might mean."

"With kids?"

"I don't know. Certainly not yet. He's not divorced." She gave me the side eye. Richard Sinclair had hinted at my representation of him in divorce court more than once. Held that up to Lulu as his true obstacle in leaving his wife as if there weren't a whole bar association full of other options.

"Don't look at me. I never think it's a good idea to represent people I know personally."

She looked down at the instruction sheet that she'd unfolded. It was bigger than a page of the *Plain Dealer* with far smaller type.

"Either way, I wanted the decks cleared so we could begin fresh." By "decks cleared" she meant a permanent split from Dr. Deborah Bloom, the age-appropriate woman he was very much still married to.

The room was getting hot. The single window faced an air shaft.

"Two people in one tiny pre-war bathroom is kind of weird and claustrophobic. What do you need to do?"

Lulu fumbled around with the instructions. She picked up the box again, maybe looking for something simpler, and a second plastic wrapped test stick fell out.

"Why two?" I asked. I'd always wondered that.

"Backup plan? I don't know. I thought it was weird, but they all had two in the box." She handed me the second test. "Why don't you take it with me?"

"What?" I waved the package. "Why?"

"You can be the control, so if mine shows up not pregnant at least I know the tests work."

I couldn't fault her logic.

"Aren't these regulated by the FDA or something?" I asked. "It's not like Joe from Rendville is whipping these up in his garage and putting them on the shelf at CVS."

"Rendville?" She squinted. I wasn't sure if that was because of the tiny print on the instructions or because of my obscure reference.

"It's the smallest town in Ohio. Read about it in my dentist's waiting room." He'd had a book on odd Ohio facts last time I was there. It was something Justin would have laughed at. *Fuck me* with my thoughts on a guy who didn't want to date me.

"Just pee on that stick," she insisted.

I guess I was going first.

A canary down a mine.

"Fine. I'll be over here doing my imitation of my mother at the pediatrician's office. I'll pretend to get a shot so you'll take your vaccination quietly."

"But for real."

"Turn around. No one needs to see these thighs. I don't want to blind you with the white."

I peed on the stupid absorbent wick and put the blue cap on it. The sound of the flush filled the room. Then Lulu and I switched places. She stuck her completed test in her velvet hoodie pocket instead of next to mine on the top of the hamper.

"Now what?" I asked. I hadn't looked at the directions, but I knew there was a waiting period. Probably somewhere between five and fifteen minutes.

"Let's open the wine I brought."

"What if you *are* pregnant?"

Lulu was already in my dining room fishing in the top drawer of my new hutch for a corkscrew before I could finish my question.

"Then this will be my last drink for a long time." She pulled the cork from the bottle.

"I'll get the glasses."

"It's a Pinot," she said, as if I were going to pull out some kind of specific glasses. I wasn't *that* classy. "I definitely needed a red," she continued, while I set two goblets on the table. "This isn't a summer party full of fizzy rosé. It may be my funeral."

We were halfway through our first glasses of the very dark and probably very alcoholic Pinot when Lulu popped up like a tipped Weeble. She fished the stick from her pocket. Brandished it like a sword.

"I'm not pregnant," Lulu crowed. "Let's get blitzed."

"Hold on. I'm the control, remember?" I went down the hall to the bathroom and retrieved the other test from where I'd left it. Two very dark lines stared back at me. My stomach plummeted to my toes. I practically ran as fast as I could, in my Uggs, back to the dining room.

"Wait." I handed her the positive test. "We must have switched."

"We didn't switch. I never put mine down."

"Except when we came to the dining room and you were looking for a corkscrew."

"But if we're both not pregnant, then it shouldn't make any difference."

I gestured toward the test I'd handed her. "Well, someone is pregnant."

"Now I know why there are two in the box. Because this is a freaking nightmare." She stalked to the living room and slipped into Air Jordans that were probably more suitable for a fifteen-year-old boy. Lulu tapped at her empty wrist. "What time does CVS close?"

"Ten? Eleven? I've hardly seen it closed."

"Let's go, then," Lulu said. "Maybe we'll luck out."

"I think I'm going to need this first," I said, then downed the entire goblet of wine in one gulp.

"Wait, what if *you're* pregnant?"

"Then this will be *my* last drink," I parroted Lulu's earlier statement.

It only took ten minutes for us to walk down four flights, visit the drugstore, and come back up.

"This time, I'm going to mark them," I said. I took the paper bag down the hall, then fished through the pen holder in the second bedroom that served as a home office/exercise room/litter box room that I never really used. Found a black Sharpie. Opened the pastel pink box and marked one of the test sticks with a C and the other with an L.

"Let's do this again, shall we?"

"What am I going to do, Casey?" Lulu's face was flushed from the wine and screwed up in real worry.

"Let's cross that bridge," I soothed. "Maybe you got a box of old tests or something that first time. Who knows how long this kind of thing is good for. Or what the false positive rate is. If I've learned one thing in the last few months, it's that science and medicine aren't always precise."

We repeated what we'd done earlier, each peeing on a stick again. I got paper towels and laid them down on the kitchen counter before pouring each of us a second glass. We settled in at my dining room table to wait.

"Why do you think Sinclair would limit your choices?" I asked. I had so many thoughts on their relationship. I kept them to myself in order to preserve our friendship. Probably during the same dentist office visit when I'd read about Rendville, I think I'd read something about keeping the lines of communication open when friends were in a controlling relationship. You wanted them to know they always had an out even if you couldn't convince them to take that out.

"He's a little set in his ways," was Lulu's weak excuse. "I just want to be able to make a decision without his influence. It's not a pair of jeans or even a house or a car or a pet...none of those choices will last a lifetime. A kid...that will. I want him to be fully clear of his marriage before we make any life decisions...together."

On cue, my pet snaked through our legs under the dining room table and rubbed against both of us. We both stroked him until he'd had enough and ran back to the bedroom where he'd once again curl up right in the middle of my duvet. Once Lulu left, I'd have to arrange myself around his highness King Simba to get a good night's sleep.

"Fair enough. Drink up. This is your last glass for a minute or eight more months."

We both finished our second glasses. I looked at the bottle which was nearly empty now. I split the last of it between our two glasses. In silent agreement we sipped until it was all gone.

A lot tipsy, I stood and stumbled over to the kitchen. I put the bottle in the bin.

"Alright. Here we go," I said loud enough for Lulu to hear through the dining room all the way into the living room where she'd wandered as if running away to the front apartment windows would immunize her against the news.

I picked up the tests and looked at the lines. One was single. One was double. The one with the single line was marked with an L, the one with the brightly glowing pink double line was marked with a C.

"Good news," I said, though my voice was anything but cheery.

I handed Lulu the L test. "You're not pregnant."

"Thank goodness." Her sigh of relief had enough air in it to fill a helium balloon. Then she looked at me. I couldn't keep it up any longer, my own face crumpled. I could feel the pressure of tears building behind my eyes. "Wait, Casey. What's going on?"

I held out the C test. She took it in her hands.

"Oh. Oh my God. *You're* pregnant. Did you...of course you didn't know. Holy mother of God."

"I had no idea." I shook my head as if that would make a baby go away. "None."

"What...wait? Who's the father? Justin or Ron?"

I closed my eyes, flashing back to two different guys on two different nights when I'd forgotten to insist on a condom. When my good-girl resolve had wavered in the face of a cute guy who was able, ready, and willing.

"I have zero idea."

ABOUT THE AUTHOR

Aime Austin is the author of the Casey Cort Legal Thriller Series. Casey is almost always in trouble. Aime's full time job? Rescuing her. Good thing Aime's got experience. She practiced family and criminal law in Cleveland, Ohio for several years—so she has the skills for the job.

When Aime isn't rescuing Casey from herself, she's hosting her podcast, *A Time to Thrill*, raising her son or traveling between Budapest and Los Angeles.

www.ingramcontent.com/pod-product-compliance
Lightning Source LLC
Chambersburg PA
CBHW030930260626
47169CB00002B/425